Russell W. Johnson

a legal thriller

ALL GUILTY ANYWAY

All Guilty Anyway
Red Adept Publishing, LLC
104 Bugenfield Court
Garner, NC 27529
https://RedAdeptPublishing.com/
Copyright © 2026 by Russell W. Johnson. All rights reserved.

Cover Art by Streetlight Graphics[1]

---

1.   http://StreetlightGraphics.com

This book is dedicated to the lawyers. The ones who taught me the skills. The ones who taught me humility. And most of all, to my good friends Bert Diener and Robby Jessup, who taught me to have fun.

PART 1

CHAPTER 1

Ivy Collins had been going to the Wake County Courthouse every day for six months, yet the deputies still made her show her bar card before admitting her to the Attorneys Only line through security. At first, she'd attributed it to her youthful appearance. Blond and blue-eyed with that frightened, fresh-out-of-law-school expression, Ivy was used to people not taking her seriously. But the husky deputy eyeing her ID that morning had checked her in at least twenty times before and ogled her ass enough that he could probably describe its every contour in his sleep. So she was pretty sure it was just part of the hazing—the numerous ways defense attorneys were treated like the visiting team inside the courthouse.

Virtually everything, from the justice center's towering hard-block exterior to its inconvenient downtown location surrounded by a maze of one-way streets with scarce parking to the imperious judges seated high on mahogany benches, down to the beefy, gun-toting men who checked the bags—all of it felt designed to make the experience as intimidating as possible.

"I really am a lawyer. Scout's honor," Ivy said, holding up two fingers.

The deputy sneered as he handed back her credentials and fired a thumb over his shoulder.

I bet prosecutors never have to deal with this crap. The assistant district attorneys practically owned the courthouse. They got reserved parking in an underground garage, were issued key fobs to unlock private entrances that bypassed security altogether, worked out of cozy offices nestled in the building's secret alcoves, and were on a first-name basis with every judge and member of the courthouse staff. Even the youngest ADAs quickly became masters of the local bureaucracy. Plus, they got to basically set the court's calendars and, in many ways, were more in charge of "the system" than even the judges. It was massively unfair.

Before law school, Ivy had been a fairly serious athlete, a five-seven point guard with a wicked crossover and a decent jumper, so she was no stranger to competition or hostile environments. But she had never dealt with a home-court advantage like that. Nor had she ever faced an opponent as fierce as the one she was set to meet that morning, the Hatchet Lady herself, ADA Eliza Wells.

Ivy slipped through the metal detector without a ding and retrieved her bag from the conveyor belt, looking back just in time to catch the deputy once again checking out her posterior.

Maybe tomorrow, I should walk in backward so he'll recognize me. Might speed things up.

As for that morning, however, Ivy was running late. She hustled across the ground floor, making a serpentine path through pro se defendants meandering toward traffic court, then managed to squeeze into an overly full elevator just as the doors closed. Twenty people were mashed into a space built for ten, and it was a sweltering North Carolina morning, which meant various levels of BO swirled together into a kind of rotten stew—an unfortunate circumstance, since Ivy was on for the long haul, headed all the way to the tenth floor.

She eyed the lighted numbers as they stopped at *every* level. Each time the elevator doors opened, the crowded conditions required an awkward, time-consuming shuffle to allow those pushed into the back to exit before newcomers came aboard. Not until the doors closed on the ninth floor was Ivy finally alone, the sole rider ascending to the Superior Court, where the major felonies were handled.

The doors opened onto a faded tile hallway. Ivy took a deep breath of the rarified air. To that point in her brief legal career, she'd worked exclusively down in District Court, mostly pleading out misdemeanors. That day was her first foray into the big time. She wielded the court-appointed case file she'd been handed that morning by her boss, Lester "the Truth" Williams, who'd assured her that the step up was nothing to worry about.

"Shoot, girl, it's all the same." Lester was a Black man in his fifties and a graduate of NC Central, an acclaimed HBCU in Durham, though the Truth liked to say his real degree came from the school of hard knocks. That morning, he had been wearing one of his tailored three-piece suits, that one olive-green, and was settling into a leather office chair while snipping the end of his morning cigar with a finger guillotine when he said, "Superior Court... District Court... It's no different, Ivy. Remember, your job's really not to fight with the prosecutor. Just find out what kind of deal they're offering and go sell it to the client. The case pleads, we get our paltry fee, the state gets their conviction, and the client gets a reduced sentence. Everybody's happy." Lester mimed washing his hands.

"But what if she's innocent?" Ivy asked.

The question caught Lester mid-puff and launched him into a prolonged coughing fit as he laughed hysterically. "Oh, that's a good one," he said once he'd caught his breath. "*Innocent.*" He rested his cigar in a glass ashtray on the corner of his desk and gave Ivy one of those looks she despised—the grizzled veteran having to explain once again how the world worked to his little white-girl associate. "Listen, Ivy, I've been doing this a long time, okay? And one thing I can tell you, without hesitation, is everybody's guilty. Everybody. Hell, we're all guilty of something."

Ivy was in no position to argue. Though she didn't consider herself naive, she was inexperienced and undoubtedly privileged. Part of the reason she'd taken the job with Lester in the first place was she had something to prove and knew there was a lot she could learn from a legit street lawyer like "the Truth," as Lester often referred to himself in the third person.

Ivy flipped open the file and started to read until Lester stopped her.

"Whoa, whoa, whoa. Slow your roll there, Nancy Drew. We don't have time for all that. Need you to get on down to the courthouse pronto. Cesar wrote down everything you need to know right here."

Cesar was Lester's paralegal and translator, who hustled up most of the firm's Latino clients. His unmistakable chicken scratch filled a Post-it note on the folder's outside cover:

Defendant—Sonia Cabrerra, 22
Felony child abuse
Victim—Hugo (son), 8.

"What's the hurry?" Ivy asked. She didn't like the idea of heading downtown on her first felony without having at least read the file.

Lester sighed, apparently getting annoyed with always having to explain everything. "We need to find out what the offer is before the prosecutor starts a trial this morning that the court administrator says is expected to last three weeks. I know this Eliza Wells. She's no joke. All focus. If you don't catch her before she gets rolling on whatever poor schmuck she's about to put away, then it could be a month before we get to talk to her. Meanwhile, our client's cooling her heels in the county jail."

Ivy checked her watch. It was already nine thirty, and Superior Court started at ten. She understood why Lester was pushing her to move. She'd really have to run if she was going to catch Eliza before her trial got going. Ivy stuffed the file into her leather bag and started for the door before asking, "Suppose they don't offer a deal. What then?"

"Trust me. The last thing the state wants is the time, expense, and uncertainty of a trial when they can get a nice and easy guilty plea. There's always a deal. Always."

THOSE WORDS ECHOED in Ivy's head as she slipped into the back of courtroom 10-C and realized she was too late. Eliza Wells was already in the midst of her opening statement for another case she was handling, laying out the particulars of a crime to a jury of twelve. Ivy thought about heading back to the office to let Lester know she'd missed her shot, but she quickly became entranced by Eliza's delivery.

The prosecutor was a humorless-looking woman in her sixties with gray hair pulled back tight. She wore little to no makeup and a long, shapeless black dress accessorized only by a single strand of pearls. Yet every eye was on her as she strutted back and forth, commanding the courtroom, stalking the jury like a predator cat. For half an hour, Ivy watched as Eliza hammered away, utilizing no notes—every fact, every picayune detail not only committed to memory but absolutely mastered. Eliza drove them like nails into the defendant's coffin.

"By the end of this trial," she said in summation, "you will have *no choice* but to find the defendant *guilty*." Eliza fired a vicious point at the defendant that sent chills down Ivy's spine. It was like a laser beam of judgment shooting from the tip of the prosecutor's finger. Guilt was an absolute certainty. Even without hearing the other side of the case, Ivy could feel it from Eliza's conviction, a righteous indignation that was palpable. She saw it in the eyes of the jury as well. They were already nodding, ready to hang the son of a bitch.

Jesus, this lady's good.

"Thank you, Madam Prosecutor," the judge said. "Why don't we take a ten-minute recess before the defense gives their opening statement."

After that, people shuffled about, some headed for the restrooms. It stirred Ivy from her reverie. She realized it was an opportunity to try to talk to Eliza about her new case—if she could muster the courage.

The prosecutor was making her way down the aisle toward Ivy, not giving her long to gin up her nerve.

Ivy cleared her throat and opened her mouth to speak, but no words came out. Eliza passed by and was about to exit the courtroom when Ivy timidly managed to say, "Excuse me, Ms. Wells?"

Eliza stopped, turned, and looked Ivy up and down, no doubt pegging her for a young wannabe lawyer in her short skirt and form-fitting blazer, both courtesy of Ralph Lauren. The prosecutor's expression morphed from a natural sneer—what Ivy would classify as "resting bitch face"—into something decidedly less pleasant, as though Eliza had just discovered a wad of gum stuck to her shoe.

"Yes?"

Ivy cleared her throat and tried to use her big-girl voice. "I'm Ivy Collins. I'm... uh... handling the Cabrerra case."

Eliza's eyes rolled toward the ceiling as she searched a mental filing system for the name among what must have been hundreds of cases.

"Cabrerra, yes," Eliza said finally. "I'm familiar with it."

Ivy nervously dug into her bag for the folder that had been sent over from the Public Defender's Office. "I'm sorry to bother you during trial. It's just that I was wondering what kind of plea the state was offering."

Eliza looked at Ivy like that was the stupidest thing she had ever heard. "Have you read the file?"

Ivy swallowed hard. "Um... just had time to skim it," she lied. "Our firm was assigned the case this morning from the court-appointed list."

The mention of the "list" brought a look of disapproval. It meant the defendant was indigent and, because the public defender's office was grossly underfunded and overworked, the case had been farmed out to a local private attorney at way below their normal market rate. Many lawyers viewed such appointments as akin to indentured servitude. Thus, a court-appointed firm had an inherent economic motivation to assign the case to their least experienced lawyer and to give it the least amount of attention possible, regardless of the case's complexity.

"I suppose you haven't seen the video, then?" Eliza asked.

"There's a video?"

"DVD. Back of the file."

Ivy flipped the folder over and, sure enough, taped to the inside cover was a shiny silver disk.

"Look, I really don't have time to discuss this right now. If you'll excuse me," Eliza said, "I'd like to use the bathroom before we start back up."

The prosecutor headed again for the door, but Ivy called after her, hating how desperate she sounded. "I just need to know what the plea deal is."

Eliza turned, shaking her head defiantly. "Uh-uh. Nope. Not on this one. No reduction. No deal."

Ivy assumed at first that it was just more hazing, like the deputy downstairs. But the prosecutor remained stone-faced.

"I don't understand," Ivy said.

Eliza huffed. "Just watch the video. Trust me. You'll understand."

CHAPTER 2

Ivy left the courthouse with nearly as much haste as she'd entered. She was desperate to get back to the office to watch the video and find out what the hell Lester had gotten her into. She walked the two blocks to where she'd been lucky enough to find a metered spot on Martin Street. There to greet her was a yellow envelope tucked beneath the wiper blade—her third ticket that month. Ivy snatched the forty-dollar citation and chucked it and her leather satchel into the passenger seat of her silver Prius and started the drive down South Saunders.

She left downtown and was almost into Garner when she pulled into a dilapidated strip mall that housed a Latino grocery store and various low-rent businesses. Among them were the illustrious law offices—plural, even though there was just the one—of Lester "the Truth" Williams & Associates—again plural despite Ivy being the only associate attorney. Beneath the marquee was Lester's cheeky tagline: *"The Truth" Will Set You Free*.

Some days, Ivy wasn't sure which was more intimidating—the courthouse or the ramshackle office where cockroaches were commonplace and the coffeemaker hadn't been cleaned in so long it looked like a science fair project. She parked between the video poker joint and the discount clothing store, got out, and tried not to look nervous as she tiptoed down the sidewalk past the taqueria, giving Raymond, the mostly harmless homeless man, a wide berth. She jumped when the bass from the speaker store kicked on, and Raymond started laughing his ass off. He toasted her with his brown-bagged bottle.

Just another little dose of embarrassment to make the morning complete.

Ivy pushed into the office, ringing the shopkeeper's bell. In the lobby was the typical motley crew of potential clients lounging around like it was a bus station. One guy was stretched across multiple chairs, snoring, a newspaper draped over his face. Meanwhile, Maria, the receptionist, was at the front desk, ignoring them. She had a telephone wedged between her shoulder and ear, talking while chomping gum and trying to type with two-inch fingernails, yet she still had enough dexterity to give Ivy the middle finger. Ivy returned the gesture and headed down the hall to the conference room, where perhaps the only DVD player still in existence was housed.

Unfortunately, Lester was using the room. He was trying to close the deal with an older, conservative-looking Black couple for what must have been a personal injury case, because the wife was wearing a whiplash neck collar. Lester had the door open because the piece-of-shit air conditioning wasn't working again. He'd set up a big rattling box fan to blow in from the hall.

Over the droning fan, Ivy heard the woman ask how long it would take to get to trial. "Won't be no need to try it," Lester said, "'cause once the insurance company sees you hired the Truth, they'll just straight scratch the check. The last thing they want is me inside that courtroom. I'm like a ninja in a necktie."

Ivy was suppressing a giggle, watching Lester kick and karate chop his shadow, when she felt a tap on the shoulder.

"What's up, boss?"

She turned to find Cesar, nattily dressed, as always, in dark slim-cut jeans, an untucked plaid button-up shirt, and a sports jacket, topped with his usual fedora, a hat only someone as cool as Cesar could pull off. Seeing him was usually the best part of Ivy's day.

"I really wish you'd stop calling me that," she said, blushing. "I'm not your boss."

"Sure you are. You're the lawyer."

He had that "Aw-shucks, I-know-I'm-model-handsome-but-am-still-humble-anyway" grin on his face.

"So what? You've probably forgotten more law than I'll ever know."

Cesar hadn't gone to college, much less law school, but he was the one person in the firm who knew everything about how the system actually worked—the jails, the courts, the bail bondsmen, all the things they didn't teach you. More importantly, he knew how to deal with the difficult clients, how to navigate all the emotions, the egos, the lies, the conflicts, the drama, the pleas of poverty when it came time to pay, and the various cons they tried to pull. Ivy liked to say Cesar had all the answers you couldn't find in a book.

"Whatever," Cesar said, still acting modest. "How'd it go with the Hatchet Lady?"

"It was a massacre."

"What do you mean?"

"No plea deal. No reduction. She seemed offended that I even asked."

Cesar's eyes widened. "For real?"

"Yeah. She told me to go home and watch the DVD that was tucked into the file. As soon as Lester clears out of the conference room, I'm going to put it on."

"Man. Let me take a look at that thing." He gestured to the file Ivy had tucked under her arm. When she handed it over, Cesar flipped it open. "I'm sorry, boss. I just had a chance to look at the charges this morning. I should have prepped you better before Lester sent you in there."

"It's not your fault."

Cesar was right about one thing. Though she didn't like to think of herself as his boss, she was the lawyer. Inexperienced or not and regardless of the reality that she was an employee who didn't choose the cases, the strategy, or the methods, in the eyes of the law and the outside world, she was the one who was ultimately responsible. Her ethics professor had made that abundantly clear in law school: "There is no Nuremberg defense. Saying, 'I was just following orders' will work about as well for you in front of the state bar as it did for all the Nazis who got executed."

Nevertheless, she still blamed Lester for that morning's embarrassment. Though it wasn't the first time she had doubted the Truth's tutelage, it bothered her enough that she finally felt the need to say something.

"Cesar, can I ask you a question?"

"Sure, boss. Shoot."

Ivy looked back at the conference room. "Not here."

"Want to step into your office?"

"You mean your office."

"Stop that," Cesar said. "It's your office now."

The firm only had two private offices, one of which was occupied by Lester, of course, and the other of which had been Cesar's before Ivy was hired and he insisted she take it. The whole thing made her uncomfortable, swooping in with her fancy degree and booting Cesar to a cubicle back by the storage closet. She'd tried mightily to resist his generous offer, but one day during her first week, she came back from court to find Cesar had moved all of his stuff out and her stuff in, even going so far as to hang her diplomas on the wall. At that point, it was hard to say no. But Ivy assumed the office switch, along with all the attention she got from Cesar, was the reason she'd received such a frosty reception from Maria, the receptionist who daily greeted her with a one-finger salute.

"After you," Cesar said. He opened the door to what had become Ivy's office, where two very worn powder-blue wingback chairs faced the desk. Ivy sat in one of those rather than circling around to her office chair because she wanted to address Cesar as an equal.

"This must be serious," Cesar said. "What is it?"

Ivy wasn't sure how to begin. Asking *Does Lester have any idea what the fuck he's doing?* didn't seem appropriate. But after the way she'd looked like an idiot in front of Eliza Wells that morning, it was what she was wondering. "I don't know," she said. "It's just...you know, Lester."

"What about him?"

"Well, the whole reason I took this job after the big-firm thing didn't work out is I'd heard Lester was some great trial lawyer."

"Okay?"

"So I get here, and Lester doesn't try shit. We've got this settlement mill running, like we're a Law-Mart or something."

Cesar nodded. "Yeah, I know. Lester used to try cases all the time. And he was good. That's for sure."

"What happened?" Ivy asked. "Because the whole time I've been here, I don't think he's ever even gone to the courthouse. He just wants to do the easy injury settlements with the insurance companies. And every criminal case we get, he tells me to plead."

"It wasn't always like that."

"What changed?"

Cesar shrugged. "I don't know."

"Come on," Ivy said. "I need to know. I'm stuck here now. There's no way in hell I'm ever going back to work with my father, and no other blue-blood firm would touch me after I've worked in a place like this." Ivy gestured to the bars on her office window.

Cesar laughed.

Ivy kept pushing. "You've known Lester a long time, right?"

"Yep. Almost ten years. Started working for him when I was sixteen."

"So you must have some idea."

Cesar rolled his head around like a boxer, stretching his neck. "Yeah, I guess."

"Come on, Cesar. Level with me."

Cesar sighed then took off his fedora, set it in his lap, and leaned in close enough for Ivy to pick up the leathery smell of his cologne, which made her heart race.

"Okay," he said. "Can you keep a secret?"

CHAPTER 3

Just as Cesar was about to spill, a sharp knock sounded on the door. Half a second later, Lester burst in, doing a celebratory strut and rubbing invisible cash between his fingers. "Just signed up a juicy one."

Ivy jumped back in her chair, feeling like a kid caught making out.

Lester raised an eyebrow, looking down at where Ivy's and Cesar's knees were nearly touching. "How'd it go with the Hatchet Lady?" he asked.

"Not well," Ivy said, relieved Lester hadn't inquired as to what they'd been talking about.

"No surprise there," Lester said. "Eliza likes to play hardball. What's she offering?"

"She's not," Ivy said. "Told me there would be no deal. She looked at me like I was an idiot for even asking." Ivy wanted to say *fucking idiot*, but since Lester was still her employer, she decided to underplay how upset she was over the position he'd put her in that morning.

"Bullshit," Lester said. "She's just fucking with you."

"I don't think so. She said there's a DVD in the file we need to watch, then we'll understand why she won't negotiate."

Lester made a face like he was trying to suck a thick milkshake through a tiny straw. "You know a lady with Eliza Wells's experience, she could be making five, ten times as much money in the private sector. So the fact that she's still in the DA's office after all these years tells you she's the most dangerous thing a prosecutor can ever be."

"What's that?" Ivy asked.

"A true believer."

Lester stroked his chin. He was always trying out some different style of facial hair but had recently shaved it all off and just had the shadow of a goatee starting to grow back.

Cesar said, "How about we go watch the video?"

Lester, always busy chasing a dollar, checked his watch. "We'll need to make it fast. I've got more clients coming soon."

The three moved to the conference room, where Cesar cued up the DVD while Lester explained that the child-victim videos were called "TEDI Bear interviews."

"Like the stuffed animal?" Ivy asked.

"Yeah, kind of. They actually do give a teddy bear to the kids, but it's an acronym too: Tender Evaluation, Diagnosis, and Intervention. They're done by an outfit with ECU in Greenville that has doctors, shrinks, social workers, and whatnot. Happens in almost every case like this involving child abuse."

Would have been helpful to know that this morning, Ivy thought.

But if her chagrin at Lester's sudden wellspring of knowledge showed, her boss seemed blissfully unaware. He explained, "The thing you've got to watch for with these is if the interviewer does anything to lead the witness. Kids are impressionable as hell. You can plant an idea in their head super easy."

Cesar fiddled with the remote, trying to get the TV on the right input. Meanwhile, Lester regaled them with the tale of the Little Rascals' cases back in the late eighties, early nineties, at the tail end of the Satanic Panic. "They involved daycare workers who were erroneously convicted of a litany of horrendous child abuse crimes based upon some bullshit 'recovered memories' some overzealous therapists created during their interviews with the preschoolers. The cases all eventually got reversed and thrown out but only after lives and reputations were destroyed."

"Wow," Ivy said. "That's awful."

"Yeah. Things have gotten a lot better since then. Those cases led to some good reforms. Now you've got reputable places like TEDI Bear who do a good job. But you still have to watch these folks, especially when it comes to interviewing the really young ones."

Cesar finally had the video playing, the image focusing on eight-year-old Hugo Cabrerra being led into a brightly colored room. Ivy's heart sank at the sight. Hugo was a gaunt, tan-skinned boy with bushy, unkempt brown hair and thick circle-framed glasses that made him look like a little Latino Harry Potter. Holding his hand was an older white woman with poofy gray bangs and a big print blouse. She introduced herself as Ms. Garber, the guidance counselor from Hugo's school.

The interviewer and police officer, who remained off camera, could be heard asking if a translator would be necessary.

"Not for this little rock star," Ms. Garber said. "Hugo has only been in the US for a short time, but he's already picked up English so well that he was a semifinalist in this year's spelling bee. Isn't that right, Hugo?"

The boy nodded timidly.

The interviewer oohed about how impressive that was before inviting Hugo to take a seat at a low table topped with coloring books and crayons.

"We need to go over a few things at the start," the interviewer said. "First, Hugo, can you tell me the difference between the truth and a lie?"

Before Hugo could answer, Lester scooped the remote off the conference table and hit fast-forward.

"What are you doing?" Ivy asked.

"Skipping to the good part."

"But I thought you said we need to watch closely to make sure they don't feed him the answers."

"No, I said *you* need to watch closely. *I've* got clients coming. You can go back over it later. Right now, I just need the *Reader's Digest* version. Oh, wait, here we go. Look, the boy's pulling his shirt up. Now, we're getting to... Oh, goddamn."

Everyone recoiled at the sight of Hugo with his Pokémon T-shirt pulled up to his collarbone, exposing a nasty series of symmetrically spaced horizontal red scars that ran from his armpit all the way down to his hip.

"Who gave you those marks, Hugo?" the interviewer asked.

The little boy trembled like a crumbling dam about to give way.

"It's okay, Hugo. You are safe, and you are going to stay safe. You just need to tell me who gave you those marks. Just tell me what you told Ms. Garber."

With that, the dam broke. Tears rolled down the boy's cheeks. He bit his bottom lip, unable to speak.

"Hugo, remember we agreed we would tell each other the truth."

Hugo nodded and released his white-knuckled grip on his T-shirt so he could wipe his tears.

"Do you know how you got those scars?"

Another nod came but still no answer.

For the first time, the interviewer stepped into view. She was a middle-aged Indian woman in a pinstriped shirt and long denim skirt, her black hair braided into a triple-wrapped ponytail. She knelt down to Hugo's eye level and held his hands.

"It's okay," she whispered. "I promise. You just have to tell me the truth. Who gave you those scars?"

Finally, the boy spoke. His voice was high-pitched and small but clear. "Mama."

They all stood silent, watching as a new deluge of tears overwhelmed the boy. The interviewer hugged and consoled him.

At that, the most inappropriate of moments, Maria buzzed in over the intercom. "Lester, your clients are here."

"Tell them it'll be a minute," he said curtly.

"But you said—"

"Just a damn minute!" Lester barked. He jacked up the TV volume. They all listened with rapt attention as Hugo recounted what life had been like since reuniting with his mother after spending his first six years being raised by his grandparents in Guatemala.

"She calls me *estupido*," he said, as though that verbal jab hurt more than the physical ones he said he frequently received from belts and broomsticks.

"What about the scars?" the interviewer asked. "How did you get those scars?"

"Mama," Hugo said. "She got angry."

"Tell me what happened, Hugo."

Again, Maria buzzed. "Lester, these folks are still waiting."

"Son of a bitch." Lester paused the video and checked his watch. "Shit. Okay, listen, Maria. The conference room is going to be occupied for a while, so go ahead and put the clients in my office. Tell them something came up with another client that is running longer than expected, and I insist on giving every person I represent all the time and attention their case deserves. Clients love that shit. I'll be with them in just a minute."

Lester didn't wait for a response before switching off the intercom and resuming the video. He, Ivy, and Cesar watched, riveted, while Hugo described an evening a few months back when his mother had been cooking in the kitchen using a large skillet with a removable metal grate. Hugo had been playing nearby with a plastic sword when he accidentally knocked the skillet to the floor. Dinner was ruined, and his mother was enraged.

"She held me down."

Hugo's lip quivered as he described how Sonia Cabrerra had given him a lesson he would never forget. With the oven mitts she was already wearing, Sonia had angrily snatched the hot metal grate out of the skillet and pressed it, searing, into the shirtless little boy's side.

CHAPTER 4

Lester stopped the recording. "Well, I've seen enough. Our lady's toast."

"What are we going to do?" Ivy asked.

Lester picked a piece of lint off his lapel. "Simple," he said. "We just need to plead that shit."

"But there is no plea bargain. That's what I've been trying to tell you."

"So what? Plead it anyway."

Ugh. Ivy wasn't sure how much more she could take of Lester's passive approach to the practice of law. "We can't just surrender," she argued. "We have to at least try to defend her, don't we? You know, like be actual lawyers and stuff." That dollop of smartass was the boldest Ivy had ever gotten with Lester, and she could tell by his expression he didn't much care for it.

"Were you even watching just now? That kid was just about the cutest little motherfucker I've ever seen. You put him in front of a jury with tears running down his face, and they will skin our girl alive." He turned to Cesar and asked about the client's immigration status.

Cesar paged through the file. "Doesn't say for sure, but I don't think she's legal. No social listed."

"Are you thinking we can agree to have her deported in lieu of prosecution?" Ivy asked.

"That's a good thought, but unfortunately, it doesn't work that way," Lester said. "We make people serve out their sentences, *then* we deport their asses. Lack of status just means our girl will get the double whammy. The state extracts its pound of flesh then turns her over to Immigration to put her on a plane. All we can do is try to reduce the amount of time she'll spend in prison before that happens. Pleading her guilty is the only option."

"Even without a reduction?"

"Hell yes." Lester stood and adjusted his suit jacket so the tip of his white shirtsleeve was exposed. "Look, sometimes admitting the truth is all you can do. I know you like to fight, Ivy. And that's good. That's what makes you a lawyer, for God's sake. You like to win. And I know you want to be that white knight who rushes in and saves the day. But in a case like this, there are no saviors. You don't get to be the lifesaving surgeon. You're more like a hospice nurse, just there to ease the suffering."

Despite the flood of metaphors, Ivy got Lester's point. Truth be told, she was actually a little relieved to hear him say it. Though it usually killed her to plead a case when a creative defense or novel legal theory presented the possibility of victory, there didn't seem to be anything like that in the Sonia Cabrerra case. Ivy would be all too happy to dump the matter if there was a way to accomplish that ethically.

"So what am I supposed to do?" she asked.

"Convince our lady to plead," Lester said. "ASAP. The sooner she rips that Band-Aid off, the better. Then just go into court and say, 'Judge, we fully acknowledge our client is a shit bag, lower than fucking pond scum. But hey, at least she admits it. She's not gonna put the state through the time and expense of a trial to prove it or retraumatize her son by making him testify.' Then you can lay out the parade of horribles that turned our client into Attila the fucking Hun. There's a sob story in her past. I guarantee it. If you want to do some lawyering, that's where it's at. Take responsibility and sell mitigation. That's the only way you're going to cut some time off this lady's sentence." Lester straightened his tie. "Now, if you'll excuse me, I've got clients waiting. You two can take it from here."

Once Lester was gone, Ivy restarted the video, and she and Cesar watched Hugo use crayons to draw a picture of the skillet his mother assaulted him with. Then the interviewer called a break and stopped the camera. When the recording resumed, she had a stack of printouts, images of different skillets found on the Internet that roughly matched Hugo's drawing.

"Take your time, Hugo. Look at these and tell me if any of them look like your mother's."

The boy considered each printout in turn, dismissed the first three, and confidently declared that the fourth one was a match.

"Are you sure?"

Without hesitation, the boy said, "Yes, I'm sure."

Cesar, who continued to study the file, slid the folder across the table. It was opened to a photocopy of Hugo's drawing next to the printout he selected—a black cast-iron Delmont grill pan with a removable grate.

"Check out the next few pages," Cesar said.

Ivy thumbed forward and realized the copies had been incorporated into a warrant application and subsequent police report recounting how a matching Delmont grill pan was recovered from the defendant's home. She turned the page and saw a series of photographs where the investigating officer had used a tape measure to show that the spacing between the horizontal scars on Hugo's side perfectly matched the metal grate.

"Shit."

"It gets worse," Cesar said.

Ivy snorted. "How could it possibly get any worse?"

Cesar spun the file around and flipped to a dog-eared page. "Check this out. After the cops find the grill pan, they tell Sonia she's under arrest and Mirandize her using a translator. Then they tell her that Hugo's going to Social Services, but first, they're going to take him to Memorial Hospital to get checked out. And she says..." Cesar traced his finger down the page until he located the exact line. "*Es donde lo llevé cuando le rompí el brazo?*"

"What's that mean?"

Cesar translated: "'Is that where I took him when I broke his arm?'"

Ivy's stomach churned. "You're sure?"

"Positive. They even made her repeat it to be certain. Then they did a subsequent interview with Hugo where he told them about a time last Christmas when his mom grabbed his arm from behind and twisted it until it snapped. Look at these." Cesar flipped farther back in the file. "They got the medical records, and sure enough, last December, Sonia took Hugo in for a spiral fracture to his right arm."

"I'm surprised they didn't call Social Services then," Ivy said.

"The record notes concern for possible child abuse, but a neighbor went with Sonia to translate and said Hugo broke his arm falling off the porch."

"Did the neighbor see it, or was she just translating what Sonia told her?"

"Doesn't say."

"Well, I'm no doctor, but a spiral fracture sounds like more of a twisting injury than something you'd get from a fall."

"Considering our lady just confessed to it, I'd say you're right," Cesar said.

Ivy groaned and buried her head in her hands.

"What do you want to do, boss?" Cesar asked.

What Ivy wanted to do was build a time machine, travel back, and go to med school instead of becoming a lawyer. But since that wasn't an option, she figured the only thing she could do was go meet the client and have an uncomfortable conversation about how she was about to spend a long time behind bars before getting shipped back to Guatemala.

CHAPTER 5

The midday sun was glinting off the razor wire curled atop the detention center's surrounding fence as Ivy and Cesar trudged down a winding sidewalk toward the entrance. Ivy had visited the jail a handful of times, but going inside that massive human lockbox still filled her with a claustrophobic sense of anxiety and made her a little paranoid she might not be let back out.

Up ahead were two gray-haired men, obviously lawyers, lined outside the gate, waiting to be buzzed in. One was a heavyset man wearing a beige seersucker and wiping his brow with a monogrammed handkerchief. The other was tall and slender with thinning slicked-back hair. He was wearing a navy blazer with chinos and loafers minus socks. Each was flipping through a file like cramming for a test, probably trying to memorize the client's name and a few relevant facts before conducting a meeting that could fundamentally determine the rest of the detainee's life.

That lack of preparation, endemic in criminal defense, was something Ivy still had not gotten used to. She was a studier, a planner, and an organizer who loved nothing more than spreadsheets and label makers. Before conducting the initial interview, she'd prefer to spend a couple of days meticulously analyzing the case file that was currently tucked under Cesar's arm. But she could hear Lester in her mind: *How long does the client need to sit in jail, waiting for you to get comfortable?* Or he would lecture her about economic realities. Most clients didn't have much money, and nearly everything pled anyway, so volume and efficiency were the names of the game if you wanted to keep the lights on. "This is America, Ivy," Lester liked to say. "You get the justice you can pay for."

Sadly, Ivy knew he was right. Before falling out with her father, she'd spent two summers clerking at his megafirm housed in one of the class-A bank buildings that scraped the Raleigh sky. She'd seen firsthand that when rich people's money or egos were on the line, they got a team of lawyers who spent years preparing a case, conducting exhaustive discovery, excessively researching, briefing, and litigating the ever-loving shit out of every scrap of minutiae long before they ever got anywhere near a jury. But in the criminal world, where the defendant was always poor and usually Black or brown, the accused often met their attorneys for the first time right before the judge called their cases and, at least theoretically, might be asked to plead or defend themselves the same day. To Ivy, the high stakes of incarceration seemed inversely proportional to the quick-draw manner in which the cases were handled.

She and Cesar took their places in line, and Ivy tried to shake off the depressing feeling those thoughts always gave her. The two older attorneys each nodded hello, Seersucker holding his glance a little longer, like he thought Ivy looked as out of place as she felt. Then came a buzz and a grinding of gears while the chain-link gate retracted.

The visitors paced single file down another long sidewalk, through a second gate that had opened in unison with the first, and up to a steel door with a thin mail-slot-size Plexiglass window. A guard, a short Black woman, opened the door from the inside and welcomed them with a half-hearted wave.

Cesar nudged Ivy. "You have your ID?"

"Oh yeah." Ivy dug into her bag for her wallet.

"I'm going to need to look through that," the guard said, pointing haughtily at Ivy's leather satchel.

One of the older attorneys smirked. They each had entered with just folders and legal pads, no briefcases to search, and had their licenses out and ready.

"Of course," Ivy said. She handed the bag over to the guard, who rifled through it while Cesar took her ID to the front desk to sign them in.

The two older attorneys were escorted back to interview rooms while the bag inspection was completed.

"Okay, here you go." The guard handed the bag back and led Ivy and Cesar to a room that was roughly the size of a phone booth. Three of its walls were painted pea-soup green. The fourth was a half wall with a thick glass window connected by a shallow metal slot to allow for the passing of papers.

Ivy fidgeted while they waited. She took a deep breath to ready herself when she heard footsteps followed by a jingling of heavy keys and the clank of a thick metal lock. Any moment, she would lay eyes on Sonia Cabrerra, the woman accused of inflicting the most horrible examples of child abuse Ivy could ever imagine. She was expecting to see a vicious beast restrained by a straitjacket and an iron mask, too dangerous to be granted an inch of freedom. But instead, what tiptoed into view was a terrified-looking young woman, barely five feet tall, who weighed maybe a hundred pounds.

This is Sonia Cabrerra?

She was pretty. Sonia had long dark hair pulled back into a ponytail and a distinguishing mole on the corner of her chin. But her eyes were bloodshot, like she'd been crying nonstop for days, and glassed over with a thousand-yard stare. Ivy did the math and realized Sonia would have been at most fourteen years old when she became pregnant with Hugo. Then as Sonia took her seat, Ivy saw something that took her breath away. Beneath her loose-hanging orange prison scrubs, protruding like a ticking time bomb, was an unmistakable baby bump.

Oh God, Ivy thought. *Another child.*

She swallowed down that thought and introduced herself. "Hi, I'm Ivy Collins. I'm your attorney. How's your English?"

Sonia held her finger and thumb an inch apart. "Little," she said. "I try... to learn. In here, I try."

Six months in lockup was probably a pretty good intensive method for language education, but Ivy couldn't afford any miscommunications. "Cesar," she said, "why don't you take over?"

"*Hola,*" Cesar said. "*Me llamo Cesar. Esta es su abogada, Ivy Collins.*"

Sonia nodded but mostly avoided making eye contact with either of them, preferring to keep her head down.

"Okay," Cesar said to Ivy, "where do you want to start?"

Ivy cleared her throat and turned on her lawyer voice. "Tell her she is facing some very serious charges. Multiple counts of child abuse."

Cesar translated, and again, the girl nodded, still keeping her eyes down.

"You are charged with one felony count for burning your son with a metal grill and a second felony count for breaking his arm."

Ivy watched closely for Sonia's reaction as Cesar translated. She was hoping to see some type of outrage, an animated defense, or at least something in the way of an explanation. Almost any emotion would have been preferable to the way Sonia simply nodded as though resigned to her fate.

"Each of the felony counts carries an aggravated range as high as thirteen years," Ivy continued, "and it's possible the judge could decide to run them consecutively or box-car them back-to-back. That means if he really throws the book at you, the total sentence could be more than twenty years in prison."

Again, Cesar translated, and again, Sonia nodded like a zombie.

Okay, Ivy thought, *time to close the deal.* "Given the evidence the state has, we think your best option is to plead guilty and hope the judge gives you a lesser sentence."

Again, Sonia just nodded after Cesar spoke.

Just like Lester said: simple.

"Our hope would be that the judge might give you less than ten, but there's no guarantee," Ivy said, ad-libbing. "The only thing I can guarantee is that if you go to trial and get convicted, the judge will give you more time than if you admit you're guilty. Judges always make you pay a price if you go to trial."

Ivy delivered the line confidently despite never having tried a case.

"Is that what you want to do?" Ivy asked. "Do you want to plead guilty?"

Cesar translated, and Sonia nodded.

"*Si?*" Ivy asked.

"*Si,*" Sonia repeated in a meek, whispery voice.

Okay, then, Ivy thought, *I guess that does it.*

She was about to call it a day when something stopped her. "When is your baby due?" she asked. Ivy had no idea how prison pregnancies were handled but thought maybe there was some kind of accommodation she could arrange.

Cesar translated and engaged in a little bit of back and forth with Sonia before arriving at an answer. "September sixth," he said.

"Do you want me to contact the father?"

This question prompted an even longer back-and-forth. Ivy could tell that Cesar was getting frustrated. Finally, he said, "It sounds like the father is out of the picture."

"Well, whether they're still a couple or not, someone will need to take custody of the child once it is born. Does she have any idea how we can get in touch with him?"

Something about the question sparked what seemed like a five-minute Spanish-language conversation. Ivy knew translation could be as much of an art as a science and that Cesar sometimes had to go over things a few times before putting them into English, but she had never seen him have so much trouble before.

Finally, she interrupted. "What's going on?"

Cesar turned up his palms. "Her Spanish just isn't very good."

Ivy did a double take. "But she's from *Guatemala*."

"Yeah," Cesar said, "but apparently, she speaks one of their native dialects. I can just barely understand her."

"Like it's a different dialect of Spanish?" Ivy knew there were subtle differences in the way some words were pronounced or typical phrases were used, depending upon where a Spanish speaker came from. She thought maybe that was what Cesar was referring to.

"No, I mean she speaks a totally different language. What the Mayan people spoke before the Spanish came to Latin America. She speaks a little Spanish, too, which is how I'm able to talk to her, but it's really rough."

The hairs on Ivy's neck stood up. That revelation could potentially give her some leverage to wrangle a plea deal after all. "Did you see anything in the police report about translation issues?"

"Not a word," Cesar said.

"And it was clearly a Spanish translator they were using?"

"Yep. No question."

"Hmm." Ivy tucked a strand of hair behind her ear. "That's interesting, isn't it?"

"Sure is," Cesar said. "Could make some hay over the confession about the broken arm. Maybe get that thrown out. But it won't help us with Hugo's testimony or do anything to explain away those burns up and down his side."

"No," Ivy conceded, "but it at least gives me something to talk to Hatchet Lady about. Maybe I can get her to agree to a reduced sentence or at least get a commitment not to actively oppose a request for leniency."

"Good idea," Cesar said.

Ivy smiled, proud of herself. She kind of felt like a real lawyer for a second.

"What do you want to do now, boss?"

"Well, for one thing, I guess I'll have to find myself a new translator. No offense, but I can't plead her guilty unless I'm sure she understands what she's agreeing to."

"Yeah," Cesar said. "But first, we're going to have to figure out what language she speaks."

CHAPTER 6

The next morning, Ivy had managed to momentarily forget about Sonia Cabrerra. She was sitting in District Court on a DUI first appearance, and court, as usual, was chaotic. Defense attorneys, overbooked in multiple courtrooms and sometimes multiple counties, were dashing in to find their clients, grab the shuck—what the court called the envelope stuffed with citation copies—touch base with whatever prosecutor was rotating through, and try to capture the attention of the judge to either plead the case or get it continued. Ivy's goal that morning was just to get her client's court date pushed back so he could complete some alcohol classes and community service before entering a guilty plea, thus meriting a lighter sentence. It should have been an easy morning. A continuance request at a first setting was routinely granted, no questions asked. There was just one rule: The defendant had to be present in court.

And just as the judge was taking the bench, Ivy received a bullshit text from her client. *Not going to make it to ct. Couldn't get a ride.*

Ivy's stomach twisted into knots. She furiously typed out a response while the judge ordered everyone to be seated. *Where are you? I'll have Cesar come pick you up.*

No response came, no matter how hard Ivy stared at the three flashing dots that seemed to mock her.

Where r u? she texted again.

Finally, he texted, *I'm sick. Can't make it.*

Ivy rolled her eyes. She'd been a lawyer long enough to know that "sick" was code for drunk or stoned.

Just then, the judge called her client's name: "Marcus. Jonathan Marcus."

Ivy stood and cleared her throat. She flashed back to law school and being called on during one of the few times she was unprepared and having to try to fake her way through the prof's Socratic gauntlet.

"Your Honor, Ivy Collins. I represent Mr. Marcus. This is the first setting, Judge, and we just need to continue it. I don't want to take too much of the court's time, so if you could just give me the return date, I'll go ahead and get out of your hair."

Ivy clicked her pen and trained her attention on her legal pad, hoping the judge would simply rattle off a date and she could scribble it down and hightail it out of there. Not until the judge ahemmed did Ivy dare look up. She found the no-nonsense eyes of Judge Jackie Walker, a Black woman in her forties who didn't suffer fools.

"Where's your client, counsel?"

Ivy looked around as though she may have misplaced him somewhere. "I, uh...apologize, Your Honor, but my client just contacted me to let me know that he is very ill and unable to come to court. But I'm here, Judge, and if the court could just—"

"What hospital's he in?"

"Excuse me?"

"Hospital. If your client's too sick to show up to my court, then he must be in the hospital. If you'll let me know which one, I'll send flowers."

Ivy felt a stupid temptation to make something up, but lying to a judge was a cardinal sin that could land her in serious trouble. Her drunk client certainly wasn't worth that.

"I... can't... answer that, Judge."

"That's what I thought. Order for arrest." The judge signed an OFA that she slid across her desk to the clerk with the speed of a blackjack dealer. "We'll see how sick your client is when the deputy shows up. Now, do you have any other clients today, Ms. Collins?"

"No, Judge," Ivy said.

"You have a good day, then."

"You, too, Judge."

Ivy turned with her tail between her legs, ready to race out of there, when she spotted Cesar in the back, motioning for her to meet him outside the courtroom. She followed him into the hall and didn't even have a chance to ask what was going on before he blurted it out.

"It's called Mam."

"What?"

"Mam. That's the language Sonia Cabrerra speaks."

"Oh right. Great," Ivy said. "Never heard of it."

"Me, neither, but apparently, a lot of people in Guatemala still speak it. Some small diaspora communities are now in DC and out in California too."

"We should be able to find a translator, then."

"Already found one," Cesar said. "Lady's a grad student in DC and can translate by phone."

"Okay. I guess that could work."

Cesar had a gleam in his eye.

"Is there more?"

"Yeah, get this. According to the translator, an interesting thing about Mam is it doesn't use any personal pronouns. *Sooo...*" Cesar mimed a drum roll. "If you were to ask, 'Is that the hospital where *I* took my son when *I* broke his arm?' or 'Is that where *I* took him when *he* broke his arm?'..."

"It would translate the same way?"

"Exactly."

The hairs on the back of Ivy's neck stood up again. For a second, she thought that revelation meant her client could actually be innocent. But then she remembered that Sonia's apparent confession wasn't the most damning evidence against her. Hugo's testimony and medical records matched. And that was just the arm. Also, translation issues couldn't even begin to address the burns on Hugo's side.

Still, the potentially mistranslated confession was significant. Ivy high-fived Cesar. "Great work."

"Thanks, boss."

"Do you think you could line up that translator for this afternoon?" she asked.

"Afternoon? I was thinking we'd go talk to her now."

"Not yet," Ivy said. "If I talk to Sonia now and she admits to breaking her boy's arm, it will take the wind out of my sails. I want to try to catch Hatchet Lady while I have reason to believe there's been at least a partial miscarriage of justice."

"Hatchet Lady?" Cesar made the sign of the cross. "Good luck."

Ivy thanked him again and promised to touch base later. Then she took the elevator up to the tenth floor, where she found that Eliza Wells had already beaten the defense into submission in the trial that had begun the day before. When Ivy walked in, the jury had been dismissed, and it appeared that the defendant had decided to plead, because the judge was going through the allocution.

"Do you understand that by pleading guilty, you are giving up certain rights, including your right to trial by jury as well as the right to appeal?"

The defendant, a young Black man, nodded sullenly. "Yes."

"And have you had an opportunity to discuss this matter with your attorney?"

"Yes."

"And has he explained the charges and the potential consequences of pleading guilty to you?"

"Yes."

"And is it still your wish to plead guilty?"

"Yes."

"And are you in fact guilty?"

The defendant looked down at his attorney, a bearded white man at least six inches shorter than his very tall client, who nodded.

"Yes," the defendant said.

"Okay," the judge responded, satisfied. "Counsel, would you like to be heard?"

The defense attorney had the opportunity to tell the judge why the defendant should receive a modicum of mercy. Ivy had once imagined herself delivering impassioned jury arguments, but she was starting to fear that the little snippet of advocacy, laying out reasons for a lighter sentence, might be the most advanced form of lawyering she'd ever get to do.

The bearded defense attorney got right to the point. "Judge, my client has admitted his guilt in this matter, but there are several mitigating factors we ask you to consider."

What followed was a halfhearted recitation of the typical criminal biography: He came from a broken home, had an absent father and overworked single mom, fell in with the wrong crowd, and got addicted to drugs. When he hit the specifics of the crime, things got a little more interesting.

"Your Honor, Jamal has no history of violent crimes and had no intention of hurting anyone. But he was strung out on drugs when this crime happened. He and his friend Mr. Sinclair decided to try to rob the victim's convenience store to get money for more drugs. It was Mr. Sinclair who had the gun. Jamal has never fired a gun in his life, and his understanding, going into this robbery, was that the gun was not loaded. That's what Mr. Sinclair told him. Obviously, that proved not to be true, because the clerk, Mr. Kim, resisted the robbery, there was a struggle, and Mr. Kim was shot and killed. My client did not pull the trigger. Never held the gun. Now, I realize that under the felony murder rule and accomplice liability, that does not matter in terms of his guilt, but we ask you to take that into account when rendering your sentence. Jamal Rawlston is not a killer, Judge. He was a troubled, drug-addicted young man who was desperate, stupid, and reckless and took part in something he will regret for the rest of his life. And he is incredibly remorseful for what happened to Mr. Kim."

Huddled together in the front row were Mr. Kim's family members, their arms wrapped around one another in a group hug, all weeping loudly. Opposite them was the defendant's mother, who sat on her side of the courtroom completely alone, crying silently while trying to maintain a sense of dignity.

The judge thanked the defense attorney for his comments then rendered his sentence. The words "twenty to life" hit Ivy like a blacksmith's hammer.

"Your Honor," the defense attorney said, "could I make just one more request?"

"Go ahead."

"My client asks if he could give his mother a hug before he's taken away."

The judge looked at the deputy, who indicated that was not typically permitted.

"I'll allow it," the judge said.

Ivy felt the urge to cry, watching both the victim's weeping family and the recently convicted man, arms shackled, as he bent over so his devastated mother could hug his neck for possibly the last time. Ivy had expected an epic song of good and evil up on the tenth floor, but what she had observed thus far seemed more like a lament about poverty and addiction and the tragic consequences of bad decisions.

After the defendant was escorted out, court recessed. Most of the trial participants moved quickly for the elevators, but Eliza Wells took her time arranging her papers and trial exhibits. She had a junior ADA with her, a "second chair" attorney, who was doing most of the heavy lifting, stacking three banker boxes full of exhibits that he placed onto a rolling cart. Eliza followed him out, walking past Ivy, not noticing her.

"Excuse me, Ms. Wells?"

Eliza stopped. She looked down at Ivy with the same dismissive sneer as the day before. "Oh, yes, Ms..."

"Collins."

"Right. Ms. Collins. The Cabrerra case."

"That's right," Ivy said. "I was hoping I could discuss it with you again."

Eliza cracked a small smile. She seemed to actually be in a good mood or what passed as her version of a good mood. "Before this case pled, I was expecting to be in trial for the next couple of weeks," Eliza said, "so you've caught me at the right time. What can I do for you?"

Ivy tried to explain her recent revelation but was too excited, sputtering and stopping a few times before finally conveying the information about Sonia Cabrerra's native language, its lack of personal pronouns, and the possibility she may have been mistranslated when admitting to breaking her son's arm.

"I find that extremely hard to believe," Eliza said.

"It's true. Mam doesn't—"

"That part may be true, what you say about her native dialect, but the translator was very confident about what was said."

"In Spanish," Ivy argued. "I could tell you I was a duck in Spanish, but it doesn't make it true."

Another small smile came. Eliza was almost pleasant. The reaction encouraged Ivy.

"Why was she questioned in Spanish anyway? It's not her native language. That's got to be some kind of constitutional violation. I bet I can get it thrown out."

"Maybe," Eliza said breezily. "But even if you could, there's still the boy's testimony. And the medical records."

Damn. Eliza might have trouble recalling Ivy's name, but she had the facts of the case down cold.

"Tell you what, though. You get your client to plead guilty to both charges—the burning and the arm breaking—and I'll recommend that the sentences run concurrently."

Electricity ran up and down her spine. That huge concession could possibly cut Sonia's time in half.

"But," Eliza said, raising a finger, "no screwing around. I want an answer by Monday, or the deal's off. I don't know if you realize it or not, but before your office got the case, the public defender sat on it for months, so it's time to make something happen on this one. I'll go ahead and put it on the calendar for Monday morning. If your lady pleads, great. But if not, you'd better get ready for trial."

Astounding, Ivy thought. Prosecutors had so much discretion, so much power over crime and punishment. A decade or more of incarceration could be shaved off a sentence just by catching a prosecutor in the right mood. But Ivy had no time for ruminating on the system's ills. She needed to act—fast.

"No problem," Ivy said. "I'm planning to meet with my client this afternoon."

CHAPTER 7

"Great news," Ivy said as she slid her cell phone through the narrow slot in the Plexiglas window so Sonia could hear the translation over the speakerphone.

Mam was a plucky language, fast paced with lots of short vowel sounds. Sonia's eyes lit up as she heard the intonations of her native tongue. She and the interpreter engaged back and forth rapidly, like bursts of machine-gun fire, and suddenly, the scared young woman was laughing and covering her mouth like a schoolgirl who'd heard a dirty joke. But then something grim took hold of her. The smile vanished, and Sonia began to cry.

"What's going on?" Ivy asked.

The translator, a woman, said, "I think she's just overwhelmed. At first, she was happy to hear someone speaking in Mam. But now she's telling me she doesn't understand what is going on. She wants to know how much she has to pay."

"How much she has to pay?" Ivy asked.

"Right."

"I don't understand. I'm court-appointed. She doesn't have to pay me anything."

After another conversation, the translator asked, "So you work for the government?"

"No," Ivy said. "I get paid by the government because we insist that everyone gets a lawyer, whether they can pay or not. But I don't work for them. I work for Sonia. I'm on her side."

As that message was translated, Sonia looked at Ivy with an expression of extreme gratitude. She clasped her hands as though praying and bowed to her attorney. Ivy realized that during their initial meeting, Sonia hadn't even understood that she was her lawyer. She must have assumed Ivy was some kind of prosecutor or other government emissary.

"She still wants to know how much she has to pay to get out of here," the translator said. "And how much to get her boy back." The translator explained, "That's how it works where she's from. If you get in trouble with the police, it usually means they are just looking for a bribe."

"Tell her that is not the way things work here."

It chilled Ivy to think of how disorienting this whole experience must be for Sonia. Ivy would certainly be scared shitless if the situation were reversed and she found herself in some Guatemalan jail, unfamiliar with the system and unable to speak the language. But a little cynical voice inside her head—which sounded a lot like Lester—wondered if maybe Sonia was just feigning ignorance. Because of the severity of the abuse, maybe it was possible she didn't understand what was going on. Ivy decided to go over the charges again to be sure.

"Please tell her she has been charged with abusing her son. Very serious charges. Burning his side," Ivy said, gesturing to her flank, "and breaking his arm."

Ivy was ready to explain how the sentences for both charges could be run consecutively but how she'd scored an agreement to run them at the same time if accepted immediately. Before the translator was halfway through the charges, however, Sonia started defiantly shaking her head. Her emphatic "No!" didn't need a translation.

The previously demure Guatemalan woman was extremely vocal, rattling off a response so lengthy the translator had to interrupt her twice to catch up.

"Ms. Sonia says the charges are not true. Apparently, she left Hugo with her mother when she first came to America, and she says Hugo got those scars while she was here and Hugo was back in Guatemala. "

"Wait a second," Ivy said. "We just went over this the other day, and she said she wanted to plead."

The translator posed the question then explained, "Ms. Sonia says she had a hard time understanding the Spanish translator you brought with you before."

"Then why did she keep nodding along like she did?"

Sonia responded to the translated question with a shoulder shrug before saying something.

"She was just being polite," the translator explained. "It's a cultural thing. Nodding just means that she heard you, not necessarily that she agrees with or even understood what you said."

Jesus. That answer hit Ivy like a bucket of ice water. The lady had nearly nodded herself into a couple of decades behind bars. Suddenly, Ivy was filled with a sick feeling she didn't entirely understand.

Part of it was fear that her client was lying and might get so entrenched in her lie that she'd miss out on the plea deal. *What would Lester do in a situation like this?* Probably, he'd cross-examine his own client, call them out on their bullshit, and force them to face reality. That seemed like a good idea, so Ivy decided to probe.

"How did Hugo get those scars, then?" she asked.

The translation and response pinged back and forth.

"It was an accident," the translator said. "He leaned against a hot grill. Like for a fire pit. It was cooling against the wall, and Hugo got burned by it."

"When?"

This answer came less quickly. "A couple of years ago. Hugo was maybe five or six."

Five or six? She doesn't know? What kind of mother wouldn't remember something like that happening to her child? Ivy's mom could pretty much recite her daughter's exact age—in weeks—for all major life events and had photo albums to boot. But not all moms were like that. Plus, if Sonia wasn't living with Hugo at the time, she might not have found out about the event until much later—perhaps not until Hugo moved to the US.

"Can anyone back this up?" Ivy asked.

A long pause came after the translator posed the question. Part of Ivy was actually hoping there would be no corroborating witness because it would make her job easier. She'd seen Hugo's gut-wrenching account. She believed every word of it and knew the jury would too. Plus, he'd identified the offending skillet, the dimensions of which seemed to match his scars. If all Sonia had to combat that was her self-serving story about the scars coming from something else, then she was screwed, regardless of whether it was true or not. Pleading guilty would still be the only option.

"Well?" Ivy asked, emboldened by the silence.

Finally, Sonia answered.

"Her parents have passed away," the translator said. "But Ms. Sonia's sister still lives in Guatemala or maybe Mexico. She isn't sure."

"Did her sister witness the accident?" Ivy asked.

"Ms. Sonia doesn't think so. But she may have seen the scars and be able to say Hugo had them before he came to the US."

Able to say or willing to say? A jury would probably just assume the sister was covering for Sonia. But since she'd been identified as an exculpatory witness, Ivy was duty-bound to at least try to contact her.

"How can I get in touch with the sister?" she asked.

The translator and Sonia engaged in some more discussion before the translator said, "That's going to be a problem. They lost touch when Sonia came to the US. The last she knew, her sister was working at a coffee plantation near the border of Mexico, but she said the workers move around sometimes to different plantations."

"There's got to be a way to call her," Ivy said.

The translator ran that up the flagpole and came back with a negative response. "She says she doesn't know how."

Ivy was nearly ready to chalk the whole story up as a lie. She wanted to keep pushing to see if Sonia would go ahead and own up to it. "Please ask her about Hugo's broken arm. What does she have to say about that?"

The translator posed the question and relayed the answer. "Ms. Sonia says Hugo fell off the steps to her trailer. That's how he broke his arm."

"Did anyone else witness it?" Ivy would have bet good money at that point that the answer was no, and that would amount to another unverifiable defense, but the translator surprised her.

"Yes," she said. "Ms. Sonia's neighbor saw it. Her name is Claudia. She's the one who went to the hospital with them to translate for the doctors."

"Does she have a phone number for Claudia?"

"She doesn't know the number," the translator said, "not without her cell phone that was taken from her. But this Claudia lives in the trailer next to where Ms. Sonia was living. You could go and see her."

Yes, she would have to. Knowing what she knew or at least had been told, it would be malpractice not to. Ivy recognized the true nature of the extreme upset swirling in her stomach. Only part of it was fear of missing out on a great plea opportunity for a guilty client who refused to admit it. The other part—the really sickening, bone-chilling part—was the possibility, however slim, that Sonia might actually be telling the truth and the suffocating responsibility that would place upon Ivy.

She started to retrieve her phone, ready to call an end to the interview, but Sonia stopped her, placing her hand atop Ivy's. She said in English two of the heaviest words Ivy had ever heard: "Please help."

CHAPTER 8

Sonia Cabrerra lay on the thin jailhouse mattress, wondering if she'd ever get a good night's sleep in that place. Forty women were in one room, assigned to bunk beds like soldiers. All night long, there was noise—talking, laughing, threatening, crying. It never stopped. Nor did the security lights that continuously illuminated the room so the guards could keep watch.

On her first evening inside, Sonia had been forced by some hard stares and head-shaking attitude to take a top bunk despite her small stature and swelling belly. Since then, her English had gotten a little better but not good enough to make any real friends or negotiate a bottom bunk. Thus, she had to become an expert on how to roll from one side of the raised bed to the other without plummeting to the floor. She was miserable.

Years earlier, during her trek from Guatemala into Mexico, Sonia'd had to try to sleep on the rocky ground of the Sierra de los Cuchumatanes, where suffocatingly hot days turned into frigid nights amid swarming insects that feasted on her flesh. That had seemed miserable at the time, but at least then, she had been free. At least then, she'd had what to that point was the most precious commodity in her life: hope.

Sonia had worked hard to cultivate it almost out of nothing, like the tiny seeds that grew into lucrative coffee orchards in the fertile soils of her rain-drenched country. She had nurtured a vision of a future far away, in a place where she wouldn't have to navigate the endemic racism toward the Mayan people or the overwhelming poverty of a country ravaged by generations of civil war, corruption, and exploitation.

That hope had given Sonia the courage to accompany her older sister, Abi, to the coffee plantation on the western edge of Huehuetenango, a place she remembered warmly because they'd been good to her there, at least at first. The old man, the one they called Jefe, with his missing two front teeth making him look impish when he smiled, had offered her fair pay and an opportunity to attend the camp's open-air school to learn Spanish. Sonia had worked hard for Jefe and done well, often keeping up with the men who harvested the coffee cherries and got paid by the bushel. But Sonia had also followed Abi on her nighttime escapades, visiting the men in the barracks, and had acquiesced to them in the same way she saw her sister do. Sonia still shuddered at how disappointed, almost jealous, Jefe had seemed when she started to show and how he'd insisted she return home to have the baby.

Sonia had been so scared then, so afraid the hope she'd worked so hard to grow would die on the vine before it really had a chance to bloom. But after giving birth to Hugo, it only intensified. She had to have enough hope for him as well. So Sonia returned to the plantation, rejuvenated, more determined than ever to make her dreams a reality and earn the money she would need to send for her boy someday soon, to ensure he would have a better life.

Jefe, however, had not looked happy to see her. The climate was changing, he said. The seasons were getting shorter. Jefe had bosses to answer to, and they had bosses, and he was having to let many workers go. Then Sonia joined a group that was making the arduous journey through the mountains into Chiapas, where the Mexican plantations were still hiring.

There, she met Juan—sweet, sweet Juan. Sonia could see him vividly, how he looked on that first day, smiling at her through rivulets of sweat pouring down his face yet still offering her his canteen before taking a drink for himself.

"*Jeeka, ma tzuula.*"

The words from Juan's lips, in her own language, had sounded like music. His mother, Sonia learned, was Mayan too. She spoke a different dialect, but it was close enough that Sonia could understand it much better than Spanish. Separated from her family, she was elated to have someone she could finally truly talk to.

Life at that new plantation was hard, though. The conditions were much worse than what she had known in Guatemala. She and those she'd migrated with were paid less than the Mexican workers and lived under constant threat of arrest or deportation if they complained—Sonia's first taste of what it meant to be an "illegal" immigrant.

Things got even worse when the Central American caravans started making the news, garnering publicity that stirred local officials to crack down, to make some examples. She told Juan about her dream of going to America, and he made it possible. He knew the men who could get them there and would even help pay her way—if they could go together.

Sonia wasn't entirely sure what that would mean, but girls like her had never been in a position to say no to men, especially not one as sweet as Juan, who seemed to really care for her.

Once across the border, they made their way to North Carolina, where Juan had a cousin who could get him a job. They would never get married but more or less lived as husband and wife as they began to build a life. It was a poor life but American poor, which was a far cry better than anything she had ever known before.

They got a trailer in Garner. Juan worked as a day laborer, and Sonia made money cleaning houses. Both were paid in cash. Juan drank too much and could be a real slob, leaving mess after mess for her to clean up, but he was more or less faithful, and they had been happy.

Sonia focused on an image of Juan—his smile, his smell, the sound of his voice. She regretted so much how things had ended with him.

Juan had known the baby could not be his. The last time they spoke, he had looked at her the way Jefe had years ago, with disappointment, disdain, and disgust. Juan refused to visit her in jail, so she had no one she could talk to in her native language. Worse, she had no opportunity to explain.

She had made so many mistakes with Juan. Even before the pregnancy, things were already so tense between them—ever since Hugo had come to live with them.

Oh God, Hugo. With him, Sonia's regrets were almost too overwhelming to think about. She had worked so hard to make enough money to bring him to America. It had been her dream that quickly turned into a nightmare. The Hugo she'd left with her mother was a sweet, smiling baby. The Hugo she got back was an angry, willful child she didn't even know and couldn't handle. Juan refused to help, of course, since the boy wasn't his. So it had all fallen on Sonia to try to discipline Hugo the only way she knew how, the way she had been raised, when a whack with a broomstick was as common as a rainy day.

In some instances, she had gone too far. Sonia had lost her temper at times—dark, angry times.

Sonia tried to push those thoughts away, afraid that if she lingered on them any longer, they would seize hold of her heart and never let go.

Somewhere across the room, a woman cried out, having a nightmare or some kind of psychotic break. People yelled for her to "shut the fuck up." Women around the room hissed various threats back and forth. Sonia had learned enough English by that point to know that none of them were being directed at her. She was safe for the moment.

Sonia turned so that she was flat on her back. In her current condition, nothing felt comfortable. She worried it would be another sleepless night, one without hope. But then Sonia thought about her lawyer, the pretty blond woman in her fancy clothes. *Maybe she could really help.* She looked very young, but she also looked smart and determined, and when their hands had touched, Sonia could see in her eyes that the woman cared. She would at least try to help. Maybe not all was lost after all.

Just then, a flurry of tiny kicks caught Sonia from the inside, right below her ribs. It took her breath for a moment. But it also made her smile. There was still hope for that baby growing inside her. She hadn't given up on Hugo, of course, but Sonia couldn't help relishing the chance she would have with the new baby to do things better than she'd done before. She placed her hand on her stomach and waited anxiously for more flutters, but the baby seemed to have found a comfortable position and gone back to sleep.

Sonia decided to try to close her eyes as well. Although sleep, real restful sleep, had mostly eluded Sonia while in detention, she had a hopeful feeling that night might be different.

PART 2

CHAPTER 9

After everything that had happened with Sonia, Ivy found it impossible to sleep the night before. She'd gone rushing back to the office, hoping to share the news with Lester and Cesar, only to find that both had peaced out early for the day, and neither answered their phone when she tried to reach them. So with no one to download with, Ivy had found herself tossing and turning, playing through a million scenarios in her mind. Not until she was about to give up on Mr. Sandman entirely did he finally show up somewhere around four in the morning, which caused Ivy to sleep through her alarm.

Thus, by the time she finally woke, showered, dressed, and made it to the office, it was nearly ten o'clock. Ivy yawned as she gave Maria the finger on her way in and was headed toward Lester's office when the receptionist stopped her.

"Wait," Maria said. "Don't go back there."

Ivy was about to ask why when she heard Lester shouting from behind a closed door. "To hell with you, then, you stubborn son of a bitch!" Glass shattered. Then Lester bellowed, "Get the hell out!"

The door to the boss's office swung open, and Cesar came storming into view, sporting a badly blackened eye and busted lip.

"What the hell's going on?" Ivy asked.

Cesar pushed past her without answering and burst through the door, out into the parking lot.

Ivy looked at Maria.

"I don't know," she said. "They've been in there yelling at each other since I got here."

Lester emerged from his office long enough to shake his head in disgust then retreated and slammed the door behind him.

Flustered, Ivy finally gathered her wits enough to dash outside after Cesar. She found him sitting shotgun in a late-nineties-model red Toyota Corolla driven by a man she recognized as Cesar's cousin. They backed out of the parking lot at speed, Cesar avoiding Ivy's gaze as they drove past.

What in the world?

Ivy wanted answers. She marched back inside, once again making a beeline for Lester's office.

"I wouldn't do that if I were you," Maria said.

Ivy ignored her and opened Lester's door without knocking.

"Not now," he barked.

"Yes, now. I want to know what's going on."

Lester rolled his eyes. "Fine. You want to know?" He seized a wadded-up paper from the wastebasket, hastily smoothed it, and shoved it in Ivy's face.

She glanced down at it, her eyes widening as she realized it was a deportation notice.

"That's what's going on," Lester said. "Your dumbass buddy let his DACA expire and didn't bother to tell me, which means I've been employing him illegally for months. Then he gets the bright idea to go drive around drunk last night, gets popped for a DUI, and is now about to get deported. They had him in an ICE hold until I got him sprung this morning."

It took Ivy a moment to absorb this news. She'd known Cesar was a Dreamer—the term he used for recipients of DACA, Deferred Action for Childhood Arrivals—the generation of undocumented immigrants brought to the US as children, most of whom had little to no memory of their "home" country and in some cases didn't even speak the language. Whenever immigration got discussed by politicos, Dreamers were the one demographic everyone had some sympathy for, even the hardliners, but that had yet to result in any legislation to aid their precarious legal circumstances.

Lester seized the paper from Ivy and stared at it in disgust. "Shit. As much as the cops hate my ass, they'll probably have ICE down here any minute to shut me down."

Ivy highly doubted that. If Lester had employed Cesar illegally for a couple of months, it was an honest mistake. The most he'd get would be a fine. It didn't explain how furious he seemed over this revelation. Lester was far angrier than Ivy had ever seen him. In her mind, Cesar was the one they should be worrying about.

"This can't happen. Cesar can't get deported," Ivy said.

"It can, and he will."

Ivy racked her rudimentary understanding of immigration law for a solution. "What if I marry him?"

Lester's face morphed into a sinister grin.

"What?" Ivy asked.

"Let's just say you're not Cesar's type."

"What's that supposed to...?" Ivy paused. Then the pieces came together. "Wait. Are you saying Cesar's..."

"Gay? You think it was a girlfriend who busted his face up like that?"

That news shocked Ivy as much as the deportation notice. Not that she cared if Cesar was gay. It had just never occurred to her. She honestly thought there'd always been some sexual tension between them.

"Want to know the worst part?" Lester asked but didn't wait for a response. "All he would have to do is drop a dime on the son of a bitch who beat him up last night, and he could get a U-Visa."

Ivy didn't know what a U-Visa was. Her expression must have indicated as much, because Lester immediately explained.

"That's the visa for victims of certain qualifying crimes. The government wants people to cooperate with the cops, so if you do, you can get immigration status. One of the eligible crimes is domestic violence, which includes getting your ass beat by your live-in boyfriend." Lester shook his head. "I told him all he has to do is tell the cops what happened, and that deportation notice could stay in the trash where it belongs."

That sounded like a great opportunity. "You told Cesar that?" Ivy asked.

"Yes. What the hell do you think I was yelling at the stubborn son of a bitch about?" Lester pointed at the shattered remains of his glass desk lamp lying on the floor.

"What did he say?"

"Won't hear of it. Won't even consider it."

"Well, maybe I can talk some sense into him."

"Good luck. I've tried for years to get him to just marry his boyfriend, who's a citizen, and who I didn't know was an abusive piece of shit. But Cesar's family is Catholic AF. They all think he just has a roommate."

"There has to be something we can do," Ivy said.

"Not me. I'm done." Lester mimed washing his hands the way he often did when condemning a client to whatever fate the state had decreed.

Ivy hated when he did that. It was hard enough to take in those instances, but to see Lester treat Cesar with the same callousness was more than she could handle. She turned to leave.

"Where are you going?"

"To find Cesar," Ivy said. Then she let loose something she'd wanted to say for a long time. "At least I'm not too chickenshit to try."

Lester's face darkened and creased into an angry mask. "You've got no idea what you're talking about," he said, pointing a finger in her face. "And you watch your damn mouth unless you want to get fired."

Ivy didn't think before responding. "Fuck you, Lester."

CHAPTER 10

Adrenaline carried Ivy about half a mile down the road before a panicked sense of regret set in. She should never have talked to Lester that way. She might have just lost her job. And as she approached the intersection of South Saunders and the entrance ramps to I-40, not knowing whether to head downtown or venture east or west, she realized she also shouldn't have set out in search of Cesar without the slightest clue where to look.

How is this possible? Cesar was a friend, maybe the best friend she had at the moment. He was Ivy's "work husband." *How is it possible that I'm so self-centered I don't even know where he lives?*

His address was something she could find at the firm, but she couldn't go crawling back there. The only contact info she had was Cesar's cell phone number, which she called and texted repeatedly without response.

"Fuck." Ivy slapped the dashboard in frustration. A car behind her honked, rudely alerting her the stoplight had turned green.

Ivy stepped on the gas and went another quarter mile down South Saunders before pulling into a BP gas station to try to collect her thoughts.

Concern for Cesar had momentarily built a kind of protective shield around her brain, allowing her to ignore the rash career decision she'd just made, but the shell was beginning to crack, and practical concerns about what it would mean if Lester fired her started to seep through. Ivy had a few thousand dollars in savings, enough to get her through the next few weeks. But then the student loan bill would come due as well as the mortgage payment on the trendy inner-beltline townhouse her parents had helped her buy back when she'd assumed she'd be pulling down a big-firm salary. Since their falling out, Ivy's father had cut her off financially, which meant she would soon be wiped out if she didn't find a new source of income soon.

God, where would I even look for a job? She'd never go back to her dad's firm, and having the taint of a place like Lester "the Truth" Williams & Associates on her résumé would make her virtually unemployable at most civil law practices. Criminal law was too grimy for the blue bloods, who looked down on its practitioners as a less-intellectual, less-sophisticated underclass of attorneys—the working class of the legal world, who didn't belong among their high-brow big-money pursuits. Before she took the job with Lester, her law school adviser had warned Ivy that once you went into criminal defense, you were pretty much stuck there. And it was an industry populated mostly by lone wolves, solo practitioners who didn't hire all that often, so associate jobs were few and far between. *Will I have to set out on my own? Put up a stupid shingle somewhere and sling together a website in the hope that someone, anyone, would be foolish enough to hire me?*

"Fuck. Fuck. Fuck." Ivy slapped her dashboard in unison with each expletive.

She took a deep breath and tried to transform her panic into some righteous anger that she could misdirect onto Cesar, as though he were somehow at fault for her current predicament. She fired off an angry text: *I just told off Lester. The least you can do is answer the phone.*

Two seconds later, her cell rang. "What the hell did you do?"

"I may have just quit," Ivy said. "I'm not entirely sure. If not, I'll probably get fired. I said 'Fuck you' to Lester when he didn't want to help you out of this jam."

"Look, Ivy," Cesar said. "I created the mess I'm in. Not Lester. It's not his fault. Go back there now and fix things with him."

"No way. I can't take it there anymore. Lester doesn't give a shit about anybody. Not the clients. Not you. Sure as hell not me. All he cares about is money."

"There's a lot you don't know," Cesar said. "Lester's—"

"An asshole," Ivy said.

"Ivy…" Cesar gave a frustrated sigh.

"Where are you?" she demanded.

"On the way to my apartment. My cousin's going to help me get my things. Make sure it's safe."

"I'll meet you there," Ivy said. "What's the address?"

"No. That's not a good idea. If Isaac's there, things could get ugly."

Ivy assumed Isaac was Cesar's boyfriend. He dropped the name so casually it made Ivy wonder if Cesar had mentioned him before and she'd just had her head so far up her ass that she'd missed it.

"I want to help," she said.

"No, thanks. I don't want you there," Cesar said flatly.

Ivy wasn't about to give up. "Listen, I'm going to keep hounding you until you sit down with me and we figure out a way to deal with your situation. Lester showed me the Notice to Appear, and I'm telling you right now there is no way I am letting you get deported. So you can cooperate, and we can meet at a time and place of your choosing, or I'll just track you down and make a scene. You choose."

Cesar chuckled. It was the first time that morning he'd sounded a little like his typical jovial self. "Okay, boss. You win. How about we meet at Don Fernando's around noon. That should give me enough time to clear out my stuff."

Don Fernando's was a "real" Mexican restaurant where Cesar and Ivy had gone to lunch together several times. The first occasion was during her initial week at the firm, when Cesar had reacted with horror at her suggestion they get tacos from an Americanized place like Chuy's or On the Border.

"Okay," Ivy said. "Don Fernando's, it is. Just don't be late."

CHAPTER 11

Ivy was the first to arrive at the restaurant. She realized it was the first time she'd stepped foot inside Don Fernando's without Cesar there to translate. But after some awkward hand gestures and a few vaguely remembered phrases from high school Spanish, Ivy managed to get herself seated and served some chips and salsa.

"*Agua, por favor.*" That was one Spanish phrase Ivy was confident about, using it in response to the waitress's drinking gesture.

When the waitress left for the kitchen, Ivy pulled out a legal pad. She knew from experience it was best to wait on the water before trying the salsa. It wasn't overwhelmingly spicy, but Don Fernando's mixed in some kind of peppercorns or something that always choked her up. She passed the time by reviewing her notes from the research she'd done into immigration options over the last couple of hours since she and Cesar had spoken.

The first thing she'd discovered was that Lester was exactly right about U-Visas. It seemed like an excellent and straightforward way for Cesar to not only avoid deportation but also obtain permanent legal status. As a victim of domestic violence, all Cesar had to do was report the crime and cooperate with the authorities, and he could be home free. If the police or prosecutor would sign a certification of his cooperation, then he'd be eligible for a visa.

The other option, which Ivy had raised somewhat flippantly in Lester's office, was to marry a US citizen, but she had discovered that was not nearly as easy a path as she'd expected. Basing her prior understanding on pop culture, Ivy had mistakenly assumed that all she and Cesar would have to do was show up in front of a justice of the peace and say "I do," and the deportation stormtroopers would magically disappear. It worked that way in the movies, anyway, like a game of tag, where getting hitched in the nick of time was like touching home base before you became It.

But Ivy's research indicated Immigration officials were actually quite hip to and vigilant about sham marriages. As a result, they required a laborious application process with extensive documentation of the courtship and subsequent cohabitation—things like joint leases, deeds, car titles, utility bills, bank accounts, love letters, cutesy couple photos, wedding announcements, and supporting affidavits from friends and family who would vouch, under penalty of perjury, to the union's bona fides. USCIS, the United States Citizenship and Immigration Service, was also known to conduct separate interviews of the spouses, asking intimate details a real husband and wife would be expected to know and failing people if the answers didn't match up. Also, anyone who'd been married for less than two years at the time of their application could only be granted conditional approval and would have to go through the screening process all over again a couple of years later to prove the nuptials had been legit.

Thus, the shotgun wedding and quickie divorce Ivy had envisioned would never fly, a reality underscored by the fact that immigration fraud was apparently a very big deal. Getting caught could mean serious fines and up to five years in jail, not to mention the loss of Ivy's law license.

The waitress returned with a large red plastic cup of ice water and, after saying something Ivy didn't understand, took out a pad and pen, ready to take down her order.

"*Uno minuto, por favor,*" Ivy said in a way that sounded more like a question than a statement.

The waitress nodded and moved on to other tables. Ivy checked her watch. *Quarter past noon.* She was about to text Cesar when he entered through the swinging saloon-style doors, wearing big aviator sunglasses to conceal his black eye.

He spotted Ivy and took a seat across from her. He had an angry vibe about him, looking defiant behind his mirrored shades as he stuffed a tortilla chip into his mouth and crunched loudly. "Okay," he said, "I'm here. What do you want?"

Cesar reached for another chip, and Ivy seized his hand. "To help," she said.

He looked at the ceiling and breathed deeply. His shoulders sagged, and his voice softened. "I know," he said. "But really, it's not your problem." He pulled his hand away.

His standoffishness offended Ivy. It made her feel like maybe the "Hey, boss" routine had all been an act, a little show for the white girl, and that only now was she getting to see the real Cesar.

"It's nothing to be ashamed of," she said.

"I'm not ashamed. Who said I'm ashamed? Did Lester say—"

"No, no, not that. I mean... I don't care if you're..."

"Gay?"

"Right," Ivy said.

"Gay," Cesar said again. "See? It won't hurt you. I'm gay. There, I said it."

He folded his arms and looked away, giving Ivy the feeling she wasn't really the one he was responding to.

"Anyway, I was talking about the immigration stuff," Ivy said.

"Oh, well..." Cesar shifted in his seat. "*That*, I actually am a little ashamed of. Not that I'm a Dreamer, just that I let my DACA expire."

"Yeah." Ivy hadn't planned to bring it up, but since Cesar had mentioned it, she had to ask. "How did you let that happen? You work in a law firm, for God's sake."

Cesar sighed. "You know that saying, 'The cobbler's children have no shoes'? I guess I got so caught up trying to take care of other people's legal stuff that I forgot to take care of my own. Just totally missed the deadline to renew. Plus, the whole thing got so confusing. One president starts DACA, then the next president cancels it, then the courts say he can't cancel it, then another court says the whole thing was unconstitutional to begin with. I didn't even think you could renew, and by the time I realized you could, it was too late. So unless Congress finally does what it's been promising to do for over twenty years and passes immigration reform, then I'm fucked. I've got a while until my removal proceeding. When it gets here, I'll probably just take voluntary departure. I've got family in Guadalajara, so I guess I'll go live there. That's all there is to it."

"Maybe not," Ivy said. "I've been reading up on U-Visas, and…"

Cesar raised a hand to stop her. "Save it," he said. "I already told Lester I'm not going there. What happened last night between me and Isaac is our business, nobody else's."

"But if he attacked you, then—"

"How do you know I didn't attack him?"

"Cesar, look at your face." Ivy gestured to Cesar's swollen lip.

He pulled away, his ego as bruised as his body. "You haven't seen the other guy," he said. "Besides, it's not Isaac's fault I decided to drive after we'd both been drinking. I of all people should have known better."

Ivy sensed some self-flagellation going on. Cesar seemed intent on punishing himself. She needed to snap him out of that way of thinking quickly.

"So you're just going to let yourself get deported? Give up on the life you've built here?"

"See any other options?"

Ivy swallowed hard. If Cesar was adamantly opposed to pursuing a U-Visa, then the only other option was a green-card marriage, but since she knew how difficult that would be to pull off and how much trouble she'd be in if it was deemed fraudulent, she was reluctant to suggest the idea.

"Well?"

Ivy fumbled for words. She feared Cesar could tell what she was thinking, that she'd considered the marriage route but wasn't sure he was worth the risk.

The waitress broke the awkward silence when she returned to take their order, which was pastor tacos for Cesar and a chicken quesadilla for Ivy. After the waitress left, they avoided returning to the topic at hand by stuffing their mouths with chips. But with each moment that passed, each scoop of salsa and crispy bite of fried cornmeal, Ivy felt more and more guilty.

"What if we just get married?" she asked.

Cesar laughed so hard he spat a wad of half-chewed chips and salsa onto the table.

"Jeez," Ivy said, "is the idea of marrying me that bad?"

"No, no, of course not," Cesar said, wiping up the mess he'd made. "You're wonderful. You're beautiful. Stunning. And a lawyer to boot. Trust me. My mother would have been over the moon if I'd ever brought home a woman like you."

"So why not do it? We could basically just be roommates. Believe me, I could use one. My mortgage payment is outrageous."

"Yeah, but Immigration's not stupid," Cesar said. "I get married right after receiving a notice to appear, and they'll know it's a sham."

"Not necessarily," Ivy said. "It's not like we just met. We've known each other long enough to be a serious couple. If Immigration asks, we say we've been dating in secret because we worked together. And yeah, sure, the NTA may have prompted us to speed things up and get married a little sooner than we planned, but the relationship is legit."

Cesar waved her off.

"Think about it," Ivy said. "We could start planning it now—save the dates, invitations, one of those big registries. Tell everyone it's real. Look, my mom just wants to plan a wedding. She doesn't even care who it's to as long as she can help pick out the flowers and all that stuff. Then we just run out the clock. Live together for a few years, long enough to get through the conditional-status period. And once you're really in the clear with a permanent green card, we get divorced just like most married people do. It will take less time than going to college or a tour in the military."

Cesar laughed. "Would you want a prenup?"

Ivy hadn't considered that.

"Relax. I'm kidding," Cesar said. "We aren't getting married. You'd be taking way too big a risk. I couldn't let you do it."

"What's the risk? Really? Nobody can know what's in our hearts and minds but us. If we live together and we say it's real, then it's real. Shit, my parents barely speak to each other, and the law says they're married. I promise you we'll get along better than they do."

"You're crazy," Cesar said.

Ivy put her elbow on the table like an arm wrestler squaring off, and crooked her little finger at Cesar. "Come on. Pinky swear," she said. "Nobody else has to know. Just you and me."

Cesar smirked and took off his glasses. His right eye was nearly swollen shut, but she could still see the earnestness conveyed there as he took her hand and kissed it. "That's really, really nice. And any guy would be lucky to marry you. But I can't ask you to do that."

"You didn't ask. I offered."

"No, Ivy."

"Yes, Cesar."

He laughed and put his sunglasses back on. "God, you are persistent."

"I've been told that before."

The waitress returned with steaming-hot plates, the food having been prepared impossibly fast.

"*Gracias,*" Cesar said as she left them. Then he said to Ivy, "Tell you what. I'll think about it."

"There's really nothing to think about. If you just—"

"Easy. You just sprang this on me. Let me sit with the idea for a little bit."

"Okay. Fair enough."

She took a bite of a wedge of quesadilla, burning the roof of her mouth with bubbling white cheese.

Cesar said, "So, tell me what this big news is about Sonia. I saw your message from last night saying there was some huge development."

"Oh, right." Ivy had spent the morning so worried about Cesar she'd almost forgotten about her imprisoned client. She spent the next several minutes catching him up on everything she'd learned from her last jail visit with Sonia Cabrerra.

Cesar was so engaged that he didn't touch another bite of his food. When she finished, he said, "Guess we'd better go talk to this neighbor. See if she can alibi Sonia on the broken arm."

"Yeah. We can go from here if you're up for it."

Cesar turned up his palms. "I don't have a job," he said. "I've got nowhere I've got to be."

That was a good point but raised something Ivy hadn't considered. She wasn't sure if she still worked for Lester and was the one who'd technically been appointed to represent Sonia. Also, Ivy hadn't made any formal appearances in the case, so she wasn't really counsel of record. But those were mainly just logistics, things she could figure out later. Besides, even if she wasn't formally Sonia's attorney, that didn't prevent her from talking to witnesses.

As Ivy pondered the best procedural way to move forward, the waitress dropped off the check. She put it in front of Cesar, who slid it in Ivy's direction.

"Hey," he said, "if you want me to marry you, the least you can do is buy me lunch."

CHAPTER 12

After lunch, Cesar excused himself to make a call, stepping away in front of a Boost Mobile store where an orange mechanical blower powered a dancing balloon man. Ivy couldn't hear much of what he said but picked up enough to glean that Cesar's belongings were temporarily stored at his cousin's home and he was under pressure to find a new place to live as soon as possible. Then something seemed to catch Cesar's attention. He abruptly ended the call and pointed across the parking lot.

"What?" Ivy followed the invisible line from Cesar's finger to the shopping center's entrance, where a gray Oldsmobile sedan with dark-tinted windows was idling between the sidewalk and a silver taco truck.

"That car," Cesar said.

"What about it?" Nothing about the old beater seemed out of place to Ivy. The tint job was clearly illegal, but that was not unusual for the kinds of rides that frequented Plaza del Toro.

"I swear I saw that same car on the way over here."

"Oh yeah?" Ivy still didn't get the significance.

"Yeah, like it followed me from my apartment."

Finally, Ivy's curiosity was piqued. "You think maybe it's Isaac?"

"No," Cesar said. "Not his car. But maybe it's somebody he asked to follow me or something."

Ivy's stomach twisted. This kind of relational drama, with the potential for violence, wasn't something she was used to. Fights in her family never got more dramatic than the occasional raised voice and more typically involved giving one another the silent treatment. But Cesar was clearly navigating a very different reality. Ivy still didn't know exactly what had happened between him and his boyfriend or just how dangerous Isaac really was.

"I'm going over there," Cesar said.

"No, don't."

Ivy tried to grab Cesar by the arm, but he moved too decisively, briskly crossing the parking lot.

"Hey!" he shouted.

The car went into motion, reversing into a jerky three-point turn, and hauled ass back behind the shopping center.

"Get back here!" Cesar shouted as he ran after it.

"Shit." Ivy tried to follow, but with high heels, she wasn't able to keep up. Within seconds, Cesar was far ahead, curling behind the strip mall and out of sight.

Ivy kicked out of her shoes and scooped them up in one hand as she hopped barefoot across the hot asphalt. She ran fast enough to keep her feet from blistering and caught up to Cesar by a dumpster that reeked of garbage baking in the summer sun. The car was nowhere in sight.

"Did you get their license plate?"

"No," Cesar said. "They were moving too fast."

Ivy put her hand on Cesar's shoulder to steady herself as she wiggled her shoes back on. The soles of her feet were scorching hot. Sweat spread across her lower back, making her dress shirt stick to her skin.

"Is Isaac, like, in a gang or something?" she asked.

Cesar looked at her like that question was insultingly stupid. "No, of course not. He's a bank teller."

"Well, why do you think he has someone following you?"

Cesar shrugged. "Who else could it be?"

That was a good question. No other reasonable explanation came to mind. With how the car had responded when Cesar went to confront the occupants, it seemed obvious that whoever it was had been watching him. *If not Isaac, then who? A disgruntled client? Maybe*, Ivy thought, but because of the timing and that they'd followed Cesar from his apartment after he moved his things out, it sure sounded like a jealous-ex-boyfriend move.

"What happened last night anyway?" she asked. "You still haven't told me."

Cesar sighed. "Isaac and I went out, and I guess I was being kind of flirty, you know—with other guys. We'd been arguing, and honestly, I was kind of trying to make him jealous. Anyway, when we got home, we got into an argument, and it got physical." Cesar shrugged like that was no big deal. "It got out of hand, and I told Isaac that was it. We were done. And I left. It was like two in the morning at that point, and I guess I was speeding and got pulled over. If it wasn't for Lester working his magic and getting me released on bond this morning, I'd still be sitting there."

"Did Lester post your bond?" Ivy asked. The Truth was usually so tight whenever it came to expenses that she couldn't imagine him laying out what had to be at least a couple thousand dollars of his own money.

"Yeah," Cesar said. "And I promised I wouldn't skip out on him. He was thinking the NTA was just pro forma at first, that there was no way they'd deport a DACA kid over a first offense, and we could get cancellation of removal. By the time we got back to the office, he was ready to call up an immigration attorney he knows. That's when I had to come clean and tell him I'd messed up and let my DACA expire. Wasn't long after that when you showed up."

"I kind of wish I'd known all that before I called him a chickenshit," Ivy said.

"You called Lester a chickenshit?"

Ivy nodded sheepishly. "Yeah. Then I said 'Fuck you' to him on the way out the door."

Cesar made a face like he'd just bitten into a lemon. "Well, hey, I'm sure we can smooth things over. Why don't we just go talk to him? He can't legally employ me, but there's no reason for you to lose your job over this."

"I don't know," Ivy said.

"Come on. He'll want to hear all about the stuff with Sonia."

"You really think he'll care?"

"Of course. You've got Lester all wrong. It's not that he doesn't care. He just cares too much and gets all burned out. Then he has to pull away for a while. Put up barriers, you know, like a defense mechanism."

Ivy rolled her eyes. She didn't buy that for a second.

"I'm serious," Cesar said. "You don't know Lester like I do."

"Well, you're going to need to enlighten me, because I've never met the person you're describing."

Cesar looked down and scratched at the top of his head like he was deciding whether or not to share something. "Yeah. I guess we never finished talking about Lester's history the other day, did we?"

"No. You had just started telling me how he used to be a real trial lawyer."

"One of the best."

"So what happened?"

Perhaps out of reflex or just some nervous tic, Cesar looked around for eavesdroppers, which seemed absurd, since they were hanging out by a dumpster in back of a shopping center.

"Okay. I don't really like talking about it, but there was this case that Lester had years ago. And this is going to sound familiar, so don't say anything, all right? Because believe me—I am very aware of the parallels and don't want to hear anything about it."

"What do you mean?"

"I mean it was a DUI case involving an immigrant."

"Oh."

"Yeah, *oh*," Cesar said. "Only this lady wasn't a first-time offender. She was charged with her fourth DUI in ten years. And they had her dead to rights. She openly admitted to the cops who pulled her over that she was drunk and willingly submitted to a breathalyzer, blowing something like a .20. So she got charged with habitual DUI and was facing serious jail time."

"What happened?"

"Well, it seemed like an unwinnable case. So the lady went to Lester, who had a reputation at that time for being able to win unwinnable cases. And once he dug into it, he determined that the lady actually had a pretty decent necessity defense."

Ivy was immediately cynical. Necessity defenses were essentially the stuff of fiction, something you learned about briefly in law school then never used.

"How could it be necessary that she drive drunk?"

"Because she really didn't want to. She'd been home all evening with no plans to leave when she and her boyfriend got into a fight."

"This *is* starting to sound familiar."

"I told you not to say anything."

"Sorry."

Cesar sighed. Telling the story seemed to really pain him. "This situation was actually different from mine because this lady's boyfriend was a for-real bad hombre who pulled a gun and threatened to kill her."

"So she *said*," Ivy interjected.

"Her kid was there and saw it," Cesar shot back. "The boyfriend chased her outside and even shot at her. She drove drunk to keep from getting killed."

"Did she drive to the police station?" Ivy asked.

"No. The guy got in his car and followed her. She was trying to lose him when she got pulled over. That's why she was so cooperative with the police. She wanted to get arrested. Thought that was the only way she'd be safe."

"Why didn't she just tell the cops what happened?"

Cesar shrugged. "She was scared. Afraid he'd hurt her kid if she turned him in."

Ivy was having a hard time believing that. If she'd been in that situation, the first thing she would have done was tell the cops what happened. But she reminded herself that her experience with and view of the police were very different from that of most of her clients. Police existed to protect people like Ivy. Still, the necessity defense was a stretch, even on those facts. It only excused criminal behavior for as long as it was truly necessary. Maybe you could drive around the block to escape a gun-toting boyfriend, but you couldn't joyride all around the city.

"Did she have a cell phone with her?" Ivy asked. "She could have called 911 while she was driving to safety."

"I told you she was scared to report this guy."

"Riiight."

"Look, do you want to play prosecutor or hear the story?"

"Sorry," Ivy said. "Can't help playing devil's advocate. Force of habit. Please continue."

"Thank you. So anyway, Lester works up the case and gets it ready for trial. Even has an expert to talk about all the trauma the lady had experienced, a long history of abuse from multiple men going back to her childhood, and how that plus the intoxication affected her decision-making. Oh, and Lester got an advance ruling that the prosecutor couldn't tell the jury anything about her prior DUIs."

"That's big."

"It was," Cesar agreed. "The ADA must have thought so, too, because they offered Lester an awesome deal."

"On a DUI? They're usually tough as hell on those, especially on a habitual."

"They weren't just rolling over," Cesar said. "They still insisted the lady serve a year of active time, but they came up with a plan. Instead of a guilty plea where she would go to prison then get deported, they proposed she come off bond and go back to jail voluntarily prior to trial. Then they would just keep continuing the case until she accrued a year of credit. After that, they would pick a favorable judge to plead her guilty in front of and agree to a sentence of time already served."

"What was the point?" Ivy asked. "She'd still get a year."

"Yeah, but it would be in the county jail, which is a whole hell of a lot nicer than prison. Plus, the prisons cooperate with ICE. The jail, at least at that time, didn't."

"Ah, I see," Ivy said. "So the lady would serve a year, but she wouldn't get deported."

"Exactly."

Jeez, that was a good deal. DUIs were one area where the prosecutors typically had very little discretion to plea bargain because there was such a strong public policy at play.

"I'd take that deal in a heartbeat," Ivy said.

"She should have. But Lester told her not to."

"Seriously?" Ivy couldn't imagine the Lester she knew ever in a million years passing up an offer like that.

"Yeah," Cesar said. "Lester was convinced they could win. He got cocky."

"What happened?"

"What do you think? She got convicted. Judge gave her four years."

Ivy shook her head. As much as she'd grown to dislike plea bargaining, she couldn't imagine rolling the dice on a trial with that kind of offer in hand.

"Did she get deported?"

"No," Cesar said grimly. "She died in prison. There was some kind of riot, and she had a stroke."

"Oh man. Lester must have been devastated."

"He was. It truly wrecked him. Before she went in, Lester begged the lady for forgiveness, swore to her he'd do whatever he could to make it right."

"Wow," Ivy said. "How do you even begin to make up for something like that?"

Cesar sniffed like he was suddenly fighting back tears. "It's not easy. But for starters, Lester gave her son a job."

CHAPTER 13

It took Ivy a moment to process what Cesar just said. "Wait. You mean...?"

"That's right." Cesar wiped his eyes. "Like mother, like son, right? I told you there were parallels."

Ivy enveloped him in a bear hug. One second, her heart was breaking for Cesar. The next, she was floored by the irony... or stupidity... that had landed him in the same position as his mother.

She pulled free and slapped his shoulder. "How could you let this happen?"

"I know. I know," he said. "Believe me. I know."

"After everything your family has been through, to—"

"Stop. I get it."

Ivy tried to steer her emotions back toward sympathy. "I really am just so sorry about your mom, though."

"Thank you. She had a hard life. There were reasons she drank like she did."

Ivy wiped perspiration from her forehead. She felt dizzy, reeling from the revelation about Cesar while standing in sweltering heat amid the oppressive odor of the nearby dumpster. "I think I need to sit down."

"Come on," Cesar said. "Let's get out of here."

They walked back around to the front of the shopping center and got into Ivy's car, where she cranked up the air conditioning.

"So, what do you say, boss? How about we head to the office and get your job back?"

Ivy puffed her cheeks and blew out a long, slow breath, not sure what she wanted to do. She might well have misjudged Lester. He obviously had some method—or at least some memories—behind his madness when it came to plea bargaining cases. And she did want to get her job back. The prospects of unemployment were still settling in but were already pretty terrifying. Ivy wasn't sure she could face "the Truth," though, so soon after cursing at him and storming out the way she had.

"Let's stick to the plan and go talk to this witness," she said.

"Don't you think that can wait?"

"No. Sonia's sitting in jail. She needs her lawyer to be on top of this."

"Yeah, but even if this witness checks out, it's not like you're getting Sonia out of jail anytime soon."

"Maybe not. But if Claudia can verify that little Hugo broke his arm in an accident, she might also be able to confirm that he already had those scars when he got here from Guatemala. And if that's the case, when I do go back to see Lester, I won't just be going hat in hand. I'll be bringing him something I know he's got to be dying for, though it may be buried way down deep."

"What's that?" Cesar asked.

"Another chance to win an unwinnable case."

Cesar stared at Ivy for a moment, not saying anything. She thought maybe she'd offended him. But then he said, "You're right. Let's go see this lady. Where does she live?"

"Good question." Ivy didn't know. Fortunately, she'd taken the Sonia Cabrerra file home with her the night before and still had it on her. She pulled it from her bag and started flipping for the police report. "Huh," she said when she found the location.

"What?" Cesar asked.

"It says Sonia lives in a trailer park in Cary."

"So?"

Cary was an affluent suburb of Raleigh that some said stood for the Concentrated Area of Relocated Yankees. It was largely populated by well-to-do folks from the Northeast who moved far enough South to escape the winters without getting all the way into the really backward parts of old Dixie. Cary consisted mostly of pristine neighborhoods full of cookie-cutter McMansions.

"I'm just surprised Cary has any trailer parks," Ivy said.

"Where do you think the people who build and clean all those big houses live?"

"Guess I never thought about it."

"Then this should be educational," Cesar said. "Let's cruise on over there."

They left the Plaza del Toro and took I-40 west for a few exits, got off on Gorman Street, and followed the GPS through a couple of turns before pulling onto a gravel road that was concealed by a dense thicket of pine trees. The unpaved street was pocked with deep, muddy, water-filled holes, and the trailers were all in disrepair—old models with discolored siding. Several had broken windows patched by trash bags and duct tape.

Sonia's trailer sat near the back, the last in a row, making it easy to determine which mobile home belonged to her former next-door neighbor. Ivy parked by a satellite dish that was propped against a cinder block and connected to the trailer by a long black cord. They got out and followed the cord onto a rickety wooden front porch where the screen door barely hung on its hinges. Ivy knocked, prompting the yap of a small dog inside.

A tiny boy of no more than three or four, wearing a pair of Superman Underoos, answered. He had thick, wavy dark hair and was holding a squirming Chihuahua with both arms, like he was hugging a teddy bear.

"*Hola,*" Cesar said. "*Está tu madre en la casa?*"

The boy didn't seem the least bit alarmed to see two strangers at the door. He nodded and carried the dog toward the kitchen, yelling for his *mamá.*

A heavyset woman in a loose-fitting V-neck T-shirt and elastic-waisted blue jeans came around a corner, slapping baking flour off her thighs.

Cesar made some introductions in Spanish. Ivy heard him drop Sonia's name and picked out the word *abogado* but didn't understand much else.

"Okay," Cesar said, turning back to Ivy. "She says she'll answer our questions."

The woman kept her eyes on Cesar. Despite saying she was ready to respond, she had a closed-off posture—folded arms—and made no move to invite them into the living room.

"Tell her Sonia has been accused of breaking her son's arm, but she says her son broke it by accident when he fell off the porch last Christmas and that Ms. Claudia here witnessed it."

Cesar went back and forth with Claudia in Spanish. "Yes," he said. "She remembers. She said she took them to the hospital."

Ivy's pulse quickened. If the witness could alibi Sonia on the broken arm, that would be huge.

"Did she actually see Hugo fall?"

Cesar asked the question. Ivy's heartbeat ratcheted up another notch when she saw the woman nod. *Holy shit,* she thought. *This is some* Law & Order *stuff here.* Ivy was actually out in the field, beating the bushes, finding witnesses, and cracking the case. *But what now?* "We need to record her testimony," Ivy announced, answering her internal question.

Cesar pulled out his phone.

"No," Ivy said. "We'll need an affidavit. Something under oath."

Fortunately, Lester had required Ivy to become a notary public for the convenience of being able to authenticate official documents in just such situations. She often notarized papers right before going into court and consequently kept her notary stamp in her work bag. She took it out along with a legal pad, thinking the affidavit would be more convincing if it was written in Claudia's own hand rather than being the kind of typed version lawyers often got people to sign that were clearly prepared by an attorney. Claudia could just put down what she saw, then Cesar could do a certified translation.

"First, let's make sure we can include some details," Ivy said. "Do you remember when this happened?"

Cesar translated the question, then the answer came. "Christmastime."

"Great. What time of day was it?"

"Evening. She says it was 'dark-like' but not totally dark."

Ivy tried to think of some other questions to tease out the details. "Did he fall off the front porch or the back porch?"

Cesar asked the question then gave Ivy a troubling answer. "She's not sure."

"How can that be?" Ivy blurted.

Cesar shrugged. "That's what she said." Claudia glanced back behind her and said something in Spanish. "She says she has to get back to cooking."

"Wait," Ivy pleaded. "Just a few more questions."

Her mind raced for ways to craft a slam-dunk affidavit that could hold up on some future cross-examination. She needed to know exactly where Claudia was standing in relation to Hugo as well as the lighting, the weather, her level of sobriety, and anything else that could have affected her ability to accurately see what happened.

"Where exactly was she when Hugo fell?"

Cesar delivered the question and came back with another troubling answer: "In her kitchen."

Ivy's insides tightened. "Did she see it through the window?" she asked hopefully.

While Cesar worked to get an answer, Ivy considered the implications. If Claudia saw the fall from her own trailer, that would not only put her a significant distance away, but it would also strain credulity, requiring the jury to believe she just so happened to be looking out her window at the precise moment Hugo tumbled off the porch and broke his arm.

Cesar said, "Now she's telling me she didn't actually see it. But Ms. Sonia told her that's what happened."

All the hope and adrenaline instantly left Ivy's body. She motioned for Cesar to come closer so she could whisper. "Is she full of it?"

"I don't think so," Cesar whispered back. "I think she believes he fell. She just wasn't actually there when it happened."

And thus she is absolutely worthless as a witness, Ivy thought.

Cesar pointed at the legal pad. "Do you still want her to sign something?"

"I don't know. I don't think so. Not yet anyway. Ask her..." Ivy paused, trying to think of any other useful information Claudia could have. "Ask her if she ever saw Sonia hit or abuse Hugo."

Cesar asked, and Claudia told them she had not.

Well, that's something.

After another follow-up question, Claudia informed them she didn't know anything about Hugo being burned, either in the United States or in Guatemala. She had never seen his scars.

Things were not turning out the way Ivy had hoped. Not sure what else to do at that point, she asked Cesar to thank the woman and get her phone number in case they thought of more questions later. He did so then told Claudia they would be in touch.

Ivy and Cesar were about to leave, defeated, when the woman called after them.

"What?" Ivy asked.

After a brief exchange, Cesar said, "She wants to know if we want to see Ms. Sonia's trailer. She still has a key."

CHAPTER 14

Ivy and Cesar tiptoed into the trailer. Claudia had assured them that Sonia's boyfriend, Juan, had not been back for some time, yet the place still felt very much lived in. It was cluttered almost to hoarder status. Crates were filled with cans of Spanish-branded foods, like maybe they'd been boosted off the back of a truck. Piles of clothes, papers, a few toys, and a mound of scrunched, mostly empty Modelo cans littered the floor. On the coffee table was an overturned pint of Jose Cuervo next to a congealed yellow pool of tequila. The whole place smelled like stale beer, and the level of filth was appalling—enough by itself to justify a child abuse charge, to Ivy's mind. But then something occurred to her.

"Hugo said his mother sometimes hit him with a broom."

Cesar looked at her quizzically. "So?"

"So does the place look like Sonia owned... much less ever used... a broom?"

Cesar took another glance around. "Good point. Maybe we should take some pictures."

Both went for their smartphones and started snapping stills. Then Ivy recorded a video, introducing herself and stating the date, time, and location, and took an imaginary audience on a tour of the trailer. The first stop was the kitchen, where the brutal attack had reportedly taken place. Its counters were cluttered, the floor grimy and narrow, but nothing seemed to disprove little Hugo's version of events. Ivy didn't bother looking for the offending grill pan, knowing that the police had already booked it into evidence.

"Let's check out Hugo's bedroom," Cesar said.

Ivy followed him into a small room that was equally filthy though considerably less cluttered. The only furniture was a rusty filing cabinet being used as a wardrobe and a stained, sheetless mattress lying on the floor in the middle of the room. Next to it, three sets of little shoes were lined up in pairs.

Ivy stopped the recording. "This is awful," she said.

"It's not a crime to be poor," Cesar reminded her.

He was right, but Ivy couldn't hold back her judgment. Everything about the trailer screamed to her that Sonia Cabrerra had no business raising a child. And she had another one on the way.

"One bedroom to go," Cesar said. "Might as well see the rest."

He led the way back through the kitchen area and passed a dining room table covered with piles of papers, a mismatched ratchet set, and some random junk. He opened the door to the main bedroom, took one step inside, then jumped back like he'd seen a rattlesnake.

"What?"

Cesar put his finger to his mouth. "Shh." He pointed inside.

Ivy peered around him. Her heart nearly leaped out of her chest when she saw it—the body of a man, naked except for a snug pair of tighty-whities, sprawled across the bed.

"Is he dead?" she whispered.

"I think he's sleeping," Cesar said, although it was the middle of the day. He called out to the man. "*Hola, señor.*"

No movement or response came.

"I really think he's dead," Ivy whispered.

Cesar moved in for a closer inspection.

"Don't touch him."

Cesar waved Ivy off as he bent down near the man's face then recoiled from the smell.

"I told you he was dead."

"Dead drunk," Cesar said. "I can hear him breathing, but he fucking reeks of alcohol."

Ivy assumed he must be Juan. Sonia had said he was out of the picture, so she hadn't focused on him as a potential witness. But his presence could potentially change everything. He might be able to alibi Sonia in the way she'd hoped Claudia could.

"I think we should get out of here," Cesar said.

"We'll need to talk to him," Ivy responded. "He's a key witness."

Cesar pointed at the leather satchel slung around Ivy's shoulder. "Give me a business card and a pen."

She handed Cesar what he'd asked for. He scribbled something in Spanish on the business card and slipped it onto the bed, almost under the man's nose.

Ivy's heart pounded from the shock of discovering Juan there, but she also felt buoyed by the fact that he was still around. If he was living there secretly, perhaps the filthy environment wasn't Sonia's doing at all. If nothing else, the empty beer cans and liquor bottle seemed likely to be Juan's.

"Come on," Cesar said, trying to steer Ivy out of the room. "If he doesn't call, we can come back when he's awake."

Ivy took a step back before being seized by another thought. The passed-out man might be more than an alibi witness, one a jury could dismiss as a self-interested liar. He could be something much, much better: a scapegoat.

If a jury ever heard little Hugo's testimony and saw those scars, they would want somebody to pay dearly for what he'd been through. Eliza Wells would have them ready to put Sonia's head on a stick unless Ivy could offer them an alternative culprit, maybe someone Hugo was too scared of to report—someone Sonia was too scared of to report. Perhaps the jury could be led to believe that the man might be the real abuser and Hugo had accused Sonia out of a mixture of fear of Juan and anger over his mother's failure to protect him from her heavy-drinking boyfriend with the barbed-wire tattoos around his sizable biceps.

All of that was utter make-believe. But if Sonia was potentially innocent and just lacked the evidence to prove it, Ivy wasn't above trying to sell the jury a line of crap in order to achieve justice. *The ends justify the means, right?* Even if Juan never came to court, she could accuse his empty chair and offer him up to the jury as a sacrifice, a boogeyman who would much better fit their preconceived notion of what an abuser should look like.

Ivy stopped backpedaling out of the room and pulled out her phone.

"What are you doing?" Cesar asked.

Ivy smiled at him and said, "Taking a picture of reasonable doubt."

CHAPTER 15

Ivy cleared her throat and tried to speak slowly and calmly in what she hoped was an earnest-sounding voice. "Lester, I'm sorry. I apologize. I should never have disrespected you like that. And it's not how I feel. I absolutely respect you. I respect the job you do for people. The way you—"

"Don't lay it on too thick," Cesar said. "Lester's bullshit detector is hair triggered."

"Fuuuck." Ivy slumped back into the driver's seat. She and Cesar had been parked outside the office for the last ten minutes, trying to rehearse her apology, but nothing sounded right.

"Look," Cesar said, "just tell him you're sorry then quickly transition into talking about the case. See if you can get him interested."

"Like he's just gonna forget what I said to him this morning?"

"Maybe. Get him talking about the next steps with Sonia. Just kind of assume you still have your job. If Lester doesn't say anything different, then go back tomorrow morning like nothing ever happened."

Ivy couldn't imagine that working. "Can't I just tell him that I know what happened with your mom's case and I get it now? That I understand why he wants to plead everything and how I was totally wrong about him?"

"No way. That will just get Lester upset. He'll think you're trying to manipulate him. Make him feel guilty."

"What's wrong with that?"

"Lester sees all the angles," Cesar said. "If he thinks you're trying to take advantage of him, he can get real nasty real quick."

"Okay, okay. No guilt."

"You can do this."

"Right. I can do this." Ivy repeated it several times like a mantra but believed it less with each successive utterance.

Cesar got out of the car and prodded her to do so as well. "Let's go."

Ivy stalled a moment longer to check her reflection in the rearview mirror and practice her sad face.

"You're beautiful," Cesar said. "Now come on."

Ivy took a deep breath. She got out and followed Cesar inside the offices of Lester "the Truth" Williams & Associates, hoping she could once again singularly embody the latter term. But her hopes for reinstatement were quickly dashed.

"Lester's not here," Maria said, filing her lengthy nails and looking smug behind the reception desk.

"Where'd he go?" Ivy asked.

Maria shrugged. "Beats me. Left right after you did this morning. I had to cancel like six appointments."

Ivy and Cesar stared at each other. Appointments, for Lester, meant money. He must really be upset.

"Maybe you should call him," Ivy said to Cesar.

He shook his head. "He told me to get the hell out. You call him."

"I'm not calling him."

"You're the one who needs to apologize."

"In person. I'm not doing it over the phone. How tacky is that?"

"Why do you need to apologize?" Maria asked, likely knowing the answer but delighting in Ivy's predicament nonetheless.

"Don't worry about it," Ivy said.

Cesar paced the lobby. "What are we gonna do? Lester's obviously not coming back today."

"Guess we'll try again tomorrow."

Cesar looked extremely put out.

"What's the problem?" Ivy asked.

He shoved his hands into his pockets and shifted his weight back and forth from one foot to the other. "I just thought if you apologized to Lester, maybe I could clear the air with him too. I know he can't give me my job back, but I was thinking he might be able to put me up for a little while. I've stayed with him before when I was between places. He's got a big old Victorian house in Durham with lots of rooms, and my cousin's place is busting at the seams, with a wife and four kids squeezed into a two-bedroom apartment."

That problem seemed easy to fix. "Just come stay with me," Ivy said. "I already told you you're welcome."

"Seriously?" Cesar asked.

"Absolutely."

Cesar thanked her profusely.

As they made their exit, Maria called after them, "Don't worry about me. I'll just be here manning the fort. Alone."

Ivy and Cesar spent the next several hours making multiple trips to transport all of his stuff from his cousin's apartment back to her townhouse. By the time they had him set up in the spare bedroom, they were both exhausted and starving. Ivy ordered a pizza, and they lounged on the couch, flipping through cable news shows while they waited for it to be delivered.

She already liked having Cesar at her place. Though there might not have been any romantic prospects for the two of them, something about him just felt like home, like she'd known him much longer than she had. Ivy smiled, looking over at her new roommate, who had drifted off to sleep.

He must be exhausted. Probably didn't sleep at all last night. Ivy was glad Cesar was comfortable enough to finally let his guard down and catch some shut-eye.

Just then, the doorbell rang. Cesar jumped.

"It's okay," she said. "You rest. I'll get it."

Ivy grabbed her purse from a side table in the foyer and was rummaging through it for her wallet as she answered the door. That was why she didn't see the gun at first. But she certainly felt the cold steel when the barrel was pressed to her forehead.

On the other end of the pistol was a man wearing a ski mask and dark clothes.

"Inside!" he commanded. "Now!"

Ivy stumbled backward, too startled to scream. The man was right on top of her, keeping the gun pressed against her head, driving her back, back, back. A second man dressed in similarly dark clothes and a ski mask entered as well. He closed and locked the door with a sickeningly loud click of the deadbolt.

The first man grabbed Ivy by the shoulder. He spun her around, ripped the purse off her shoulder, and shoved her in the middle of her back with enough force that it caused her to fall onto her knees. Then he seized her by the collar, scooped her up, and more or less dragged her into the living room. In the meantime, the second man had bolted past them with both arms extended, pointing his gun, yelling, "Down on the ground, motherfucker! Move!"

Cesar was already face down on the living room floor by the time Ivy was marched into the room. Another shove, and she was right there beside him, her face buried in the carpet.

"Keep your fucking head down!" the first man shouted. "Don't look at me."

Seconds felt like hours. Ivy closed her eyes as tightly as possible, her breathing loud and labored, as one of the men hovered over them, standing watch and alternately pressing the gun against the backs of their heads while the other crashed about the house.

CHAPTER 16

Not until long after Ivy had heard the sound of the front door slamming, followed by the squealing tires outside, did either she or Cesar dare look up. Eventually, however, they ascertained that it was truly over. The place was ransacked, and they were both in shock, but the men were gone.

She and Cesar sat there hugging each other, both crying, until mustering the courage to go next door and ask a neighbor to call the police, as their cell phones had been stolen.

Two officers responded—a Black man and a white woman, both of whom were polite and patient, especially considering the lack of helpful information the victims were able to provide. Ivy had gotten the best look at the men and was hard-pressed to describe either. Both were maybe six feet tall-ish. Though they were both wearing masks, the skin around their eyes and mouths must have been visible, yet she couldn't even be sure what race the men were. All she really remembered seeing was the gun.

Ultimately, the only promising piece of intel came from the pizza delivery driver, who, upon his subsequent entry into the neighborhood, had seen a dark older-model sedan speeding away.

When the officers relayed that to Ivy, she immediately thought about the car she and Cesar had seen earlier that day, the one Cesar said followed him from his apartment.

"Oh my God, that was—"

"Probably nothing," Cesar said, shooting her a look of death.

"What?" the female officer asked. "Anything could be helpful."

Cesar answered for them quickly. "It's probably a coincidence," he said, "but earlier today, outside the law office where we both work,

I saw a car kind of like that, and it just seemed suspicious, like maybe somebody was watching us or something."

"Did you happen to get the license plate?" the male officer asked.

"No," Cesar said. "I couldn't even tell you what kind of car it was. Buick, Oldsmobile, something like that. Like I said, it's probably just a coincidence."

"Maybe," the female officer said, "but it could be an angry client or something. You should keep an eye out. Let us know if you see anything else suspicious."

She was looking at Ivy, who wanted to say a lot more but took Cesar's hint that he didn't want it blowing back onto Isaac. And as she thought about it, the possibility of the assault being the work of Cesar's ex-boyfriend didn't make much sense. She could see Isaac sending someone to keep tabs on Cesar or maybe to rough him up, but to rob him seemed off.

"It's strange," the male officer said. "Most burglaries happen during the day, when no one's home. An armed invasion like this at night is risky. I'm surprised more wasn't taken. Doesn't seem worth it. Just look at all the stuff around here." The officer pointed out the flat-screen TV and expensive stereo sitting right there in the living room.

Ivy and Cesar had done a hasty inventory when the police got there, and although the burglars had made quite a mess, tossing the place, the only things they could tell were missing were their cell phones, which had both been on the coffee table, and Ivy's purse.

The more Ivy thought about it, the more it bothered her. She could understand the thieves forgoing heavier, bulkier items in the interest of haste, but her laptop was in her work bag, lying on the far side of the couch, right there in the living room, and she had a whole drawer full of jewelry in her bedroom that hadn't been touched. She started rethinking the possibility that maybe the whole thing had been a terror attack by Cesar's ex-boyfriend, when she realized the officer was staring at her suspiciously, as though expecting an explanation.

"Wait. You don't think we're making this up, do you?" she asked. If only she'd gotten that doorbell camera her parents had suggested, she'd have proof.

Before the officer could answer her question, a knock on the door made both Ivy and Cesar jump. The female officer opened it.

There, filling the door frame, was Charles Collins III, six feet four and built like a grizzly bear. Ivy's father also had a loud, gravelly voice to match a grating personality and thus was always a dominating presence, but as he pushed his way past the officers toward his little girl, he loomed even larger than normal.

"Ivy," he said. "You're okay. Thank God." He was still wearing a jacket and tie like he'd come straight from the office despite the late hour. At any point earlier that day, Charles Collins would have been the last person Ivy wanted to see, but after the evening's trauma, she wanted to melt into her father's protective embrace.

He stopped her, seizing her by both shoulders with stiff arms and examining her like he was buying a horse. "You're sure you're not hurt?"

"Yes, yes, I'm fine," Ivy said, taking a step back. "How did you—"

"Ms. Myerson next door. She texted your mother, saying you'd used her phone to call the police. Something about a break-in." As he spoke, Ivy's father surveyed the scene and quickly locked onto Cesar, who was seated on the couch. "Is this the perpetrator? I want him prosecuted to the fullest extent of the law." Ivy's dad beckoned for the officers to jump into action.

The male officer began, "Uh, sir—"

Charles wheeled around and shut down whatever excuse he was about to receive. "You should know that the district attorney is a close personal friend. I'm happy to call Bill about this myself if I have to. Now get over here and—"

"Dad," Ivy said. "This is Cesar. He's my friend. We work together. He was held up too."

Charles Collins turned up his nose. "I see," he said, raising an eyebrow. Then he addressed the officers. "I demand to know what's going on. What have you got?"

The police briefed him on the situation as though he was their commander. When they covered the part about the suspicious car Ivy and Cesar had seen outside the law firm, Charles began nodding like it all suddenly made perfect sense. He pointed at his daughter. "I told you, didn't I? You go to work in a sewer like that, and what do you expect? But you had to go and prove your little point. To think that—"

"Dad, please," Ivy said. "Could we talk about this later?"

Charles growled. He did not enjoy being interrupted.

"We were actually just wrapping up," the male officer said. "Why don't we go ahead and get out of your way."

The police suddenly seemed in a hurry to get going. Charles Collins III often had that effect on people. Once they'd said their goodbyes and made their exit, Ivy's father resumed staring down Cesar. He cleared his throat loudly, suggesting it was time for the young man to depart as well.

Cesar began, "Oh, I...um..."

"Could we talk outside?" Ivy asked. She took her dad by the arm and led him out the front door, hoping to avoid having to explain that Cesar was living with her.

They stood on the front stoop in the thick summer night air. Ivy waved at the female officer, who was seated in her cruiser, filling out paperwork.

"It is time to put an end to this nonsense, Ivy," her father said. "You are quitting that ridiculous job tomorrow and coming to work with me."

"No, Dad. I'm not."

"Oh yes, you are. It's where you belong."

"Since when? You didn't even want me to work there."

Charles looked appalled by the suggestion. "I never said that."

"Sure you did. You didn't even want me to go to law school."

"Erroneous!" Charles shouted. "Entirely erroneous! I merely mentioned—one time—that nursing might provide a more reliable job market, not to mention a much healthier lifestyle."

That line of argument had been a familiar refrain throughout their relationship. Ivy's father had an uncanny way of passing off his chauvinism as chivalry. The same thing had happened when Ivy attempted to follow in her dad's footsteps by going out for basketball, only to have the old man suggest that cheerleading would be less likely to lead to injury. Ivy could bring up a ton of other examples, but the one thing she'd come to accept about her dad was that there was no reasoning with him. Charles Collins III was often wrong but had never once been in doubt. The only way to effectively deal with him was not to deal with him. It was one of the reasons well-heeled defendants hired him. He was so aggressive and disagreeable that many plaintiffs' attorneys preferred to settle cheap or drop a case altogether rather than have to endure a long, dragged-out, bare-knuckles legal brawl with Ivy's father.

"Look, can we talk about this later?" Ivy asked. "I've had a really long day. I'm exhausted. Please, just go home and let me get some rest. We'll talk tomorrow."

"Absolutely not," Charles said. "This has gone on long enough, Ivy. Your mother and I haven't heard a peep from you in six months. Now, I demand to know what this is all about."

"Like you don't know."

"I most certainly do not."

Ivy didn't even know where to begin. That her father pretended not to know why she was angry with him was nearly as infuriating as the reason itself.

"I want answers," Charles said. "Enough of this damn silent treatment."

At that inopportune time, Cesar chose to come outside. "Is everything okay?" he asked.

Charles sneered. "I think it's time for this boy to leave."

"I'm not a boy," Cesar said, puffing out his chest. "And I'm not going anywhere until I know Ivy is okay."

"Excuse me?" Charles's eyes bulged, and his nostrils flared. Ivy was afraid her father might actually turn violent. He was pushing sixty and in terrible shape, but he was still considerably larger than Cesar and had a volcanic temper.

Cesar wasn't backing down, though. "You heard me. I'm not a boy. And I don't like how you're talking to Ivy. Now, I heard her ask you to leave."

Charles Collins III glared like a ram about to charge. "And just who exactly is it you think you are to talk to me like that?"

Ivy answered before Cesar could. "I'll tell you who he is," she said. "He's my fiancé."

PART 3

CHAPTER 17

The news of Ivy's engagement did not go over well. In fact, the police officer who'd been lingering in her vehicle, completing her report from the break-in, had to intervene to keep the peace and eventually forced Ivy's father to leave. Before he did, however, he reiterated that Ivy was cut off financially, which emphasized the importance of smoothing things over with Lester.

She woke up the next morning determined to do exactly that. Upon going downstairs to the kitchen in search of coffee, she found Cesar, already awake, staring at his laptop and eating a bowl of Apple Jacks.

"Morning, boss."

Ivy yawned and said, "No more *boss*, okay? I'm your fiancée, remember?"

"Stop saying that. I'm sure it was fun to piss off your dad last night, but I told you I'm not going to do some sham marriage."

"It wouldn't be a sham," Ivy insisted. "Just a platonic marriage. No law against that."

Cesar put up a hand. "Enough. Please. It's really sweet you're willing to do that for me, but I'm not putting you in that position. Besides, it sounds like I may have another option."

Cesar swiveled his laptop around so Ivy could see an email he'd received from Lester at five-thirty that morning.

Sorry for losing my shit yesterday. Just brought back a lot of stuff. For you, too, I imagine. Anyway, I think we can work something out with your immigration situation. I owe you that. Come on by the office today around 10:00, and let's talk.

"That's great," Ivy said. "Maybe he emailed me too." Ivy retrieved her laptop from the living room, placed it on the table, and logged into her Gmail account while Cesar dug back into his bowl of cereal.

"Anything?" he asked.

Ivy hit Refresh on her inbox a couple of times before conceding that there was nothing there from Lester.

Cesar gulped down a bite of Apple Jacks. "Well, that's okay. I'm sure we can work things out with him. Why don't you go get ready, and we'll head over there?"

Ivy agreed. She showered and dressed, the whole time rehearsing conversations with Lester in her mind but unable to settle on exactly what to say.

When they got to the office, the Truth was there waiting to greet them. He flashed his high-watt smile when Cesar entered but turned it upside down as soon as Ivy emerged from behind.

"Why don't you have a seat?" he said to her then beckoned for Cesar to follow.

Ivy plopped down on a hard plastic chair in the lobby and sat for nearly an hour without a phone to distract her, enduring verbal jabs from Maria about how it was like she'd been called to the principal's office.

"You think you'll get expelled or just suspended?" she kept asking.

Ivy was about to tell her for the tenth time to piss off when Lester and Cesar finally reemerged, smiling, laughing, and engaging in a sideways hug. Then Lester scowled and ominously crooked a finger toward Ivy.

Here we go.

She trailed Lester into his office and took a seat. As soon as he shut the door, she tried to launch into the apology she'd rehearsed. "Lester, I'm s—"

"Save it," he said.

"Excuse me?"

"I said save it. You're not sorry. You said what you meant to say, so let's not bullshit each other, okay?"

"No, really, I didn't mean it. I—"

"Sure you did. You think I'm a chickenshit for settling cases the way I do."

Ivy didn't know what to say. She'd never been very good at lying and had no poker face at all. Fortunately, Lester didn't give her an opportunity to try.

"Maybe you're right," he said. "Maybe I have gone soft. Played it too safe."

Ivy was shocked to hear him admit that.

"Cesar told me what you offered to do for him to help with his immigration situation, and I have to say that's just about the dumbest damn idea I've ever heard. The two of you can get yourselves into a whole mess of trouble."

"But we have to do—"

Lester silenced her with a hand. "Don't worry about Cesar. We're working something out. Me and him have a plan he can tell you about if he chooses to. But right now, we're talking about you."

"Okay."

"I am impressed you were willing to stick your neck out for him like that, though."

"Sooo, does that mean I still have my job?" Ivy asked, smiling and playing it cute.

"I don't know. I'm just not sure about that, Ivy."

"Oh?" That was not what she'd been hoping to hear.

"I'm trying to figure out why you'd still want to work here. Cesar told me about the whole scene with your dad. I mean, I knew you had that connection to the big firm. Always figured you were wanting to get some experience on your own, working here for a year or so, before taking the cushy job with Dad. But now it sounds like your whole reason for being here is just some kind of 'Screw you' to the old man."

"Maybe," Ivy said. "Maybe at first."

"Yeah, that's what I thought."

Lester swiveled his laptop around. He had the web page for Charles Collins III's bio pulled up. "It says your dad started out in the DA's office."

"He did five years there to get his trial experience. Almost had a perfect conviction record. Just one loss. Any guess who it was to?"

Lester flashed a smile. "I was trying a lot of cases in those days. To be honest, I don't even remember your dad."

"Well, he remembers you," Ivy said. "Told me the only consolation to losing was that you were the best trial lawyer he ever saw."

Lester shrugged modestly. "Look, Ivy, I feel you. I really do. But I don't want to be a pawn in some family drama. And I'm going to tell you right now you don't want to live your life like it's some kind of dare, just doing a thing to prove you can. Because this life isn't easy. Adrenaline and ego will get you through a decade or so of being a trial lawyer, but eventually, you'll wake up and realize you fucking hate it. You'll hate the constant stress, the sleepless nights, the asshole clients, the power-drunk judges, the never-ending motherfucking deadlines, and knowing that every second of every day, no matter what you're doing, there's always a hit squad of assassin litigators out there who are just as smart and educated and motivated as you are who are spending every waking moment of every single day trying to figure out how to fuck you up on some case. This is a business full of killers, Ivy. People who'd slit your damn throat just to get an attaboy or a little gold star. But by the time you wake up to that reality, it will be too late. You'll have a mortgage and a spouse or, worse, an ex-spouse, and a couple of spoiled, ungrateful kids who will all have their hands out, wanting private school and cars and Xboxes and shit, and you'll realize you're stuck. You won't know how to do anything else that makes the same kind of money. You'll be the one serving a life sentence."

It didn't take a whole lot of insight for Ivy to realize that Lester was talking about himself. She appreciated the sage advice. She really did. But her mind was made up.

Ivy pointed at her father's bio. "Charles Collins III," she said, reading off his full name. "You know, his dad, my grandfather, was a federal prosecutor before becoming a district court judge. That was Charles Collins Jr. Charles Collins Sr., my great-grandfather, was a justice on the Supreme Court."

Lester shrugged. He knew all about her lineage. "So you're a legacy."

"No," Ivy responded. "My dad was a legacy. He's very proud of those three little *I*'s after his name. So much so that all he ever really wanted in life was to have a son to keep the line going. Before I was born, he used to refer to his future child as I-V, like the Roman numeral. Then he was disappointed with a girl, who he couldn't rightly name Charles. But I guess he and my mother had been jokingly referring to me as I-V for so long that the name stuck. So now I'm Ivy, named after a weed, with a permanent reminder on my driver's license that I'm not the kid my father wanted."

Lester fished around inside a lacquered redwood humidor at the corner of his desk and retrieved his morning cigar. "That's heavy," he said.

"Yeah. So anyway, I got into law school despite my dad's suggestion that I shouldn't bother and scored the clerkship with his firm then fought my way into the litigation department, even though he tried to steer me toward contracts. Then last summer, I got approved under the third-year practice rule to be able to argue motions in court so long as I had a licensed attorney supervising. So I went to my dad to sponsor me, and you know what he said?"

Lester snipped the end of his cigar and lit it with a match. "No. What'd he say?"

"He said I was wasting my time. That I just didn't have what it takes." Ivy did an impression of her dad's deep, dictatorial voice. "Litigators have to get their hands dirty, Ivy. They need to have moxie, gumption, chutzpah—or whatever other code words he used for testicles."

Lester took a puff and blew out a cloud of smoke. "Okay, so?"

"So I don't like people telling me what I can't do."

Lester pointed his cigar at Ivy and nodded like he identified with that sentiment.

"And there's something else too," Ivy said. "Something that really matters."

Lester took another puff. "All right, let's have it."

"I'm afraid that if I don't come back to work here, you'll plead Sonia's case without really giving her a chance, and I think it's possible she might be innocent."

Ivy could immediately tell she'd offended Lester, who rolled his eyes before staring at her for what felt like a long time. Finally, he put down his cigar and leaned forward.

"Okay, counselor. As long as the client's best interests are mixed up in your motivations somewhere, I guess I can live with the rest of it."

"So does this mean I've still got a job?" Ivy smiled sweetly.

"If you're sure you want it."

Ivy didn't stop to think. "I'm sure," she said.

Lester considered her for another moment then laughed. "Just don't start asking for no damn raise or nothing."

"Wouldn't dream of it," Ivy said.

"Okay, then." Lester extended his hand, and Ivy shook it.

CHAPTER 18

Once Ivy's employment status was secured, the meeting with Lester quickly turned into a strategy session for the Sonia Cabrerra case. Ivy caught him up on all the developments while he studied the photos of Hugo's scars.

"I'm no expert," he said, "but those look recent to me. They've still got a purplish color to them."

That wasn't what Ivy wanted to hear. She had a feeling she was about to get her arm twisted about settling.

Lester said, "Let's say you're able to find someone who will testify the kid already had those scars before he came to the US. You'll have to get the jury to believe the kid made it up. And he sure looked to me like he was telling the truth."

"Whose side are you on?" Ivy asked, only half joking.

"Look, I'm just trying to keep it real here. You've got to be tough on your client sometimes. It's a whole lot better for you to break her down in private than to let the prosecutor do it in open court. People will try to sell all kinds of bullshit, mostly to themselves. All I'm saying is that before you let this plea deal go, you need to put the screws to this Sonia and see if she holds up."

"Okay," Ivy said. "How do I do that?"

"Go meet with her again and cross-examine the shit out of her. She says she's innocent, then tell her she's got to prove it. Where's the evidence? Who can back up her story? If the boy's had these scars for years, then where're the photos of him at the swimming pool that will show it's true? Where're the family members from Guatemala to corroborate it?"

"Right," Ivy said.

"I'm not saying she has to plead," Lester told her, "but she needs to understand that if this story is bullshit, it will get exposed, and she'll have to face the consequences. You need to give her a little advance taste of what Eliza Wells is going to dish out."

Ivy was thinking through how to do that when a rapid knock sounded on the door and Cesar rushed in. He pointed at Lester's desk phone and, without asking, scooped up the handset and pushed the button for line two.

"*Señor? Pardón. No. No. Por favor. Un minuto, por—*" Cesar's shoulders sagged. When he held the receiver away from his ear, a busy signal bleated loudly. "Shit," he said.

"What was that?" Ivy asked.

"That was the boyfriend. The one we left the card for in Sonia's trailer."

Ivy felt a rush of excitement. "What did he say?"

"To never contact him again. Said he's moving to Texas to take a job. I asked him if he would come back to testify for Sonia, and he said he doesn't care what happens to her or her kids."

"*Her* kids? Isn't the baby on the way his kid too?" Ivy asked.

Cesar turned up his palms. "I don't know. The way he said it..."

He and Ivy stared at each other for a quiet moment, both thinking the same thing.

"Well," Lester said, "if he's not the daddy, that would explain the attitude."

That prompted Ivy to do some quick math. "Cesar, how far along would you say Sonia is in her pregnancy?"

"I don't know. I don't think she's ready to pop, but she's definitely showing. Why?"

"I'm just trying to think how long she's been in jail already. Eliza Wells said the public defender's office had this case for months before it was assigned to us."

Cesar stroked his chin. "What are you saying? That she got pregnant in jail?"

Ivy shrugged. "If not, it must have been right before she was arrested. The window's pretty tight. And with Juan's reaction and Sonia's insistence that he was out of the picture, maybe... I don't know. I mean, the jail is coed, right?"

"Yeah," Cesar said, "but they keep the women and men separated."

"They don't keep them separated from the guards," Lester said.

Ivy and Cesar both stared at him.

She hadn't considered that. "You think..."

"Hey, I have no idea. But crazy shit happens. Probably worth finding out."

"Guess that's one more happy topic we'll need to discuss." She said to Cesar, "Lester wants us to go browbeat Sonia before we pass on the plea deal Eliza Wells offered."

Cesar looked at Lester. "You didn't tell her?"

"That's your business," Lester said. "You can fill her in if you want."

"Fill me in on what?" Ivy asked.

"Well, I guess there's no reason I can't tag along on a jail visit, right? I mean, as long as you don't pay me for it."

"It's a free country," Lester said.

Ivy demanded to know what they were talking about.

"Come on," Cesar said. "I'll explain on the way."

CHAPTER 19

Cesar insisted on driving, which proved to be an annoyance because he kept his focus more on the road than on sharing details of his and Lester's conversation.

"It's really nothing earth-shattering," he insisted. "Lester can't employ me, but he looked back at his records, and since I've never taken a vacation in all the years I've worked for him, he says that under the Wage and Hour Act, he's required to pay me for all the PTO I accrued when I did have work authorization. So..." He grinned. "I'm basically getting paid to take a sabbatical while I sort out my immigration stuff."

Ivy couldn't believe he sounded so breezy and was referring to his looming deportation as though it were just a little bureaucratic wrinkle to be ironed out.

"That's the part I want to hear about," Ivy said. "What's his plan for your 'immigration stuff'?"

Cesar remained noncommittal. "Still working it out. Lester's setting me up with an attorney he knows."

Okay, finding an immigration attorney sounded like a step in the right direction, but Ivy was hoping for a little more detail. "What about our plan?" she asked. "Should we still—"

Cesar shut her down with a gesture, the abruptness of which kind of hurt Ivy's feelings. "Lester doesn't want us to do anything until after I meet with the attorney. Need to make sure we have a solid plan before pulling the trigger on anything else."

"Okay, I guess that makes sense. When do you meet with this attorney?"

"I don't know. Soon."

"How soon?"

Cesar laughed at her persistence as he pulled into the detention center. He parked close to the gates and turned to face her after he cut off the engine. "Don't worry so much. I've got a feeling it's all going to work out."

Ivy wished she could say the same but figured if Cesar wasn't worried about it, she could at least be justified in pushing his problems out of her mind long enough to focus on Sonia. While Cesar got them buzzed in, she pulled a legal pad out of her bag and remained in the car to make some notes on questions she needed to ask. Ivy wrote down the things Lester had mentioned as exculpatory evidence Sonia would be expected to produce if her defense was going to hold up. Prior photos of Hugo with his shirt off, showing the scars, would be the best thing. Second would be witnesses who could attest that he had the marks when he'd first come to the US. Then there was still the broken arm. Sonia's next-door neighbor, Claudia, had said she didn't actually witness Hugo's fall. Ivy decided she would conceal that information from Sonia at first and lay a trap for her the way a prosecutor would. She would ask Sonia to describe exactly what had happened and who was there to see if she would place Claudia clearly at the scene then confront her with what Claudia had said to see how Sonia responded. If she couldn't produce any evidence that Hugo's scars were preexisting, and if Sonia lied about Claudia witnessing the broken arm, then it would be time to lean on her hard to take the plea deal.

Cesar tapped on the windshield to get Ivy's attention and pointed at the detention center's retracting outer gate. She got out and followed him down the walkway. When they were buzzed through the main door, Ivy took a seat on a bench inside to continue with her notes while Cesar checked them in.

She tried to think of reasonable answers to her own questions.

Why did no one at school ever notice the scars, like in gym class?

"My son is in elementary school. They don't change clothes for gym."

Why aren't the scars documented in Hugo's pediatrician records?

"Hugo doesn't have a pediatrician. Where I'm from, primary care and wellness visits aren't really a thing."

But Hugo had to get vaccinated before he could enroll in school, right?

"Yeah, sure, they gave him some shots. They didn't strip him down."

How about at the hospital when he broke his arm? All those records don't say anything about scars.

"That's because they were focused on his arm. The nurses left the room when Hugo changed into his gown."

And there's no one who's ever seen Hugo with his shirt off?

"Why would anyone other than me have seen my son with his shirt off?"

Not even at the swimming pool?

"You've seen where I live. We aren't exactly members of the country club."

What about Juan? He lived with the boy. Surely he's seen him with his shirt off at some point.

"Yeah, sure, Juan has, but he's mad at me and doesn't want to help."

"Shit," Ivy grumbled. She didn't know what was worse—how awful such answers would sound at trial or the fact that they could all actually be true.

As she was pondering those things, Cesar came back from the check-in window shaking his head.

"Bad news, boss."

"What do you mean?"

"Sonia's not here."

That was the last thing Ivy had been expecting. "Well, where is she?"

Cesar bit his bottom lip before answering. "She's in the hospital."

CHAPTER 20

Ivy immediately assumed the worst.

"What happened? Was Sonia attacked?"

"No," Cesar said. "It has something to do with the baby."

Oh god, the baby. Ivy hadn't thought about that. Maybe Sonia had gone into labor. It seemed early for that, but Ivy was no expert, and some babies came early. "Is Sonia okay? Is the baby okay?" At that moment, it dawned on Ivy for the first time that it wasn't just Sonia's life for which she was responsible. It was the baby's too.

"I don't know. Somebody's supposed to come talk to us," Cesar said.

They sat there stewing for another thirty minutes, during which Ivy kicked herself about not giving the baby more thought before then. She should have asked more questions like: *When is the due date? Boy or girl? Who is the father?*

That last question seemed especially prescient after Juan's angry refusal to testify on Sonia's behalf and reference to "her kids."

Finally, a steel door buzzed open, and a mid-forties Black woman wearing a sharp-looking navy-blue pantsuit stepped out into the waiting room. She was the first person Ivy had ever seen smile inside the detention center.

"Claire Haskell," the woman said when she offered her hand first to Ivy then to Cesar. An ID badge identified her as Claire Haskell, PhD. It made an impression on Ivy that she hadn't introduced herself as Dr. Haskell.

"I'm the correctional psychologist here," Claire explained. "I've taken kind of a special interest in your girl. She gave us quite a scare last night."

"What happened?" Ivy asked. "No one's told us anything. Is the baby okay?"

"The baby is okay for now," Claire said, "but we thought Sonia was going into preterm labor. She woke up screaming about what turned out to be Braxton-Hicks contractions. False labor. But when we got her to the hospital, the doctors found several other issues of concern."

"Like what?" Ivy asked.

"Preeclampsia, dangerously high blood pressure. It can lead to serious issues, even death for both mother and child. Often shows up in the sixth month of pregnancy, which, as I'm sure you know, is right where Sonia's at."

Ivy did not know that—another point of shame, which she tried not to reveal by asking how the condition could be treated under the circumstances.

"That's the thing," Claire said with a sigh. "I'm kind of what passes for a social worker around here, and I've tried to look out for Sonia. I've made sure she gets extra milk, prenatal vitamins, folic acid, et cetera. The accommodations here for pregnant women are actually better than most detention centers, but that isn't saying much. A woman with Sonia's condition needs to be home, in bed, in a comfortable environment, with as little stress as possible."

Ivy brushed back her hair and blew out a long breath. "I don't suppose you want to let her out," she said with a hopeful smile.

"Well, that's what I wanted to talk to you about. Is there anything you can do about getting her bail reduced?"

Ivy looked at Cesar to get his opinion. "She's already got it knocked down to ten thousand unsecured," he said, nodding. "No way a judge is going lower than that with these charges."

"I see," Claire said.

"Could she just stay in the hospital until the baby is born?" Ivy asked.

"I wish," Claire said. "But outside medical services are heavily scrutinized here. The state has to pay not only for them but also for an extra guard to accompany the prisoner throughout the duration of the visit. I've pushed things already, arranging for Sonia to stay last night for observation just so she can get some real rest, but she'll be transported back here this afternoon."

"Jesus," Ivy said. She couldn't imagine carrying a baby, much less doing so behind bars.

"We're in a real race against time here," Claire explained. "Preeclampsia creates a serious risk for premature birth and a whole host of congenital issues. Sonia needs to rest and keep her blood pressure controlled to give the baby as much time as possible to develop."

Ivy felt so frazzled she wanted to pull her hair out. "Is there anything else you can do here? Some special accommodation?"

Claire turned up her palms. "We're just not real well equipped for this kind of situation. We're overcrowded and underfunded. There are some facilities for nursing mothers and their newborns, but they're all full. Sonia's not our only pregnant guest. This happens a lot more than you might expect."

That was the last thing Ivy wanted to think about—all the pregnant women behind bars and the nursing mothers. *How does that work?* she wondered. *Do they let the infants come in and suckle like a calf for an hour before slapping Mom into shackles and sticking her back into gen pop?*

Claire smoothed the sides of her hair. "I just thought that under the circumstances, with the baby's life at risk, a judge might consider house arrest or something."

Ivy looked at Cesar, who shrugged.

"Can't hurt to ask," he said.

It actually could hurt, Ivy realized. It could make her look stupid in front of the judge and Eliza Wells. But that was obviously of much less concern than Sonia's current predicament.

"I'll see what I can do," Ivy said. She'd be willing to risk embarrassment with a novel motion to address the terms of Sonia's pretrial confinement. But the thing that worried her most was that any delay or action other than accepting the current plea offer might cause that window of opportunity to close. She needed to at least explore with Sonia the possibility of pleading before she allowed that to happen. It was Thursday, and the detention center did not typically allow visitors Friday through Sunday.

"It is really important that I speak with Sonia today," Ivy said. "She's on the court calendar for Monday, and we have important things to discuss."

Claire pursed her lips. "That could be difficult. Visitation is over at one thirty, and there's no telling what time Sonia will be discharged and brought back over here."

Though Claire promised to pass along the message, Ivy wondered how logistically difficult it could be for Sonia to get phone access in a window of time when their Mam translator would also be available. Moreover, she feared the conversation would be monitored. All calls out of the detention center were recorded. Once she identified herself as Sonia's attorney, anyone listening in was supposed to stop the recording, but who knew if that actually happened? All that brought up another paranoid thought: *Just how much has Sonia told this state-funded shrink, with her limited knowledge of Spanish?*

"I appreciate your helpfulness and looking out for Sonia," Ivy said, "but I am curious what exactly your involvement with my client has been thus far."

"I'm glad you asked. That's something else I needed to bring up. I previously had a written authorization from the public defender to meet with Sonia, and I was hoping I could get the same from you. I assure you my role is purely as a counselor. I get paid by the state, but I'm bound by patient confidentiality. With Sonia's permission, I can share things with you, but that's as far as it goes."

Ivy wasn't sure she believed that and wasn't certain she'd be in favor of it even if she did. Once Eliza Wells knew there was a trove of therapist's notes about Sonia's deepest, darkest secrets, she might try to concoct some rationale for piercing through the privilege and having a judge compel their production.

"That's a question that's probably above my pay grade," Ivy said. "It's something I'll need to discuss with my boss."

Claire nodded. "Please do ask him. Sonia has been through an awful lot, and I think the counseling could be very beneficial to her, especially with a proper translator. We've done our best. We're both conversational in Spanish but certainly less than fluent, so it's not ideal."

That's good, Ivy thought. Everything up to that point had been in Sonia's second language, which meant if she'd admitted anything too damaging, Ivy would at least have the mistranslation angle to argue, in addition to confidentiality, to try to keep it from Eliza Wells or, worse, a jury.

"I'll get back to you about that," Ivy promised. "In the meantime, please just have Sonia call me."

CHAPTER 21

By four p.m. on Friday, Sonia still hadn't called, and Ivy was freaking out. If she didn't talk to her client before Monday morning, she might not get a chance until the deputies perp-walked her, shackled in her orange jumpsuit, into the courtroom. And the conversation they needed to have wouldn't be an easy one. It would require browbeating Sonia to reveal the weaknesses of her case and perhaps convincing her to plead guilty.

Ivy had been trying all afternoon to get the Hatchet Lady, Eliza Wells, on the phone to beg for an extension and to see if maybe they could set up the potential plea for later in the week. But in the entire history of jurisprudence, no prosecutor had ever actually been at their desk when the operator took the call, and leaving a message in the general mailbox was like shouting into a black hole.

Meanwhile, Cesar was "on sabbatical" back at Ivy's townhouse, unpacking and settling in, and Lester wasn't any help at all. The boss rolled into the office late for a meeting and had stayed busy ever since, twice waving off Ivy and telling her he'd get to her by the end of the day, which for Lester usually meant four to four thirty-ish.

Ivy was pacing outside the conference room while Lester finished up an injury consult. She was determined to ambush him with questions the second he emerged.

At four twenty-five, he came out, juggling two cell phones, trying to conduct a two-way negotiation as he went right past Ivy toward his office. She followed, waiting for any break in the conversation that would allow her to get in a word.

"Just hang on," Lester said to the phone in his left hand. "I got the son of a bitch on the line." He held that phone down to his side, unmuted the phone in his right hand, and immediately started shouting. "Fifty thousand is fucking insulting! No way my client's taking a penny less than a hundred. No. No. Hell no. I won't let them take less than a hundred on this case. It'd be malpractice. They should take my license away. I..." Lester paused because the client, who was on the left-hand phone, could overhear him and was shouting to get his attention. "Hold on," Lester said. He muted the right-hand phone then said to the left, "What's the problem? Yes, I know you'd take fifty, but I'm trying to squeeze a little more out of this guy. Just trust me. We'll have this done in a minute."

As Lester switched back to the right-hand phone, Ivy caught his eye and waved to get his attention. He nodded for her to follow him into his office as he resumed negotiating.

"Yeah, that was my client on the other line. He's mad as hell that I'm even talking about a hundred." Lester was silent for a minute as he walked around his desk and plopped into his swivel chair. "Meet in the middle? Seventy-five?" Lester groaned as though the thought of settling for that amount made him physically ill. "Man, you are killing me. Even at ninety, you'd be picking my pocket. Might as well walk in here with a gun and put it to my head and... Eighty thousand?" Lester gave a long, loud sigh. "Hold on." He muted the right-hand phone then told the client, "Good news. We've got a deal at eighty. Whoa, whoa, hold up. Don't get greedy on me now. No way. Listen, your case sucks. It's dog shit. The fifty K was a gift. The extra thirty is just because I'm a great fucking lawyer. Yeah, that's what I thought. You're welcome. Call you when the paperwork's ready."

Lester ended the call with his client and held up his pinky finger to let Ivy know he needed one more minute then wrapped things up with whoever he was talking to on the right-hand phone. "Maaan, it kills me to do it, but against my advice, my client has decided to take your paltry offer of eighty K. Yeah, send me a check and release, and we'll get it wrapped up. You too. Later."

With that, Lester dropped both phones onto his desk like smoking six-shooters and wiped his brow. "Whoo. I think it's Miller time."

Ivy gave him her nervous smile, all teeth. "Could I go over a few things with you first?"

Lester rolled his head around, stretching his neck, obviously tired and ready to cut loose with his weekend routine. "Okay, hit me."

Ivy dove into what had happened with Sonia—the hospital, the preeclampsia—and was starting to work her way into the fact she had no idea what to do on Monday morning when the case was called and Eliza Wells expected her to either plead or be ready to proceed.

But before she could get too far down that road, Lester made a big *T* with his hands. "Time out," he said.

Ivy caught her breath as Lester asked her how much time she had already spent on Sonia's case. "Today? Kind of... all of it."

Lester didn't look happy about that. "All of it?"

"Well, yeah. I've been researching and drafting a motion to try to get her pretrial release. That took all morning. Then I've been trying to get Eliza Wells on the phone to see if she'll hold the plea offer open past Monday. Then I spent the last couple of hours just kind of brooding about it. How am I supposed to concentrate on anything else?"

"How about the rest of the week? How many cases have you worked on besides Sonia's?"

Ivy knew there had been at least one or two others but was having a hard time remembering what they were.

"You do realize that Sonia's is just one of many cases we've got, right? Not to mention the one that will pay us the least. You've got a ton of things assigned to you that need just as much attention."

Ivy started to protest, but Lester raised a hand. "Listen, I know it's hard to manage a caseload. I do. I'm just asking, 'Could working on the things that actually pay the bills be a factor in how you choose to prioritize?'"

"Yes, of course. But what about Monday?"

"What about it?" Lester asked.

"What am I going to do about Sonia?"

"Sounds to me like you've already done it."

"But I haven't even talked to her about the plea."

"You tried to, didn't you?"

"Yeah."

"You left a message for her to call you, right?"

"Yes, but she hasn't."

"Well, that's hardly your fault. If she calls, great. If not, try talking to her on Monday morning."

"But this is the kind of thing that will take a while. I know Sonia's knee-jerk reaction will be to reject any plea."

"Then that's her choice, Ivy. Listen, girl. Remember what I told you on your first DUI plea where the judge threw the book at the guy and you came back here all depressed? You're not the one who poured the liquor down his throat, and you aren't the one who made him drive. He made those choices. Feel bad about your own fuckups, not somebody else's."

Lester started looking around for his briefcase.

"But if Sonia decides to go to trial, what do I do about the preeclampsia?"

"You got your motion all written up on that, right?"

Ivy did but had no idea whether it was any good or had a chance in hell of succeeding. "Do you maybe want to read it?" she asked.

"Nope," Lester said. "I'm sure you did a great job. Right now, there's a barstool down at Barrister's calling my name. I may just go find me the next ex-Mrs. Williams tonight."

Lester, the thrice-divorced lawyer, stood and started out the door.

"But if we don't plead, they're going to ask us to set a trial date and do a scheduling order and all kinds of things I've never handled before," Ivy said as she followed him.

Lester turned, put a hand on her shoulder, and said in a voice that sounded genuine, "Just do your best, Ivy. Whatever you decide, I'll support you."

CHAPTER 22

When Eliza Wells finished reading the motion, she handed it back to Ivy without any reaction. The prosecutor, seated at the counsel's table with a stack of files to her right, resumed making some notes on her legal pad. "I'll oppose it," she said without looking up. She was so matter-of-fact that it invited no debate. Ivy had started to turn back toward the defense table when Eliza said, "Should I assume that the plea offer is rejected?"

"No," Ivy blurted. "I just haven't had a chance to fully explore it with my client."

Eliza gave her a disapproving look.

"There're translation issues. And she's been in the hospital, and—"

"It's today or never," Eliza said. "Either she pleads, or we pick a firm trial date."

"But—"

"I'll put you on last this morning to give you a chance to talk to your girl, but if she's going to plead, it needs to be today." Eliza turned and looked around the courtroom, which was filling up with lawyers and witnesses. She waved to a dark-haired woman in a black skirt and flowing red blouse and beckoned her to come forward. "I had to bring in a translator from Charlotte," Eliza explained. "The only court-approved Mam translator in the state. She can help you talk to your client in one of the conference rooms over there."

The thought of using the state's translator made Ivy a little uneasy, since she didn't know what the attorney–client privilege rules were in such a situation. But having someone there in person, as opposed to Ivy's translator on phone standby, would probably improve the dynamic for what would be a tricky conversation.

"Thank you," Ivy said.

"Sure. After calendar call, you'll have maybe ten, fifteen minutes to confer. But I can't stress enough that this is your only opportunity. After today, I start getting ready for trial. Understand?"

"I understand," Ivy said.

A heavy metal door for the prisoner hold swung open, and two deputies marched in a row of six detainees, who shuffled like penguins. Sonia was second from the last, by far the shortest in the line, her shackled hands protecting her baby bump as she walked. When Sonia caught sight of Ivy, her eyes lit up.

God, I'm in over my head. Ivy knew serious action was necessary. She just wasn't sure what it was: browbeat Sonia to plead or take the case to trial and convince a judge to give her client in-home confinement in the meantime. The answer, she decided, was both: to try to get her to plead, but if she wouldn't, then argue her motion.

"All rise." The bailiff called the courtroom to order as Judge Bingham entered from a rear door behind the bench. He was a balding Black man with a closely cropped salt-and-pepper beard and horn-rimmed glasses.

The judge spoke in a quiet, deliberate voice as he instructed everyone to be seated and called the calendar. When he reached *State v. Cabrerra*, Ivy stood, unsure of what to say.

Eliza Wells spoke for her. "Judge, we may have a new plea offer extended in that one, so I'd like to hold it open to give defense counsel time to talk to her client."

The judge motioned to the deputy, who directed Sonia to stand and led her into the jury-deliberation room. Ivy turned, searching for the translator, whom she had not yet had a chance to speak to. She was pleased to see that the translator was already making her way down the aisle toward the front of the courtroom. "Thank you," Ivy whispered to her as the judge moved on to the next case on his list.

The deputy stood outside the jury room. Inside, Sonia was seated at a long conference table surrounded by twelve chairs. Ivy thanked the deputy and closed the door.

"I'm Marisol," the translator said, offering her hand. "What part of Guatemala is your client from?"

Ivy had no idea. She couldn't name the capital of Guatemala, much less its different regions. "Not sure. Maybe we should ask her?"

Marisol and Sonia engaged in what appeared to be some friendly Mam banter before the translator explained, "She's from the Huehuetenango Department."

"Department?" Ivy asked.

"It's just what they call the different parts of the country. Huehuetenango is in the western highlands, on the border of Mexico. I was just telling her that my grandmother is from that same area."

The polite thing at that moment would have been to ask more about Marisol's background, but they didn't have much time. She decided to dive right in and started asking her client for other witnesses or evidence that could prove Hugo's scars were preexisting. Sonia had nothing. Her parents were no longer living, so they couldn't testify about the accident. She and Hugo had been reunited for only a relatively short time, so she didn't have any photos of him with his shirt off, and she couldn't think of anyone who had seen the scars, except for maybe Juan, who she was adamant would not be willing to help.

Once every door on that topic was slammed shut, Ivy moved on to the broken arm.

"Please tell her that I talked to her neighbor, Claudia, who said that she did not actually witness Hugo fall and break his arm. She says that Sonia just told her that was what happened, then she drove them to the hospital."

Before the translator finished, Sonia was shaking her head back and forth.

"She says Claudia is lying. They were both on the porch, talking, when Hugo fell."

"But why would she lie?" Ivy asked.

As the question was translated, Sonia hung her head. She mumbled a response that the translator had to ask her to repeat. She did. Then Marisol went and sat down next to Sonia and put her arm around her.

"What?" Ivy asked.

Marisol said, "She says that Claudia must know."

"Know what?"

Sonia and Marisol spoke to each other again before the translator explained. "Claudia's husband, Tomás. He would sometimes come over to Sonia's trailer when Juan was at work. Tomás knew they didn't have papers and said he would turn them in to ICE if she didn't do what he wanted."

Marisol didn't have to say any more. Ivy got the picture.

"Is Tomás the baby's father?" she asked.

Sonia responded to the translated question with a shame-filled nod. She wrapped her arms around her stomach and began to cry.

"Is that why Juan is unwilling to help? He knows the baby isn't his?"

Before Ivy could get the translated answer, a knock came at the door. The deputy poked his head in. "They're ready for you."

Ivy's anxiety level ratcheted up. "Just two more minutes, please."

The deputy closed the door, and the translator reported the answer to the previous questions. "You are right about Juan. She told him the truth after she was arrested. She says there's no way he'll help her."

"Okay, here's the thing," Ivy said. "I believe you. I do. But I don't know how we can win this case. Hugo's testimony is very convincing.

A jury is going to believe him. Plus, the police were able to match up his scars to the grill pan they found in your kitchen. They'll also say you admitted to breaking his arm and Hugo told them that was what happened. The medical records also show that he had a spiral fracture, which is consistent with a twisting injury. So if all we have is your account, without a single witness who can back it up and say that Hugo got those scars in Guatemala or that he fell and broke his arm accidentally, then it doesn't matter what I believe or even what the truth is. You are going to lose, and you could get the maximum sentence. This is your one chance to take the state's offer. You can plead guilty and probably cut your sentence in half. If you pass it up, you won't get this opportunity again."

Ivy watched Sonia intently as the translator spoke. After she was done, Sonia sat quietly. Her stoicism amazed Ivy. If faced with a similar decision, she imagined she'd completely unravel.

Another knock came at the door. The deputy looked in and said, "We need you now."

"Okay," Ivy said, "we're coming."

Before she could prod Sonia for an answer, the tiny woman said something to the interpreter. Ivy waited for the translation, knowing that no matter what it was, plead or go to trial, she'd spend many nights ruminating over Sonia's decision. What she never imagined, however, was the sheer terror she felt when the English words came, conveying a response much more terrible.

"She wants you to decide."

CHAPTER 23

"I understand we have a plea agreement," the judge said after everyone had taken their places.

"That's right, Judge," Eliza Wells said. "Defense counsel has informed me that we do."

Ivy brushed her hair out of her eyes and took a deep breath, praying to God she was doing the right thing. Sonia had been fitted with headphones that would allow the proceeding to be translated to her in real time. She watched the judge with her thousand-yard stare, seemingly numb to the reality of what was about to happen. After some pro forma presentations from the lawyers and the allocution—the judge's formal warning prior to accepting a guilty plea—Sonia was about to be sentenced to as much as ten years in prison. She would permanently lose custody of her children, both Hugo and the one on the way. And once it was over and she had served her time, she would be deported back to Guatemala. It was all so heavy, pressing down on Ivy's chest, suffocating her. She couldn't believe that she, a twenty-four-year-old, six months out of law school, was the one making the call with the stakes so high.

"Very well," the judge said. "Madam Prosecutor, if you could please summarize the factual basis for the plea."

Eliza Wells began going through the overwhelming evidence of guilt. It should have bolstered Ivy's resolve that she was doing the right thing, but it didn't. She was already kicking herself for being a coward, asking if she was doing it just to let herself off the hook from having to try the case and risk the embarrassment of an inevitable loss. Or maybe it was because she feared Sonia's case could actually be won if she had a real lawyer.

Fuck. No first-year attorney should ever be in this kind of position.

Ivy felt like a total fraud, a kid playing dress-up among the adults. Imposter syndrome was a theme in her life. She was always scraping and grinding to try to achieve, both on the basketball court and in the classroom, the kinds of accolades that had come so easily to her brilliant, uber-competitive father. It had resulted in a résumé and persona that Ivy often feared were a house of cards. What was worse was that Ivy believed everyone in the courtroom could see it and just didn't care because she was making their jobs easier, performing her proper function as a cog in the settlement machine that kept the wheels of justice turning.

When Eliza Wells finished explaining how officers had recovered a matching grill pan in Sonia's home, she said, "The detective told Ms. Cabrerra they were taking her son to the hospital, and in response, she said, via a translator, 'Is that where I took him when I broke his arm?'"

A chill ran through Ivy's body. Eliza hadn't mentioned that the translator was working in Spanish, not Mam, and that Sonia was speaking her second language. There was no reference at all to the defense position that she had been misquoted.

Maybe that didn't matter or was something Ivy could point out when it was her turn to speak. But the chill turned into a massive gale-force wind of arctic air when Eliza talked about how medical records confirmed that the boy had suffered a spiral fracture to his arm.

Ivy couldn't believe she hadn't thought of it before. It suddenly seemed so obvious.

"Medical records." She didn't even realize she'd said it out loud until everyone looked at her.

"What was that, Ms. Collins?" the judge asked.

"Oh... I, uh..." Ivy fumbled for words.

Eliza Wells was staring daggers into her, obviously displeased by the interruption. "Defense counsel will have her turn to speak in just a moment," Eliza said. "Now, as I was saying, Judge—"

"No, wait," Ivy blurted.

"Yes, Ms. Collins?" The judge did not appear nearly as annoyed as Eliza Wells over her lack of decorum. He looked more confused.

Ivy was both embarrassed and scared, almost to the point of paralysis, but she found a way to push all that aside and trust her instinct, to stop thinking altogether and do what she needed to do. "I'm very sorry for the interruption, Judge, but I need one more minute to confer with my client before we proceed any further."

Eliza Wells started, "Judge, if I could just—"

The judge cut her off. Most of the jurists Ivy had seen up to that point were a little like schoolteachers, occasionally drunk on the power of their position and preeminently concerned with maintaining order, especially in the unruly world of District Court. But Judge Bingham was obviously a man whose focus was fairness.

"Counsel said she needs another minute," he said calmly. "Talk to your client, Ms. Collins."

The interpreter, Marisol, was seated behind Ivy and Sonia. She leaned in close so they could whisper among the three of them. Ivy didn't have much time, but there was something she needed to know before they went any farther down the irrevocable road.

"Please ask Sonia if she knows whether her parents took Hugo to the hospital when he was burned."

The translator asked then delivered the answer. "She doesn't know whether they did or not."

Dammit, Ivy thought. "Well, ask her if they took him to the hospital, what hospital it would have been."

Again, the translator asked and came back with an answer that was no help. "She isn't sure. She says she never went to a hospital before coming here. Even when she was born, it was at home."

"Marisol," Ivy said desperately, "you know about this area. If someone was hurt, is there a hospital that the villagers would take them to?"

Marisol furrowed her brow. "I mean... Huehuetenango does have hospitals. Several. If someone was really hurt, a child, I think they would take him."

Sonia said something that Marisol translated. "She wants to know why you are asking."

"Because Sonia may not know anyone who can testify that Hugo got those scars in Guatemala, but if I can find medical records that say he did, then that changes everything."

"Ms. Collins?" the judge prompted. "Are we ready to proceed?"

"No, Judge," she said, spitting out the answer before she lost her nerve.

Eliza Wells sighed and crossed her arms.

Ivy again felt an impulse to crumble into dust but pushed forward anyway. "Your Honor, I apologize to the court for this, but I have not had this case for very long, and although we were inclined to enter a plea, I have realized that there is another key area of investigation that I need to undertake before I can, in good faith, recommend this plea to my client. I would ask that the plea offer be held open for a short period of time so I can complete this last aspect of due diligence."

"Well, whether to hold the offer open is up to the state," the judge said. "Ms. Wells?"

Eliza looked ready to spit fire. "Judge, if the defendant is not pleading today, then the offer is revoked and won't be extended again. I've made that very clear to Ms. Collins."

"Ms. Collins?" the judge said. "I can't force the state to hold their offer open. Now, having heard that it will be revoked if not accepted today, is it still your wish not to proceed?"

"Yes?" Ivy had no idea whether Sonia was even telling the truth, much less if medical records that could prove it were out there. By passing up the plea, she was taking a total shot in the dark, pushing all her chips into the middle of the table before the first card was dealt. But something inside her told her it was the right thing to do. "Yes, Your Honor," she reiterated more forcefully.

The judge shook his head. "Okay. But before you let this opportunity go, I want to make sure your client understands that she is facing some very serious charges that carry the potential for a lengthy prison sentence. Now, if this plea *were* to go forward, I am prepared to follow the state's sentencing recommendation, which would result in a significantly reduced sentence from the maximum one that could be imposed if the defendant were to be convicted at trial of all charges. Now, I don't say that to try to pressure you, but I know there is a language barrier here and we are utilizing the services of a translator, so I just want to make sure that your client understands what is happening and that it is indeed her desire to forgo this plea offer, knowing it will be revoked and that there may not be any other plea offers in the future. Do you understand that, Ms. Cabrerra?"

Sonia looked surprised to be addressed directly by the judge. She glanced around then nodded once the question posed to her was translated.

"I need you to answer with words, ma'am, so we can get it on the record."

Sonia spoke, and Marisol reported, "She says yes, she understands."

The judge bit his bottom lip, obviously concerned. "Okay, Ms. Cabrerra. Then I just need you to confirm that you do not wish to plead at this time and would rather risk a trial."

After Marisol translated, Sonia mumbled something that would have been unintelligible even if it were in English.

"What was that?" the judge asked.

Marisol had to ask Sonia to repeat it then responded, "She says she trusts her lawyer."

CHAPTER 24

"Very well," the judge said. He looked back at Eliza Wells. "Well, Madam Prosecutor, unless there are any other cases I've missed, I guess we can stand in recess."

"That's all for today, Judge."

He was about to gavel the session closed when it dawned on Ivy that she hadn't raised her motion about pretrial confinement. With all the knee-shaking brinksmanship over the plea offer, it had nearly escaped her mind.

"Wait, please, Judge, there is one more thing."

Judge Bingham looked back at her, surprised by yet another last-second revelation. "Yes, Ms. Collins?"

A lot of judges would have been pretty annoyed with Ivy at that point. But if Judge Bingham was put out, he was doing a good job of hiding it.

"Since we are not pleading, I, uh, have a motion." Ivy looked frantically around the table for where she'd set her motion, suddenly forgetting what it was titled. "It's a motion about bail." She flipped frantically through her case file and finally found where she'd jammed the papers she'd spent all weekend writing and revising. "May I approach, Your Honor?"

The judge waved her forward. Ivy walked nervously across the well of the courtroom and handed the motion up to the judge. She wasn't sure if she should go back to the counsel's table or stand there and wait for him to read it. She waited a minute but then felt stupid and slinked back next to Sonia.

"Okay, yes," the judge said, placing the paper down on the bench. "I noticed that the defendant is expecting. Your motion is well put, Ms. Collins. What do you say about this, Ms. Wells?"

Eliza pounced at the question. "The state opposes the motion, Judge. As you've said yourself, these are very serious charges, and contrary to the defense motion, we believe the defendant is a flight risk. She is an undocumented immigrant who is in this country illegally. She didn't need a passport to come here, so she doesn't need one to leave, and because of her international roots, flight is a substantial risk. But the bigger issue here, Judge, is the health of the unborn child."

"That's what Ms. Collins is arguing," the judge said.

"Yes," Eliza said. "She's right about that being a relevant concern, but she is wrong as to the solution."

"What do you mean, Ms. Wells?"

"What I mean is that Ms. Cabrerra has no money, Judge. She has no family. Apparently, she has no friends of any means, because she hasn't been able to raise bail. And she also has no place to live. The trailer she was living in was being rented by her boyfriend at the time, who our investigators have learned has moved out of state and reportedly wants nothing to do with Ms. Cabrerra. Currently, Ms. Cabrerra is housed, she's fed three meals a day, she's supplied with prenatal vitamins, and she has access to medical care that is paid for by the state. Those accommodations exist only while she remains in custody. And there is simply no reason to believe that the unborn child, much less Ms. Cabrerra, would be better off outside of detention, where she would be homeless and destitute. She is exactly where she needs to be."

The judge nodded, indicating he considered Eliza's argument persuasive. "Ms. Collins, tell me how your client would be able to meet her needs if I were to grant your motion. Where would she go? Who would care for her?"

Ivy was flabbergasted. Eliza's argument had taken her completely by surprise. She'd been expecting her to demonize Sonia, not make an argument for her well-being. It just seemed so self-evident to Ivy that Sonia would be better off out of jail that she'd never considered any of the issues Eliza had raised.

She looked to her client for answers. "Do you have anywhere you can stay?"

Sonia shrugged. Through Marisol, she said, "I would have said Claudia's, but I guess that's no longer possible."

It occurred to Ivy that she'd never even discussed the motion with Sonia. She'd just assumed her client would want it. Maybe Sonia agreed that being behind bars at the moment was the best thing for her.

"Do you want me to withdraw the motion?" she asked.

Sonia shook her head animatedly at the translation. "No," Marisol reported. "She needs to get out as soon as possible. She says she can't have her baby in jail because they will take her away."

Her. It was the first time Ivy had heard any mention of the baby's gender.

"Well, Ms. Collins?" the judge asked.

Shit, Ivy thought. She wanted to say she would just take in Sonia herself and pay for whatever she needed, but that was ethically prohibited. She might be willing to do it regardless, but she couldn't tell the judge that in open court.

With little foreknowledge of what she was about to say, Ivy started freestyling, just speaking from the heart. "Your Honor, if this motion isn't granted, then Ms. Cabrerra will have her baby in jail, and as soon as the doctors clear it, she'll be ripped away. Now, Ms. Cabrerra has already been separated from her son for six months, and she's presumed innocent, Judge." Ivy hesitated, hating how naive that sounded, like a first-year law student waxing eloquent about their love for the law or calling anything they considered bad policy "unconstitutional." She resumed more forcefully, saying, "I believe she *is* inno-cent."

The judge raised his eyebrows, and Ivy realized how unconvincing that must have appeared, considering they'd gathered that morning so Sonia could plead guilty to those very crimes.

"I know how that sounds, Your Honor, since we were just about to plead guilty, but believing someone is innocent and risking a maximum sentence over whether you can prove it are two different things."

The judge nodded, acknowledging the point.

"Well, we have decided to take that risk," Ivy said. "You now know the offer we are passing up to try to prove Ms. Cabrerra's innocence. That should show you how strongly I feel about it. And if Ms. Cabrerra is found innocent of these charges, she not only will have been unjustly incarcerated the entire time, and she will not only have been wrongly separated from her son, but she'll be forced to endure a *Handmaid's Tale*-type horror of giving birth behind bars only to have that crying baby ripped from her as well."

The judge smiled. "*Handmaid's Tale*-type horror," he said, seeming to enjoy the phrase. He sighed and leaned back, placing a hand atop his head.

"Your Honor, could I interject something?" Eliza Wells asked.

The judge gestured for her to speak.

"The argument Ms. Collins has just made is not really an argument for pretrial release."

"It's not?"

"No, sir. It's an argument for a speedy trial. Ms. Cabrerra does not have the wherewithal to meet her or her baby's needs outside of her current detention. I think that point is fairly well established. The argument of innocence and what will happen if the baby is born before she has her day in court is really an argument for a speedy trial—to give her a chance to exonerate herself as soon as possible. And the state is happy to accommodate that. In fact…" Eliza paused to flip through some papers. "If you want to retain jurisdiction over the matter, there's an open slot next month when we could tee up this case. I propose denying the defense motion so that Ms. Cabrerra can continue to receive state services in the interim while setting the case for trial a month from today. That would be the best of both worlds here, so to speak."

State services. It irritated Ivy how Eliza could throw that out there like Sonia was simply getting food stamps or Medicaid instead of being caged like an animal.

But the judge was nodding along like he was in complete agreement. "How about that, Ms. Collins? I am going to deny the motion, but I am willing to go ahead and set this case for trial next month."

Ivy was ready to decline that out of hand without even looking at her client. She had absolutely no idea how long it would take to prepare the case for trial but was fairly certain that doing it in a month was insane. Before she could answer, however, Sonia started talking loudly. Ivy turned to silence her, and Marisol said, "She wants the speedy trial. Very much, she wants it."

Ivy whispered to them, "No, Sonia, it's not a good idea. It's not enough time."

Sonia apparently understood without the need for a translation because she reacted to Ivy's words as though they smelled bad. She seized Ivy's hand and spoke to her directly in heavily accented English. "Please. I want the trial. I want it now." Tears welled in Sonia's eyes as she gestured to her very pregnant belly.

Ivy couldn't say no.

"Are we agreed, Ms. Collins?" the judge asked.

Ivy took a deep breath before answering. "Yes, Your Honor. I guess we are."

CHAPTER 25

"A month?" Lester sounded like he was about to choke on his cigar as he swiveled back and forth in his office chair.

"Yes," Ivy said. "Sonia insisted upon going to trial before she gives birth."

"That's one month? Like in thirty days?"

"Uh-huh."

Lester laughed wickedly. "I'd normally want at least six months to prepare for a case like this. But honestly, it may be best to just get it over with. The sooner, the better."

"Why's that?"

"Because all that really matters is whether you can come up with some medical records to support your girl's story. If not, then you could take all the time in the world to prepare, and it wouldn't make a difference."

Ivy suspected that was true. "If there are medical records, then you think we can win?"

"Sure," Lester said. "You find records showing the kid got those scars back in Guatemala, and you've exposed him as a liar. Eliza might even dismiss the whole case if that happens. But all of that is a gargantuan-size if."

"So what do we do if it turns out there are no records?"

"In that case, you'll just go in there and do your best and get your ass kicked."

"Me?" Ivy said. She'd assumed it would be a *we*.

"Yeah, you."

"You're not going to help?"

"Hey, I thought the girl should plead," Lester said, holding up his hands. "You're the one who decided to take it to trial. So congratulations, counselor, you've got yourself a trial. It'll be good for you to get your nose bloodied. Good learning experience."

Ivy was shaken to her core by the notion of trying the case by herself. It had never occurred to her that Lester might force her to go solo with something so big. She knew he'd make her do all the grunt work but figured that at the end of the day, he'd step in for the high-level stuff.

"I can't try a case like this. I've never done a trial. Ever. I had one semester of trial advocacy in law school, and I kind of sucked at it."

Lester placed his cigar in the ashtray and checked his watch, which meant he had a client meeting and was losing patience with the conversation. "Look," he said. "Unless these magical medical records are out there, you could have Johnnie Cochran, Clarence Darrow, and Oliver Wendell motherfucking Holmes try this case, and it wouldn't make any difference."

Ivy felt like a calf being led to slaughter. "But you said that whatever I decided, you'd support me."

Lester stood and put his hand on Ivy's shoulder. "And I do support you," he said, smiling. "Go get 'em, girl."

He left the room on the way to his next appointment. Ivy followed him out into the hall, but Lester ducked quickly into the conference room, loudly greeting some new clients. Out in the lobby, Ivy could hear Cesar's familiar cheerful voice as he chatted up Maria in Spanish.

"Hola, boss," he said upon seeing her.

"Thought you were on sabbatical," she said.

"I am. But it turns out sabbatical is Latin for not having shit to do. So I figured I'd come in and volunteer my time. Got anything needs doing?"

"Actually, yes," she said, thinking that someone with Cesar's finesse, tenacity, and Spanish skills would be the perfect person to try to track down Hugo Cabrerra's Guatemalan medical records.

She was about to fill him in, but Maria rudely waved a pink slip of paper at her. "Your shrink called."

"Shrink?"

"Yeah, some psychologist named Claire Haskell. Didn't want to leave a message but gave me her number and said it was real important you call her back."

Ivy took the message slip and noticed the number didn't have the detention center's standard 986 prefix, which meant Claire Haskell had left her private number.

"I told her not to waste her time, that we already know you're crazy, but she insisted she needed to speak with you," Maria said.

Ivy gave Maria the stink eye and motioned for Cesar to follow her back to her office. They each took a seat, and she caught him up on that morning's aborted plea hearing.

"So you don't know if these records exist?" he asked.

"That's right."

"Jesus, Ivy. You're taking an awfully big risk."

"Well, the die is cast. Either the records are out there, or they aren't. If they are, then I need you to find them."

"And you don't actually know what hospital Hugo would have gone to?"

"No, but how many can there be?" Ivy had no real concept of how big Guatemala was but imagined something the size of maybe Rhode Island.

"I don't know. Probably a bunch," Cesar said. "A lot of hospitals down there are more like what we'd think of as urgent care. I bet there's a ton of them they could have gone to."

Ivy hadn't considered that. But she also knew there was no point in worrying about it. If there were a thousand places Hugo could have gone, then they'd just have to call every single one. She decided to take a page out of Lester's book and offer platitudes in lieu of actual assistance. "That's why I need you on this. The whole case rests on it, and I know that if there's anyone who can pull this off, it's you."

Cesar smiled, clearly seeing what she was doing. "Fine," he said. "I'll try to track down these records. But what are you going to do?"

That was a good question. When it came to trial prep, Ivy really didn't know where to begin. She looked down at the message slip she'd placed on her desk. She picked it up and said, "I'm going to find out what this shrink is calling about."

CHAPTER 26

Ivy called Claire Haskell using the new iPhone she'd purchased over the weekend. Claire picked up on the third ring. She told Ivy she had cut out of work a little early and was on her way home. Claire proposed they meet at a nearby coffee house called Miriam's. Ivy agreed to be there in fifteen minutes.

Ivy still wasn't sure what to make of the therapist, but she didn't think it was a coincidence Claire had called with such urgency right after that morning's court appearance, at which the defense had decided to take the case to trial. *Is she a spy?* Ivy wondered. *Is she someone Eliza Wells wants to probe Sonia's secrets to try to elicit a confession?* That notion had the hairs on the back of Ivy's neck standing up. *But why the offsite meeting?* It gave Ivy the impression that maybe whatever Claire Haskell wanted to talk to her about was something she didn't want advertised to her employer.

When Ivy got to Miriam's, Claire was already there, seated at a black metal outdoor table, sipping an iced coffee. She waved when she saw Ivy approaching.

"I've always wanted to try this place," Ivy said. "I need to get out of the office sometimes to concentrate. This looks like it could be a good place to pore over a court file for a few hours."

Claire stood and shook Ivy's hand. "I can highly recommend the iced chai latte. Would you like one?"

"Not right now," Ivy said. "My nerves are kind of shot after court this morning. I don't think caffeine is a good idea."

"Yes, I heard you're taking Sonia's case to trial."

"Good news travels fast." Ivy held Claire's gaze, wondering exactly how that information had already made its way to a state psychologist. It raised her suspicion that Eliza Wells was behind all of it.

"Sonia asked to speak with me when she got back from court this morning," Claire explained.

"You can't speak to my client without my permission," Ivy snapped.

That was exactly why Lester always said clients' families should do whatever it took to bail their loved ones out of jail—sell the car, mortgage the house, take out a loan, donate blood—anything to free the accused from a detention center that often equated to one big confession machine. The moment a defendant invoked their right to counsel, the state wasn't constitutionally allowed to interrogate them any further. But that just meant the cops wouldn't do it themselves. Instead, they'd stick the defendant in a cell where they'd be surrounded by chatty guards and snitchy inmates twenty-four hours a day. And lo and behold, they would stumble into a jailhouse confession by the time of trial.

Claire held up her hands in mock surrender. "I understand that," she said. "And that is exactly what I told Sonia. But she is extremely troubled right now and said she would very much like to resume our sessions."

Ivy's Spidey sense was tingling, her synapses on fire with suspicion. She came right out with her accusation. "You mean so you can get her to confess?"

Claire looked shocked. "No, no, no. I assure you that is not my goal."

"Riiight."

Claire scratched the top of her head. She had a troubled expression. "Ms. Collins, we're getting off on the wrong foot here. Please, have a seat for a minute, and let's talk. Just person to person, okay?"

Ivy sighed and slumped down into one of the black metal chairs.

Claire sat and sipped her drink. "Are you sure I can't get you anything?"

"No, thank you," Ivy said, annoyed at what she viewed as another disarming tactic. She was willing to hear the lady out, but she wasn't about to drop her defenses.

"Very well." Claire took a deep breath, closed her eyes, and clasped her hands as though saying a silent prayer. "Ms. Collins, I understand your hesitancy to let me counsel Sonia. I do. But with the public defender's permission, I've already been meeting with her for months, and I can assure you that my only goal is to help Sonia."

"Is that right?"

"Yes, it is. Ms. Collins, I am a Christian woman. Now, I don't know if that means anything to you. For a lot of folks, it's come to mean all kinds of wickedness. But to me, it means that I feel called to help these women, most of whom have been used and abused and kicked around their whole lives."

"And you want so badly to help Sonia, this one lady out of the hundreds you have over there, that you came all the way out here to make this personal plea?"

Claire remained silent for a moment, and Ivy thought she had her. She'd exposed the bullshit. But when Claire spoke, her response surprised Ivy.

"Actually, no," she whispered. Claire looked around as if checking for eavesdroppers. "The reason I wanted to meet is I think I can help *you*."

"Help me how?"

Claire had a canvas satchel sitting by her feet. She reached down into it and retrieved a manila file folder. "When I spoke to Sonia this morning and found out you were going to trial, I had her sign a consent form that would allow me to share this with you." Claire pulled a sheet of paper from her file that she handed over to Ivy. "Here's a copy for you. Sonia has asked that I share anything and everything about her treatment with you. She is quite adamant that she never burned Hugo, though I will tell you she does regret quite a lot when it comes to him. I don't know what kind of witness she would make, because she freely admits to losing her temper with the boy on several occasions and punishing him harshly—the ways she was punished growing up in Guatemala. Things that don't fly here, if you know what I'm saying."

Ivy wasn't sure whether that was good news or not. Sonia's professing her innocence in the matter of the burns was helpful, but she noted that Claire hadn't said anything at all about the broken arm, and that concerned her.

"Thank you for the offer," she said, "but I don't think having you analyze my client right before her trial is a good idea."

Ivy stood to leave, considering the meeting to be over.

"Please wait," Claire said, raising her voice, then looked embarrassed by her volume.

"What?" Ivy asked.

Claire leaned forward and whispered conspiratorially, "The information I can give you isn't about Sonia."

"No?"

"No," Claire said. "It's about Hugo."

CHAPTER 27

"Hugo?" Ivy didn't understand. Claire worked at the detention center. She would never have met with Sonia's son. *What helpful information could she have about him?*

"Yes," Claire said. "Sonia and I have talked a lot about him. And while I can't officially diagnose him, there are a number of compelling traits he's exhibited that I think could explain quite a lot."

Now this is interesting. Ivy had long known that one of the biggest challenges in Sonia's case would be how to convince a jury that sweet, adorable little Hugo had made up such vicious lies about his mother. She sat back down.

"Okay," Ivy said. "You have my attention."

"Good. Tell me, have you ever heard of histrionic personality disorder?"

"No. What is it?"

"It's on the spectrum with some others you may have heard of: narcissistic personality disorder, borderline personality disorder, antisocial personality disorder. Typically, it doesn't really manifest until the teenage years or early adulthood and is much more commonly diagnosed in women than men, though that may just be due to cultural bias. Clinicians are loath to ever diagnose such a thing in a child as young as Hugo, but the way Sonia has described his behavior, it really seems to fit. And he's got the risk factors."

"Such as?" Ivy asked.

"Early-childhood trauma. Being separated from his mother. Being raised by grandparents in an overly permissive environment where he was basically given free rein. And I suspect some genetic component too. The way Sonia describes her sister, Abi, she sounds exceedingly promiscuous in a really unhealthy, attention-seeking kind of way. And all the women of their family—Sonia's mother, her sister, even Sonia herself—seem to have real difficulty with mood regulation. They're prone to fits of rage when frustrated."

The fits of rage were the last thing Ivy wanted to hear. She was still struggling with how anything Claire had to offer could be helpful to Sonia's case.

"I still don't understand what it means. How does a person with histrionic disorder behave?"

"Think of narcissism," Claire said. "We've all become familiar with that one. A true narcissist has a giant hole inside them, a hollowness that they can never fill. They do their best to plug it with the admiration of others, but that's only a temporary fix. They constantly need more and more. And they're so fundamentally wounded with this sense of inner shame, which is too great for them to ever acknowledge or process, that they tend to lack empathy for others, viewing them merely as a means to their emotional ends."

"Okay, sounds a little like my father," Ivy said, only half joking.

Claire smiled at the aside. "Well, histrionic disorder is similar, but it's more tied to an overwhelming fear of abandonment. These are people who need to be the center of attention, pretty much at all times, not so much for their egos but just to feel safe. Otherwise, they're terrified that the people they care about or depend upon will leave them."

That made some sense to Ivy. She could certainly see how a boy with Hugo's background could have abandonment issues. His mother had left him shortly after his birth and was a virtual stranger to him until they were reunited a little over a year ago. She still wasn't sure how it could explain Hugo inventing the burn story, though—if, in fact, he had invented it.

"And you really think Hugo has histrionic personality disorder?"

"Like I said, I haven't treated Hugo, so I can't formally diagnose him. And I would never diagnose a child that young anyway. But there's a lot of smoke there. And the thing about people with histrionic personality disorder is the desperate ways they will act when they perceive that they are about to be abandoned. We're talking extreme dramatics—outrageous outbursts, threats of suicide, violence, and concocting grandiose fabrications of victimhood."

"Like telling people your mother held you down and branded you with a skillet?"

"Exactly," Claire said.

Wow. Ivy felt chills. If true, it could really explain a lot. She had no idea how she could ever get any of it in front of a jury, but she felt more and more like the truth was coming to light.

"There's something I don't get, though," she said.

"What's that?" Claire asked.

"If Hugo was afraid of his mother abandoning him, then why make up a story that would pretty much ensure their separation?"

Claire shrugged. "I know it seems contradictory, but that's often how these things play out. With histrionic personality disorder, there's usually this vicious push and pull in relationships. They'll lash out at their loved ones one minute then desperately beg for forgiveness the next. Plus, let's not forget we're talking about a very young child whose concept of reality and consequences hasn't totally developed. All I expect Hugo would be aware of is that he was hurt by his mother and wanted to hurt her in return. And he needed attention. I doubt very much he thought it through any more than that."

"Jeez." Ivy leaned back. Suddenly, she did feel like she could go for a drink but not of the caffeinated variety. "Are you willing to testify?"

Claire sat up abruptly. "Oh no. No, no, no. I can't testify for you. I could lose my job. Not to mention, as I said, this isn't a formal diagnosis. Just a hypothesis, if you will."

"Great," Ivy said. "Then what am I supposed to do with all this?"

Claire turned up her palms. "You're the lawyer," she said. "I can't answer that. But..." Claire slid Sonia's file folder across the table. "I am authorized to give you this. Maybe get your own expert to look at it. My hope is that there's something in there that will be useful."

Ivy took the file and tucked it into her bag.

CHAPTER 28

That evening, Ivy met up with Cesar for dinner at an Italian restaurant that specialized in brick-oven pizzas. They shared one with pepperoni and banana peppers while Ivy told Cesar about her meeting with Claire Haskell.

"This is great," he said while folding his pizza slice in half. "We've got the little bastard."

Ivy wasn't ready to start referring to Hugo as "the little bastard." Even if he had made up an incriminating story about his mother, he was still just a kid and one who'd gotten off to a really tough start in life.

"You know what I mean," Cesar said, reading her expression. "This could explain Sonia's side of things."

"It could," Ivy agreed. "But the jury will never hear it."

"Why not?"

Ivy explained that Claire was unwilling to testify and that they would likely need an expert who had actually treated Hugo for such testimony to be admissible anyway. "What do you think the chances are of Lester springing for our own forensic psychologist?" she asked sarcastically.

"Yeah, I see your point. Don't suppose the state would pay for it."

"Maybe if we'd put in the request a year ago. But since we're a month out from trial, the best we could do is pay for it up front and hope to get reimbursed pennies on the dollar somewhere down the line."

Cesar nodded, knowing as well as Ivy that Lester would never authorize any advance expenses in a court-appointed case.

"Well, I've got some good news," Cesar said.

Ivy's heart fluttered. "Oh my God. You found the records?"

"No, not yet. But I did find Sonia's sister, Abi."

Ivy had almost forgotten about her but instantly realized how smart it was for Cesar to think to contact her. As Sonia's only living adult relative, she was likely their best source of information.

"How'd you find her? Sonia said they'd lost touch."

"Found her on WhatsApp. She's living in Guadalajara and was really sorry to hear about the trouble Sonia is in. I asked her about Hugo, and she said that her parents told her the same thing, that they were cooking over a fire pit and set the metal grate against a wall to cool, and Hugo leaned against it."

Ivy's heart was racing. *This is huge.* But she felt the need to manage her expectations. *Would scars from the metal grate used with a fire pit match those from a skillet pan?* Maybe the sister was just telling Cesar what he wanted to hear. Ivy decided to probe.

"Did you tell her what Sonia said and she agreed with it, or did you just ask her if she knew what happened?"

She watched as Cesar pulled out his phone and scrolled back through his conversation.

"I told her Sonia said Hugo was burned while living with her parents in Guatemala and asked if she knew anything about that. Then she told me what her parents told her."

That was kind of a mixed bag. It would have been more compelling if Cesar had just asked if Abi knew how Hugo got scars along his side so as not to suggest the answer. Instead, he had fed her the basic story about it occurring while he'd lived with his grandparents. But Abi had apparently supplied some details on her own that matched up with Sonia's. In sum, Ivy considered it to be fairly convincing, but it was also inadmissible hearsay. Unless Abi had witnessed it firsthand, she'd never be able to testify about what her parents told her happened.

"Did she ever see the scars herself?" Ivy asked.

"No," Cesar said.

"Shit." *Another brick wall.*

"But Abi said she is pretty sure her parents took Hugo to the hospital and also thinks she knows which one."

Ivy slapped the table so hard it rattled the silverware. Patrons at nearby tables turned to stare, but she didn't care. "Oh my God," she said, clutching her chest. "Cesar, this is so big. Thank you, thank you, thank you."

Finding those records would be not only an enormous relief but also a huge validation. Ivy would be a hero, a real lawyer.

"I've been trying and trying to call them," Cesar said, "but nobody ever picks up. I'm a little afraid they may no longer be operating. The shit with the cartel in that area is super bad. Like open-warfare-with-the-government bad."

And just like that, Ivy's mental images of glory were dashed, flattened like an anvil dropping down on a slapstick cartoon character.

"I wish I could just go down there. This is the kind of thing that if I could go in person, I bet I could get those records," Cesar said.

Ivy suspected that was true. As crafty and resourceful as Cesar was, if those records existed, he'd have the best chance of anybody of coming back with them. But traveling to Guatemala was out of the question because of his immigration situation.

"If you leave the country, you won't be able to get back in."

"Yeah, I know."

Ivy stopped to think. Cesar might not be able to go, but there had to be someone who could. "What about Sonia's sister? Could she get the records?"

"She lives in Guadalajara."

"So?"

"So that's in Mexico."

Ivy hadn't grasped that. She also had no sense of how far that was from Sonia's hometown in Guatemala. Other than a college spring-break trip to Cancun, she had never been south of the border and knew little about the geography. "Is it far?" she asked.

"Yes. It would be like asking someone in Seattle to drive to Dallas. And like me, she'd have to cross an international border and risk not being able to return."

That was frustrating, but Ivy wasn't about to give up. "What if we hired somebody down there, like a private investigator?"

Cesar nodded. "Yeah, that could work. If we can find someone."

"Well, let's at least give it a try."

"You think Lester will spring for a PI?"

"Who cares? I'll pay for it myself. This is too important. Just tell me how much it will be."

"Okay," Cesar said. "I'm on it."

They resumed munching on their pizza, Ivy cutting hers with a fork while Cesar continued to eat his folded, grease-dripping slices like a sandwich. The talk of international travel brought Cesar's looming deportation to mind, and Ivy realized she hadn't asked about it in a couple of days.

"So, have you met with the immigration attorney Lester was setting you up with?"

"Talked to him on the phone," Cesar said. He kept chewing like the immigration issue was no big deal.

"And?"

Cesar swallowed and took a long drink of water before responding. "And I think we've got a pretty good plan. I'm feeling good about it."

Ivy was pleasantly surprised to hear that, having thought Cesar's options for staying in the country were bleak. "Well, are you going to let me in on it?" she asked. "Are we getting hitched or what?"

Cesar laughed. "No, no. No need for a green-card marriage. I think I've got this."

"Got it how?"

Cesar reached for another slice from the pie, but Ivy stopped him by placing her hand atop his.

"What's going on?" she asked sternly.

"Relax." Cesar pulled his hand back. "It's no big deal. I'm just going to go ahead and apply for a U-Visa."

Wow. Cesar was full of surprises. He had been adamantly opposed to pressing charges against his ex-boyfriend, so Ivy was surprised to hear he had changed his mind.

"I thought you weren't willing to report Isaac to the authorities."

"I'm not."

Ivy was confused. "Then how...?"

"Duh," Cesar said, holding a finger gun to his head. "The other night? We were both robbed at gunpoint, remember? That's a felonious assault. My attorney says it's U-Visa all the way. I just need the police to sign off on the certification, and I'm home free."

Cesar went in again for a slice of pizza. Ivy felt a sense of relief that his immigration dilemma seemed to be solved. She was thankful something good could come out of their harrowing experience, which had traumatized her in a way she still hadn't even begun to grapple with, other than to know she'd be triple-checking the locks and sleeping with the light on for many nights to come. But suddenly, the tumblers inside her brain clicked into place, and she saw what was happening.

"Cesar," she said, "let me see your phone for a second."

He stopped mid-bite. "Huh?"

"Your phone," Ivy repeated.

Cesar swallowed hard. "Why do you want to see my phone?"

"Because I do. Just for a second."

"But why?"

"Why not?"

"I don't understand."

"Why don't you want me to see your phone?"

"Because it's my private property. I don't go snooping through your phone."

"I'm not going to go through it. I want to see what it looks like. Just hold it up."

"No."

"Show. Me. Your. Phone," Ivy growled.

"Fine." Cesar held up his phone up for a second then pulled it back under the table before Ivy could get a good look. "Happy?"

"A little slower, please."

"This is stup—"

"Now."

Cesar rolled his eyes and held up his phone long enough for Ivy to see a diagonal crack across the top of the screen.

"Brand-new phone, and you've already got a crack in it," Ivy said.

That Saturday, she had invited Cesar to go with her to the Verizon store where she'd bought a new iPhone to replace the one that had been stolen. She hadn't thought much of it at the time when Cesar said he'd already taken care of his, but now she was very suspicious.

"Yeah, I'm a klutz," Cesar said unconvincingly. "Dropped it, like, an hour after I got it."

"Turn it around," Ivy said.

"What?"

"Let me see the back of it."

"Why?"

"Just do it."

Cesar held up the phone and flipped it around quickly, but it was long enough for Ivy to appreciate its scuffed edges and recognize the cover.

"That's your old phone," she said. "The one that was stolen."

Cesar made a weak attempt at looking aghast. "No, it's not. That's crazy. I just got this."

Ivy wasn't buying that for a second. "Cesar, I've seen you on your phone a billion times. That's your old phone, and I want to know how the hell you've got it when it was stolen the other night."

Cesar looked at the ceiling like he was trying to think up an excuse but then gave up. "Okay, it's not what you think."

"Really? Because I'm thinking you got somebody to rob us so you could apply for a U-Visa. And you used me so you'd have a witness."

Cesar's face turned stark white. He got emotional, looking like he might cry, and reached for Ivy's hand. She pulled it back.

"I swear that's not it. That's not how it happened. Not... totally."

Ivy crossed her arms. She was as mad as hell. If Cesar wanted to cook up some immigration scheme, fine. She'd even been willing to marry him to help. But having someone break into her house and put a gun to her head? *That is seriously fucked up. And why didn't Cesar let me in on it? Why all the theatrics, acting just as traumatized as I was?*

"Please believe me," Cesar said. "I would never do that to you."

He actually sounded sincere. Ivy started to ask, "If you didn't do it, then who?"

But before she could verbalize the question, she realized the answer. Lester.

CHAPTER 29

Ivy left Cesar at the restaurant and sped across town. She got on I-40 and made the twenty-minute drive to Durham in just over ten. Lester lived in a historic olive-green Victorian close to downtown, near the old Durham Bulls stadium made famous by Kevin Costner and Susan Sarandon. Ivy parked on the street and marched angrily across the yard and onto the wraparound porch, where she banged on the door. Lester answered wearing a silk monogrammed bathrobe and holding a .38 snub-nosed revolver.

"Goddamn, Ivy. You can't come up here in the middle of the night, knocking like a damn debt collector. I almost shot your ass."

"I'm getting used to having guns pointed at me thanks to you."

Recognition was all over Lester's face. He didn't bother trying to deny it.

"Cesar told me everything," Ivy said.

Lester tucked the pistol in the pocket of his robe. "Come on inside. Let's talk."

Ivy wanted to tell Lester to go fuck himself, but she found herself following him through his seventies-style man cave replete with cheesy statues, animal-skin rugs, and velvet paintings of naked women. He led her past an indoor Zen garden with a trickling water feature then down into a recessed living room with shag carpeting, a maroon suede couch, and an impressive wet bar in the corner.

"Okay," Lester said. "Go ahead. Get it out of your system."

Ivy was infuriated by his nonchalance. "I'm not really sure where to start. As I was driving over here, I was thinking that maybe I should just call the cops and tell them about the shit you and Cesar pulled."

Lester moved to the wet bar and poured himself a tumbler of whiskey from a crystal decanter. He glared at Ivy. "First of all," he said, "Cesar had nothing to do with it. He just put the pieces together once I got him onto the U-Visa plan. I told him what was up, and he was grateful. Just asked for his phone and wallet back. Speaking of which...."

Lester stepped behind the bar, where an autographed portrait of Richard Pryor hung next to a shelf lined with Donald Goines novels. Lester removed the portrait, revealing a wall safe. He punched in a code, and the door swung open. He reached in among stacks of cash and jewels to retrieve what Ivy recognized as her purse and cell phone.

"The second thing you need to know is that you weren't part of the plan. Cesar was the target, but you and he were pretty much inseparable, so... shit happens. Here, you can have these back." Lester placed Ivy's belongings on the bar and closed the safe.

Ivy didn't move to retrieve her phone or purse. She wasn't sure she even wanted them. Taking them back felt like it would somehow make what Lester had done okay, like—no harm, no foul.

"Do you have any idea how fucked up I am over what happened? I've slept maybe two hours a night since. Every time I close my eyes, I see that gun being pressed against my head."

Lester grimaced. "Yeah, I'm sorry about that. The gun was necessary, though. The presence of a deadly weapon is what makes it a felonious assault. If it makes you feel better, it wasn't loaded."

It occurred to Ivy at that moment that Lester actually may have been the masked man, though she still had a difficult time picturing what the assailants looked like. All she could see was the gun.

"Were you...?"

"Me? Shit no. I was down at Barrister's with about fifteen witnesses all night long."

Of course he was. Lester would know how to cover his tracks with a rock-solid alibi in case anyone ever got suspicious.

"So who were the goons?"

"Just some folks who owed me a favor. And that's all you'll ever know."

Ivy shook her head in disgust. "I thought we were supposed to defend the criminals, not join them."

"Well, if you'd told me about your criminal immigration marriage-fraud scheme, maybe I wouldn't have had to pull mine."

Lester looked satisfied, like he'd scored a point. Which was bullshit. Ivy might have been willing to enter into a sham marriage to help out a friend, but what Lester had done was dangerous. Even if the thugs were instructed not to hurt anyone, there were a thousand ways it could have gone bad.

"There were no victims with what I was planning."

Ivy was pissed that Lester wasn't more apologetic. He should have been begging for forgiveness.

Instead, he said, "Look, sometimes, for the right client, an attorney has to be willing to risk it all. I just—"

"Can we cut the whole Jedi-Zen-master, attorney-training bullshit? What you did was a crime. It was at least three crimes. And someone could have been hurt, maybe even killed."

"You gonna turn me in?"

Ivy was really seriously considering it, though she was as happy as anyone that Cesar had a solution to his immigration problem.

"No," she said finally.

"Good." Lester took a sip of his drink, the first sign that evening that he was at all nervous.

"I'm going to blackmail you," Ivy said.

Lester gulped down the liquor. "Come again?"

"I'm going to blackmail you," Ivy repeated. "I won't turn you in but only on one condition."

"Which is?"

"You help me try Sonia's case."

Lester took another sip of his drink and stood silent for a moment, processing what she'd said. "You do know blackmail's illegal, right?"

"Hey, I learned from the best," Ivy said. "Besides, sometimes, for the right client, an attorney has to be willing to risk it all."

Lester raised his glass to her then set it on the bar. He paused there for a moment, eyes closed, thinking. Then he crossed the room to an antique writing desk, where he retrieved a legal pad and pen and handed them to Ivy.

"What's this for?"

Lester said, "If we're gonna try this fucker, we've got a lot of work to do. You'll need to take notes."

PART 4

CHAPTER 30

The weeks leading up to the trial went by in a blur. Every morning, Lester came into the office with a new idea, another motion that needed to be filed, research that needed to be done, loose ends that needed to be tied up. Each time, Ivy dutifully recorded his latest burst of brilliance and diligently got to work, all the while knowing the most important aspect of their trial prep was what Cesar was working on—trying to find Guatemalan medical records that would show Hugo's burn injuries occurred while he was living apart from his mother.

With the help of Sonia's sister, Abi, Cesar had identified the hospital where Hugo most likely would have been taken, but they were unable to get someone to return a phone call or respond to multiple letters. Just days out from trial, Cesar was still unable to confirm that they had ever treated Hugo, much less that they had records saying what Ivy hoped they would say. He had, however, finally found a private investigator who guaranteed he could get any records that existed—for a price.

"A thousand dollars?" Lester shouted when presented with Cesar's ask during that morning's prep session.

"No," Cesar said, laughing. "A thousand in Guatemalan money. It's like a hundred bucks US."

"Oh, okay," Lester said. "Wire him the funds, then, but make sure he understands he's got until Monday morning to get those records in our hands, or we've got to try this case with our pants down."

"I'll make sure he gets that message."

"Get going, then. Time is of the essence."

Cesar saluted and left Lester and Ivy alone in the conference room. Lester closed his eyes and started rubbing his temples. Ivy had never seen him so stressed.

"You okay?" she asked.

"Yeah, yeah, just tired." For the last few weeks, Lester had abandoned his usually lackadaisical working style while he and Ivy had done double duty, working around the clock to prepare Sonia's case while also holding down their normal caseload.

Lester commented, "All those trials you see on Court TV are rich white people who can pay their lawyers enough to shut down their practice and spend all their time on one client. But trying something like this for a poor person who doesn't have two nickels to rub together while keeping the lights on in your damn office is a whole different thing."

Ivy had come to realize that as well, though at the moment, she was too nervous to be tired. That afternoon, a pretrial hearing was scheduled that would largely determine the case's outcome.

The defense Lester and Ivy had constructed was basically a three-pronged approach. The first and most important aspect was Cesar's assignment of finding medical records that would prove Sonia had not burned Hugo. Without those, "the case is pretty much cooked," Lester liked to say, though Ivy discouraged him from using that unfortunate pun.

The second part of the defense had to do with the broken arm. Ivy had filed a motion to exclude Sonia's supposed confession about breaking Hugo's arm and consequently to have the charge dismissed. In just a few hours, she'd get a chance to argue her motion before Judge Bingham.

The third part of the defense was Lester's baby—convincing the jury that sweet little Hugo could have made up such horrible stories about his mother. To do that, he'd hired a forensic psychologist to evaluate Hugo and offer the opinion the prison psychologist, Dr.

Claire Haskell, had tipped them off to but been unwilling to testify about herself—namely, that Hugo suffered from trauma and psychological issues that could explain why he'd falsely accused his mother.

Lester had been adamant about his choice of therapists. Dr. Saul Eli was a semiretired shrink in Chapel Hill he affectionately referred to as "a real defense whore." Back in the day when Lester was regularly trying cases, he'd used Dr. Eli in several murder trials. "The guy never saw a killer he didn't think was clinically insane."

"Great," Ivy said.

"It makes sense if you think about it," Lester argued. "Well-adjusted folks don't usually go around croaking people."

Dr. Eli had proven to be reliably defense oriented, producing a report that would certainly help their case—if he was allowed to testify. That was the other motion scheduled for that afternoon: Eliza Wells's motion to exclude Dr. Eli's testimony. At least Lester was handling that one.

Ivy was feeling pretty rattled. She believed they had slung together the best defense possible with such limited time and resources, but like all three-legged stools, if one support got knocked out, the whole thing could topple. And if things didn't go well that afternoon, and if Cesar's PI didn't deliver, they could lose not one but all three legs and end up flat on their asses.

"Are you okay?" Lester asked.

The answer was no. Ivy felt like someone had dropped a barbell onto her chest. It was like she couldn't catch her breath. She kept imagining herself getting in the courtroom and suddenly losing the ability to speak.

"Maybe you should handle both motions today," she said. "There's so much riding on this."

"Nah," Lester said. "You got this. You've done all the research on the confession, and you'll probably be better at arguing the law than me anyway. I'm more of a facts man."

"Are you sure? Because—"

"I'm sure," Lester said. "I have total confidence in you."

That made Ivy feel the pressure even more.

"Okay," she said.

"Hey." Lester pushed her chin up with his thumb. "I think some-body needs to ring the bell."

Ivy groaned. Cesar had told her about the stupid ritual from back in Lester's swashbuckling trial-lawyer days—ringing a boxing bell before going to court. She'd thought it was a joke until Lester had brought the bell in a few days earlier, claiming it was one that was used in a Sugar Ray Leonard fight back in the eighties.

"Come on," Lester said. "We need to get you fired up." He circled behind Ivy and started massaging her shoulders.

"Okay, okay," Ivy said, shrugging him off. "I'll ring the bell." She stood and crossed the room to the credenza where the bell sat next to a humidor of Lester's Cuban cigars.

"Hold up. Not like that." Lester pulled out his phone and started playing "Eye of the Tiger." "You've got to get loose first." Lester bounced to the music while shadowboxing. "Try it. Let me see some combinations."

"I'm wearing heels," Ivy complained.

"Then kick them off."

"Seriously?"

"Seriously. We need to get you pumped up."

Ivy slipped off her shoes and started going up and down on her toes.

"Come on," Lester said. "You can do better than that. Throw some punches."

Ivy gradually put a little more effort into it until, in spite of her-self, she started to feel the blood and adrenaline flowing. She popped a couple jabs and hooks and even an occasional uppercut.

"Hatchet Lady's not gonna know what hit her, right?" Lester yelled over the music.

"Right," Ivy responded.

"I want to hear you say it."

"Hatchet Lady's not gonna know what hit her."

"Come on. Yell that shit!"

"Hatchet Lady's not gonna know what hit her!"

"She's got to deal with Ivy fucking Collins!" Lester yelled. "Come on. Let me hear it."

"She's got to deal with Ivy fucking Collins!"

"Like you mean it!"

"She's got to deal with Ivy fucking Collins!"

"Okay," Lester said, stopping the music. "Now you're ready. Go ring that bell."

CHAPTER 31

As soon as Judge Bingham called the courtroom to order and turned the floor over to Ivy, she came out swinging. "Your Honor, this is the defendant's motion to suppress an alleged confession and to dismiss count two of the indictment. I know you are familiar with the facts of this case from our prior hearing, Judge, so I won't belabor those."

Ivy wanted to get right to the point and also wanted to gloss over the horrific allegations. In summary, she said, "Once the police made the decision to arrest the defendant on the charge presented as count one of the indictment, they attempted to Mirandize her with the help of another officer who is fluent in Spanish. Then they told her that they would be taking her son to Memorial Hospital, at which point the defendant is reported as responding in Spanish, saying, 'Is that where *I* took him when *I* broke his arm?' This led to a subsequent interview with the child, where, after some prompting, he alleged that his mother had previously broken his arm by twisting it. Thus, the alleged confession also led to a search for medical records at Memorial, which showed that the boy was previously treated there for a broken arm, which, according to those records, was reported as resulting from a fall. The problem with all of this, Your Honor, is it was done in Spanish, which the defendant doesn't speak."

The judge gazed over his reading glasses at Sonia, whose name and appearance pegged her as a likely Spanish speaker. The courtroom bailiff snickered. Ivy did her best to not let that disrupt her momentum.

"What I should have said is that she doesn't speak Spanish well, Your Honor. It's not her first language. Ms. Cabrerra is from a remote part of Guatemala where they still speak an ancient Mayan dialect called Mam."

"One more time, please," the judge said.

"I'm sorry?"

"The name of the language."

"It's called Mam, Your Honor."

"Did you say Mam, like 'Yes, ma'am?'"

The bailiff snickered again.

"That's correct, Judge. Spelled M-A-M."

"Okay. I've never heard of that before. Please continue."

Ivy felt knocked off her stride. Judge Bingham apparently wasn't as familiar with the case as she'd expected. Because he'd presided over the prior hearing where Sonia had nearly pled guilty via a Mam translator, Ivy thought the judge would already have known about the unusual language. But Judge Bingham presided over a lot of cases. And unlike federal judges who had clerks to summarize files and do advanced research on the legal issues, state court judges often came into hearings cold, with little to no advance knowledge of what the cases were about, and were then expected to make important, life-changing rulings on the spot, based largely upon the oral presentations of the lawyers. That meant the persuasive skills of the attorneys went a lot farther in determining outcomes than the facts and the law might otherwise dictate. Or as Lester liked to put it, "There really is no law. There's just whatever you can convince a judge of."

Ivy took a sip of cold water from a Styrofoam cup and started again. "I'd never heard of Mam before either, Your Honor. But I have an affidavit here from Ms. Marisol Davies, who is a certified translator fluent not only in Mam but also Spanish and English. She attests to one of the unique aspects of Mam, which is that it does not contain personal pronouns. So if a Mam speaker was trying to say, 'Is that where *I* took him when *I* broke his arm?' or 'Is that where *I* took him when *he* broke his arm?' it could very easily get translated the same way into Spanish then English."

The judge nodded. He could see where she was going.

"My client, via a proper Mam translator, adamantly denies breaking her son's arm. She says that *he* broke it when *he* was playing and fell off her front porch, which is consistent with what is reported in the medical records. So there are a lot of constitutional problems here. First, because the Miranda warnings were given to the defendant in English and Spanish—two languages she has very limited proficiency in—the warnings were not effective, and thus, any subsequent confession violated her rights under the Fifth, Sixth, and Fourteenth Amendments to the US Constitution as well as Article One, Sections Nineteen and Twenty-Three, of the North Carolina Constitution. A defendant has to make a knowing, intelligent, willing, understanding, and voluntary waiver of her Miranda rights in order for a subsequent confession to be admissible. In addition, Your Honor, the confession in this case really was not a confession at all but rather a mistranslation. If a Mam speaker is translating something into Spanish, there is really no reliable way to know who the personal attribution was to when she talked about the broken arm. She could just as easily have meant to say that the boy broke his arm, which is what the medical records say. For those reasons, the alleged confession should be suppressed."

Next was the part where Ivy started waxing eloquent about the law to make the leap from suppression of the confession to dismissing the charge entirely. "The right against self-incrimination is one of the bedrock principles of our legal system, Your Honor. It's one of the things that sets us apart from other countries, how we keep from becoming one of those oppressive regimes where bogus or coerced confessions can be used to convict innocent people or political opponents. And it's a right that is constantly under assault, so it must be jealously guarded by the courts. That's why the law requires not only that the confession be suppressed but also that any other evidence that it led to also be suppressed as fruit of the poisonous tree. Otherwise, the state would benefit from its constitutional violation and have a perverse incentive to repeat such abuses in the future. Applying the fruit-of-the-poisonous-tree doctrine in this case requires the dismissal of Count Two in its entirety because the so-called confession is what led to all subsequent evidence related to that charge."

With that, Ivy took her seat, feeling pretty good about her presentation but fearing she might have laid it on a little too thick with the constitutional stuff. Lester gave her a thumbs-up under the table, a welcome jolt of affirmation. Then Ivy gripped the arms of her chair as she waited to see how Eliza Wells would respond.

Her expectation was an impassioned legal argument. But Eliza surprised her by calling a witness to the stand, Amelia Diaz, the police officer who'd translated Sonia's confession. After going through some preliminary questions covering Officer Diaz's background and experience, Eliza moved into the events at issue.

"Officer Diaz, at any point during your conversations with the defendant, did you ever get the impression that she was having any difficulty understanding you?"

"Not at all. The entire time we spoke, she appeared to me to be a very natural, completely fluent Spanish speaker."

Ivy could see the righteous indignation burning in Eliza's eyes as she nodded along with the officer's answer. Eliza was a true believer, all right. Lester had often said that the secret to being convincing was to be convinced, and in that moment, there was no doubt the prosecutor one hundred percent believed that all the "mistranslation" business was a colossal crock of shit.

"At any time, did the defendant ever ask you to slow down?"

"No."

"Did she ever ask you to repeat anything?"

"No."

"Did she ever ask you to explain what something meant?"

"No, ma'am."

"Did she ever do *anything* or say *anything* to indicate that she was confused about what you were saying?"

"Not at all."

"How about when the defendant spoke to you in Spanish? Did you ever have any difficulty understanding her?"

"Not in the slightest. Her Spanish was excellent."

Ivy grabbed a pad of sticky notes and scribbled a message to Lester. "This is bullshit." When Cesar had first spoken to Sonia, it had taken him all of thirty seconds to realize her Spanish wasn't very good. There was no way the police interpreter didn't realize the same thing. Ivy started kicking herself that she hadn't brought Cesar along to testify as a rebuttal witness. She had thought the point about the language issue would go largely unchallenged, that Eliza would focus her argument more on the law than on the underlying facts. But Ivy was quickly learning that Eliza Wells didn't let anything go unchallenged.

Lester shook his head like he wasn't surprised. He, much more than Ivy, expected cops to lie.

Eliza asked, "Officer Diaz, when you told the defendant that her son was going to be taken to Memorial Hospital to be evaluated, do you remember the exact words she said to you in Spanish?"

"Yes," Officer Diaz said. "I wrote it down." Referencing the police report, she read aloud, *"Es donde lo llevé cuando le rompí el brazo?"*

"And what does that mean in English?"

Officer Diaz turned and faced the judge as she answered, "'Is that where *I* took him when *I* broke his arm?'"

The judge stroked his chin. There was nothing new about the information. Ivy had already told the judge all about what was said, but the way the officer delivered the line gave it a dramatic, revelatory effect.

"Did you repeat the question to make sure you had accurately understood the defendant?"

"Yes," Officer Diaz said. "Her answer kind of shocked me, and I wanted to be absolutely sure, so I asked her to repeat it, and she said the same thing again. Then I even asked her a third time with hand gestures, pointing right at her then miming like I was breaking somebody's arm to be sure she meant what she was saying, and she nodded affirmatively."

Ivy leaned over and whispered to Lester, "There's nothing in the report about hand gestures."

Again, Lester looked unsurprised. "The bitch is testi-lying."

All of a sudden, Ivy's heart pounded as she realized the officer was about to fudge her way past Ivy's motion and condemn Sonia in the process. "What do I do?" she whispered.

"Hang her ass with it," Lester said.

"How?"

"Just like you said. It's not in the report."

CHAPTER 32

Ivy had never conducted a cross-examination of a real, live witness before, much less attempted to tear down a police officer who had come to the stand armed with not only weapons of lethal force but also the blue uniform, the state imprimatur of credibility. Police officers were to be believed. They were the beleaguered, underpaid public servants who risked their lives on the front lines of societal decay, forced to mix with and clean up after the worst of the worst in order to protect decent, law-abiding citizens. At the very least, they were owed the benefit of the doubt from the people they served. At least, that was what most jurors thought.

Not criminal defense attorneys, though. "Testi-lying," Lester's term to describe Officer Diaz's performance on the stand, was commonly used by the defense bar to refer to the way police officers, practiced in testifying as part of their job, could skillfully slant, obscure, and even invent facts in order to ensure a conviction. What that meant for Ivy was that she couldn't just come right out and ask why the gestures Officer Diaz described—pointing at Sonia and simulating the breaking of her boy's arm—weren't contained in the report. Because if she went right to it, she could expect a smooth, reasonable-sounding, well-prepared excuse. Instinctively, Ivy knew she had to lay some groundwork to set the trap.

"Officer Diaz, since you are fluent in Spanish, is it common for other officers to ask you to translate for a witness or suspect?"

"Yes, it happens all the time."

"And when you translate, is a report typically made?"

The officer gave Ivy a look that could have been either confusion or suspicion. "There's not a separate report for the translation."

"But your translation would be included in whatever police report was being generated for that interaction. Is that correct?"

"Yes, but I am not always the one who writes the report," Officer Diaz said.

"Well, you are the one doing the translation, right?"

Eliza Wells shot to her feet. "Objection. Asked and answered."

Judge Bingham glanced disapprovingly at the prosecutor. His expression indicated that she was technically right, but he wasn't inclined to be quite so strict and would allow Ivy some latitude to build momentum with her questions. "Overruled. The witness can answer."

"Could you repeat the question?" Officer Diaz said.

"Yes," Ivy said. "My question was: Even if you are not always the one writing the report, are you the one doing the translation?"

"When I'm translating, yes, obviously."

A snicker from the courtroom deputy got Ivy doubting herself, but a nod from Lester encouraged her to keep going.

"Your translations are about important matters including police interrogations and witness interviews as part of official investigations. Correct?"

"Yes, that's right."

"So even if you do not personally write all the reports, I'm sure you at least review the portion of the report summarizing your translation to ensure that it is accurate."

Officer Diaz hesitated before responding. She was caught in a sticky situation. By that point, she had to know Ivy was going to point out things she'd testified to that were not contained in her report, but if she said she didn't even bother to review how her translations were recorded, it would expose her as not sufficiently caring about their accuracy.

"I do my best," she said.

Ivy started to ask her if she'd reviewed the report of her translation in this case, but she assumed Officer Diaz would just say she didn't remember. It seemed for a second like a dead end, but the thought sparked an idea for another line of questioning.

"Officer Diaz, how many reports would you say you write in a year?"

"Me personally?"

"Actually, let's include both reports that you write as well as ones that contain a recitation of your translations."

Officer Diaz shrugged. "Couldn't tell you."

That kind of response was designed to thwart the question in hopes the questioner would move on. Ivy needed to stick to the point until she got an answer.

"Can you give me an order of magnitude?"

"It really just varies," Officer Diaz said. She sounded entirely reasonable, just a public servant having to sit patiently through some inane questioning by another smart-aleck lawyer trying to pull one over for their scumbag client.

"Are we talking hundreds of reports a year? Thousands?" Ivy asked.

"Not thousands."

"Hundreds, then?"

"I wouldn't say 'hundreds' plural."

"Then maybe about a hundred reports a year that you have either authored or that contain information about communications where you served as the translator. Does that sound accurate?"

Officer Diaz looked at the judge, like he should step in and get the lawyer to stop annoying her, but Judge Bingham stared back, waiting for an answer.

"I guess it's somewhere in that ballpark," she conceded.

"Okay," Ivy said. "Is it also true that when you are making a report, you don't know whether or not you will ever be called to testify about what's in that report?"

"Yes."

"And if it's a report that you are called to testify about, you don't know *when* you might be called to testify. It could be weeks, months, or even years later. Correct?"

Officer Diaz studied her fingernails as she answered, "Yes, that's generally true."

"So you've got to make sure the reports are as detailed as possible because it's very likely you won't have a clear recollection of the events when and if you are ever called to testify about them?"

Officer Diaz responded, "Yes, but a lot of times, cases do stick out in your mind. It's not uncommon to recall something that just didn't make it into the report because you didn't think it was important at the time, but it turns out to be important later."

Shit. That was a good answer. It flustered Ivy for a second, and she needed to pause and take a sip of water to regain her composure. When she finished, she said, "Officer Diaz, when you went to the defendant's home, it was to translate for officers investigating allegations that Ms. Cabrerra had burned her son with a metal grate. Is that right?"

"Yes."

"In fact, you were there to carry out a search warrant and look for that metal grate, right?"

"That's right."

"At the point that you first arrived at the defendant's home, there was no indication that the boy had also previously suffered a broken arm at the hands of his mother. Correct?"

"Not at that point."

"In fact, as you testified on direct, it wasn't until after you read the defendant her rights and told her that her son was being taken to the hospital that the first mention was made about his arm being broken. Correct?"

"That's right. She said, 'Is that where I took him when I broke his arm?'" Once again, Officer Diaz delivered the statement with a dramatic flair, but that time, it seemed a little gratuitous and had less impact.

Ivy had a copy of the police report on the table in front of her and read from it. "Actually, what she said was '*Es donde lo llevé cuando le rompí el brazo?*'"

"Yes. Those were her exact words."

"Her exact words that you wrote down?"

"Yes."

"Is that your handwriting there in that part of the report?"

"Yes, it appears to be."

"And you also wrote down that you repeated the question to be sure you heard her right, and she repeated the same answer, '*Es donde lo llevé cuando le rompí el brazo?*'"

"Yes, I did."

"So you were very careful to write down the exact words of both exchanges, but you didn't write down anything about asking a third time and using hand gestures, which you now say you pointed at the defendant and mimed her breaking an arm to make sure she meant what she was saying?"

Officer Diaz took a moment to flip through her copy of the report, as though she didn't know damn well there was nothing in there about that.

Thirty seconds of pointless scanning passed before she nonchalantly said, "I don't see that specifically written out in here. This is one of those instances where I have a clear recollection of it. I guess I didn't write that part down because it didn't seem important until this issue about the pronouns came up."

Damn. Another good answer. A complete fucking lie but a good one.

Lester tugged at Ivy's sleeve, and she bent down so he could whisper to her.

"If she was so confident that Sonia's Spanish was good, then why did she need to do the gestures?"

Ivy patted his hand. That was a great point.

"Officer Diaz, you testified on direct that the defendant appeared to you to be fluent in Spanish. Correct?"

"Yes, absolutely."

"You said you had no difficulty understanding her and that she did not appear to have any difficulty understanding you. Correct?"

"No difficulty at all."

"Then why did you feel the need to repeat your question twice and even act it out with gestures to make sure you understood what she was trying to say?"

Officer Diaz took a minute to consider her answer. She obviously hadn't appreciated that contradiction before. Judge Bingham leaned toward her, seeming interested in what she would say.

"I guess I was just surprised is all. I mean, what kind of a mother would break her child's arm and just admit to it like that?"

Though it was another good answer, it wasn't convincing, in Ivy's opinion, but probably the best the cop could have done under the circumstances.

Ivy knew she needed to stay on the attack. "It wasn't because you were concerned that maybe the defendant wasn't accurately saying what she was trying to say?"

"No."

Before Ivy could ask her next question, Lester passed her a sticky note on which he'd written out a question. Ivy read it, but it didn't make sense to her. Lester motioned for her to bend down then whispered, "Whenever I get an answer that everybody knows is a lie, I always ask this. Trust me."

Ivy decided to do just that. She faced the officer and asked with an appropriate amount of incredulity, "Officer Diaz, are you being as honest with your last answer as everything else you've testified to?"

Before the officer could answer, Eliza Wells was on her feet, objecting. "Argumentative, Your Honor."

"Sustained," the judge said, which meant the witness didn't have to answer. But Ivy realized she didn't need her to. The point was made.

Ivy started to ask another question, but Lester tapped her under the table then whispered, "Cut it off there."

Again, Ivy listened to her boss. "No more questions, Your Honor."

She sat and whispered to Lester, "I was just going to establish that she doesn't speak Mam or know anything about its lack of pronouns."

"Not necessary," Lester assured her. "You did a great job. When you get in a zinger like that, it's best to just sit down. Let that be the thing that hangs in everybody's mind."

CHAPTER 33

Eliza Wells didn't do any redirect on Officer Diaz. Instead, she called another witness, Detective Reed, the lead investigator on Sonia's case and a twenty-year veteran of the force, who talked in convincing detail about how typical it was, once a credible charge of abuse was made, to then look for other instances of abuse.

"By the time a case gets on our radar, the abuse has usually been ongoing for a long time," Detective Reed explained. "So after an initial arrest, it is standard procedure to start looking into other chargeable events."

"How would you have gone about looking for other chargeable events?" Eliza asked.

"First, we would have conducted additional interviews with Hugo and asked him about any other instances where his mother had hurt him. Basically, the exact same thing we did after the defendant admitted to breaking her son's arm."

Ivy objected. The judge sustained, but Detective Reed immediately cleaned it up. "Sorry, Your Honor. I guess I should have said, 'after it appeared to us that the defendant had admitted to breaking her son's arm.'"

Ivy objected again but was overruled.

Eliza started driving her point home. "Based upon your decades of experience conducting investigations like this, is Hugo's statement about his mother breaking his arm something you would have learned even if she had never said anything to you at all?"

"Objection," Ivy said. "Calls for speculation."

Judge Bingham thought for a moment. "Overruled. The witness can answer as to the type of information he would typically expect to find."

Detective Reed turned to look at the judge. "Your Honor, it is my absolute one hundred percent belief that even if the defendant never said a word to us, we would have ended up in the exact same place. We would have learned about the broken arm from Hugo, and we would have scoured his prior medical records, looking for other potential instances of abuse."

"Thank you," Eliza said. "No further questions."

⎯⎯⎯ ◈ ⎯⎯⎯

IVY ATTEMPTED TO CROSS-examine Detective Reed, but it was mostly rambling and ineffectual. His testimony gave Eliza all the ammunition she needed to counter the fruit-of-the-poisonous-tree argument with the concept of inevitable discovery as far as Hugo's statement and the medical records were concerned. It presented Judge Bingham with the perfect opportunity to split the baby on Ivy's motion by suppressing the confession but allowing the remainder of the charge to go forward.

"At least you got a split decision," Lester said when they were back at the office, discussing the day's events. "I got TKO'd."

After Ivy's motion was decided, Eliza Wells had argued her motion to exclude Lester's forensic psychologist, Dr. Eli. It was a knock-out of a key witness for the defense but only a "technical one," according to Lester, because it was more because of Eliza's procedural maneuvering than anything having to do with the witness's credentials or the merits of his analysis. Once Lester agreed to help try the case, he had immediately retained Dr. Eli and filed a motion requesting an opportunity to evaluate young Hugo. But Eliza opposed it and ran out the very short clock until Lester decided he needed to go ahead and disclose his expert's report in order to meet the court deadlines, even though he had yet to perform a forensic interview. In terms of the ubiquitous boxing metaphors, that was akin to leading with your chin. It left the defense wide open to the criticism that Dr. Eli had made his diagnosis based purely upon a records review without actually talking to Hugo. That, combined with the wealth of literature and professional wisdom discouraging, if not outright prohibiting, formally diagnosing a child so young was all the reason Judge Bingham needed to keep Dr. Eli's opinions far away from the jury.

As the defense team staggered out of the courthouse on the Friday evening before trial, Ivy returned to her image of their case as a three-legged stool, realizing that two legs were gone. The only remaining hope teetered on the possibility that Cesar could find some Guatemalan medical records that would save the day.

On the walk to the car, Ivy pointed that out to Lester and asked him what they were going to do.

"I think we should go get drunk," Lester said.

That logic seemed unassailable to Ivy, so they walked another block down to Barrister's, an English-style pub that catered to the local trial lawyers. It had a side-alley entrance, and its walls were covered with framed neckties hung in honor of attorneys who'd scored big verdicts. The place was one of Lester's regular haunts, where he had a usual table beneath six framed neckties. Ivy pointed at the one closest to them, which displayed a black-and-silver tie with a bold zigzag pattern. She read the bronze plaque. "'Not Guilty Verdict—*State v. Morgan*.'"

"That one was a bogus murder rap," Lester said. "Guilt by association. Tony Morgan was a fourteen-year-old kid who accepted a ride home from some guys he knew from the neighborhood, not knowing they'd come across some rival gang members and decide to do a drive-by shooting. Tony had nothing to do with it, just in the wrong place at the wrong time."

"And you got him acquitted?"

"Yep."

Lester smiled. Ivy could see the pride in his eyes. She imagined that saving an innocent person's life had to be the most terrifying yet satisfying experience a real lawyer could ever have.

"God, that was a long time ago," Lester said. "Tony's a high school principal now, down around Atlanta somewhere. Still sends me a Christmas card."

The story got Ivy thinking about how Lester had once cynically declared that all defendants were guilty. Looking up at the framed necktie, she knew there had been a time when that wasn't the case.

"It is hard to believe," she said.

"What? That I could win a big case?"

"No, that anybody would ever wear that tie."

Lester laughed. "Hey, it was the nineties."

A waitress came by their table, and Lester ordered a whiskey, while Ivy asked for a glass of merlot. As they awaited their drinks, Cesar showed up.

Please have good news, Ivy thought.

"Okay, I've got good news and bad news," Cesar said. "Which do you want to hear first?"

Lester wanted to start with the bad.

"No, it works better the other way," Cesar said. "The good news is there is a medical record for Hugo."

Ivy slapped the table with excitement. Electricity surged through her body at the possibility that the case could be rescued.

"Yeah," Cesar said, beaming. "My guy got to a lady who works in the hospital, and she confirmed that a Hugo Cabrerra was admitted there about four years ago. The timeline fits."

"When can we get the record?" Ivy asked.

"That's the bad news."

Ivy held her breath as she waited for Cesar to explain.

"It seems that they don't have Sonia listed as Hugo's mother. They have a Magda Cabrerra on the file."

"That must be the grandmother," Ivy said.

"Yeah, that's what I figured too. Anyway, the hospital isn't willing to release the records based upon the authorization we sent from Sonia. That's why they haven't been responding to us."

Lester couldn't understand what the problem was. "Just send them the fucking birth certificate."

Ivy and Cesar gave each other knowing looks. Ivy explained that Hugo didn't have a birth certificate. He had been born at home, and his birth was never registered. They didn't have any definitive documentation to prove that Sonia was actually his mother.

"This is bullshit. There's got to be a way," Lester said.

Cesar took a seat and leaned in, whispering, "My guy says his contact there will smuggle out the records for us, but he'll need another thousand to pay her off."

"Fine," Lester said. "That's like a hundred bucks, right?"

"No," Cesar said. "This time, it's a thousand US dollars."

Lester sighed.

"I'll cover it," Ivy said.

"No, no. That's okay. We've come this far. We need to see it through. In for a penny, in for a pound." Then Lester started laughing.

"What?" Ivy asked.

"I'm just imagining putting in for reimbursement with the state, telling them we had to pay a thousand dollars to grease some flunky in Guatemala."

"It will be well worth it," Ivy said. She was getting excited again, feeling like there could actually be a light at the end of the tunnel.

"Now, you're sure this guy's not bullshitting us, right?" Lester asked Cesar.

"He knew the date and the grandma's name. I don't think there's any way he's just making it up."

Lester took a sip of his whiskey and gave Cesar a nod. "Wire him the funds. And tell him we need the record ASAP. Even sooner than that. The trial starts Monday, for God's sake."

Cesar scratched the back of his head. "Yeah, that's the thing. My guy's contact inside the hospital doesn't work again until Monday. He says that's the earliest she'll be able to get it."

In unison, Ivy and Lester set down their drinks and stared at each other. They'd built their entire case around the presumption that the record was out there, since there really was no defense without it. They could probably get through jury selection without knowing for sure whether they could produce the record at trial but not the opening statement. Lester was adamant that you never, ever promised the jury something in the opening unless you were one hundred percent sure you would be able to get it into evidence.

What made it worse from Ivy's point of view was that she had been assigned to deliver the opening, since it was something they were able to script and rehearse. Lester would take on the aspects of the trial that required adapting on the fly, such as jury selection, the closing argument, and some of the more combative cross-examinations. Ivy had already practiced the opening they'd planned, to the point that it was entirely committed to memory. She didn't have time to learn a new one.

"Relax," Lester said, reading the panic on her face. "If we get the record in time, you'll do the opening you've prepared. If not, I'll handle it."

"Handle it how?"

Lester shrugged. "I can always use the archer story."

"What's the archer story?" Ivy asked.

"You don't know the archer story?" Lester was incredulous. "That's Criminal Defense 101."

Ivy couldn't tell whether he was serious. She looked at Cesar, who shrugged.

"No, I don't know the archer story," she admitted.

"It's what you use when you're basically fucked and don't have anything else to talk about other than reasonable doubt," Lester said. "Hopefully, you'll never have to use it, but if we don't have that record come time to start the trial, then you're gonna hear it."

CHAPTER 34

Friday night ruined Saturday. Instead of trial prepping, Ivy spent most of the day too hungover to focus. The only substantive thing she accomplished was to shop for some decent maternity clothes for Sonia to wear during the trial.

That left Sunday for a frantic final dash to get ready. Ivy, Lester, and Cesar convened at Lester's house to go over jury selection, the first and perhaps most important part of the trial.

"Most lawyers get jazzed about closing arguments," Lester said, waving a smoking cigar like a wand as he spoke. "But if you ask me, the parts of the trial come in the order of importance. Pretrial motions matter most because they determine what evidence gets in. We already got our asses kicked there. So next is jury selection. Determining who sits in that box determines how they'll view the evidence. Following that is the opening statement, where you've got to frame the case in a way that will play to the jurors you've chosen. A trial is a competition between two stories, two explanations of the evidence. You've got to give the jury a theme—a prism—through which to interpret things your way. Then through the examinations, you've got to get the witnesses to fit your theory. By the time you get to closing arguments, most people have already made up their minds. All you can really do at that point is try to give the jurors who are on your side the arguments they'll need to stand up to the others when they go back into the jury room to deliberate."

"Okay, so what kind of jurors do we want in this case?" Ivy asked.

Lester puffed on his cigar. "That's just it," he said. "I don't know who's good for this. Can't see any clear preference as to gender. Women might be more inclined to identify with a female defendant, but they might also judge Sonia more harshly. A Hispanic juror might identify with Sonia or more strongly with Hugo or come to the courtroom with some kind of bias against Guatemalans or people of Mayan heritage that we'd have no idea about. Then you got politics. Liberals are normally a defense favorite, but even that could backfire because those folks are all about protecting the vulnerable, which Hugo certainly was. I just don't know."

"Maybe we should have hired a jury consultant," Ivy said.

Lester swatted that notion away. "They don't know shit. All this juror-profiling stuff is really just generalities anyway. At the end of the day, you've got to look people in the eye and go with your gut."

"Well, we've got to do something to prepare, right?" Ivy asked.

Lester stubbed out his cigar in an ashtray on the bar. "Yeah, I guess so."

When they were at court that Friday, they had stopped by the clerk's office and obtained a list of all the people who'd been summoned to jury duty—fifty names. Lester picked it up from the antique secretary desk in the corner of his living room and handed it to Cesar.

"Take this and run the names through the voter registration website and write down the political party for each. I figure if we've got nothing else to go on, all things being equal, we shoot for Democrats and Black folks, just 'cause they're probably less trusting of the police."

"Got it," Cesar said.

"And if you finish doing that, start googling the shit out of them. Take notes on anything interesting you find on Facebook or LinkedIn or whatever."

"What should I do?" Ivy asked.

"I'll need you taking careful notes during jury selection," Lester said. "I'll ask the questions, and you write down the answers. Then we'll huddle up and talk about it before we make any decisions on which jurors to exclude."

"But what about now?" Ivy asked. "Should I split up the list with Cesar?"

"No," Lester said. "You just work on your opening."

Ivy had already rehearsed her opening statement a gazillion times. She'd done it fast, slow, and every speed in between. She'd even done it with accents just to keep things fresh, delivering the jury speech in a Southern drawl, a British accent, and occasionally with the exaggerated flair of a Pentecostal preacher.

"I think I've got that part down," Ivy said. "What's worrying me are all the things you can't plan for."

Lester shook his head. "You've got to roll with the punches, Ives. It's like Mike Tyson said. 'Everybody has a plan until they get punched in the mouth.'"

Ivy didn't want to hear that. She was a planner. For that reason, Lester had agreed to do the cross-examinations of the police and social workers during trial, where things were sure to be adversarial. Her role, after the opening, would be limited to two cross-examinations. One would be the doctor who'd treated Hugo for his broken arm. Ivy believed that would be fairly straightforward, since the doc was essentially a neutral witness. But the other would be massively tricky: the cross of Hugo himself. That was at Lester's insistence. He said they would need a soft touch in dealing with the boy, and he just couldn't help crossing every witness like they were an axe murderer.

"Well, I don't know about Mike Tyson," Cesar said, "but if we get that medical record tomorrow, it is sure going to knock Eliza Wells for a loop."

"From your lips to God's ears," Lester said.

The men appeared to relish that thought, while Ivy remained fixated on just how much of the eventual outcome was out of her hands—even out of Lester's hands despite all his experience and natural aplomb. They would use every ounce of their abilities, their intelligence, their training, their moxie, and their mad-dash preparation to try to guide events toward a favorable outcome, but they couldn't control what the witnesses would say, how the judge would rule, or what the jurors would think. They couldn't even control whether they would get the medical record they desperately longed for, much less if it would say what they needed it to. All they could do was all they could do.

Ivy stood and started gathering her things. "You ready?" she asked Cesar, who had ridden there with her.

"Where are you going?" Lester asked.

"I think I know what I need to do."

"What's that?"

"Pray," Ivy said.

She wasn't joking. Although she wasn't especially religious, usually attending church only around the holidays and mostly not knowing how she felt about the tenets of the faith she'd more or less inherited from her parents, that night after arriving back at her townhouse, Ivy found herself down on her knees in her bedroom, hands clasped, begging God to help her and to help Sonia.

CHAPTER 35

Ivy got to court early on Monday to meet with Sonia and assist her in changing out of her prison jumpsuit into something more presentable. Finding appropriate maternity clothes was a challenge, but Ivy had procured several nice outfits, including the pink Ann Taylor dress and thin white cardigan she'd brought for the first day. Sonia seemed pleased with their fit and to be wearing something normal again. She nodded her thanks to Ivy, who squeezed her client's shoulder before they entered the courtroom along with the female deputy who would keep close watch on Sonia throughout the trial.

Lester and Cesar had arrived by that time and were huddled at the counsel's table. As she approached, Ivy heard Cesar say, "I'm working on it."

"What's going on?" she asked.

Lester had his arms folded, looking pissed. "No records."

Ivy's heart dropped.

Cesar said, "My guy's contact inside the hospital is sick. She no-showed for work this morning."

"I think this PI is jerking our chain," Lester said. "Or else this lady is jerking his."

"I really don't think so," Cesar insisted, but he sounded less than sure. "I'm going to get more information. Just let me talk to him again, and I'll check in with you at the break. Maybe his lady will be feeling better and can go in this afternoon."

"Sure, for another thousand bucks," Lester said.

Ivy's stomach churned. She feared Lester was right and they'd been scammed.

"Just don't give up yet," Cesar said. "I'll find out what I can."

Lester waved for him to go on.

As Cesar exited the courtroom, Eliza Wells entered, rolling a stack of banker boxes full of documents and exhibits. She nodded curtly to the defense lawyers.

Lester gave Eliza his brightest smile and a big wave like they were the best of friends. As he did so, he whispered to Ivy behind clenched teeth, "Where's the kid?"

"I don't know."

The week before, Lester, with a translator's assistance, had emphasized to Sonia that she should look for opportunities to make eye contact with Hugo throughout the trial. Let him peer into her sweet soul and see how much she loved him. The hope was that he wouldn't be able to condemn his mother once he had to face her.

"Maybe they aren't planning to have Hugo testify," Ivy said. "They may just try to admit the video of his interview."

"Like hell," Lester said. "Our client has a constitutional right to cross-examine his lying ass."

Before they could continue their discussion, the bailiff called the courtroom to order. Judge Bingham entered and also took note of the fact that the victim was not present. He asked Eliza Wells about it.

"Your Honor, given the victim's age and the nature of the accusations, we think it's best if he is not present, at least through most of the trial. It is our hope not to retraumatize him any more than absolutely necessary."

The judge nodded sympathetically.

Lester jumped to his feet. "Your Honor, I think the defense is entitled to know whether the boy is going to testify, because otherwise, we oppose the entry of any video interviews or statements he's made. All of it is inadmissible hearsay."

Eliza had obviously expected that and was ready with her response. "Your Honor, there are multiple exceptions to the hearsay rule that apply here. Statements contained in police reports meet the business records exception. Statements contained in medical records are information provided for the purpose of medical diagnosis. And the clinical psychologist who interviewed Hugo is an expert witness who can testify about the basis of her opinions."

Lester looked flustered for a second and started snapping his fingers, trying to remember the name of something. "Confrontation Clause," he blurted. "It's right there in the Constitution, Judge. A defendant has a right to confront her accuser. They can't hide the kid behind records and experts."

"Your Honor," Eliza fired back, "the Constitution doesn't say anything about bullying and intimidating an eight-year-old child. The court has wide discretion to protect juvenile witnesses."

"Protect, not exempt," Lester said.

"Okay, okay," Judge Bingham said. "Tell you what. I figure the most we're going to get done today is to pick our jury and hopefully deliver opening statements. We'll plan to start with the state's evidence at ten tomorrow morning, so I'll expect you all to be here at nine with briefs about the law on this issue, and we can take it up at that time. Now, unless there's anything else, I've got fifty people crammed into the juror assembly room who I know would very much like for us to get started."

Judge Bingham instructed the bailiff to bring in the potential jurors. The lawyers took their seats and prepared for the voir dire—a Latin phrase meaning "to speak the truth." Each side could question jurors about experiences they'd had or beliefs they held that might make them unsuitable to decide the case. Ivy pulled out a chart she'd created by taping two sheets of paper together landscape style and dividing them into two rows of six squares, numbered one through twelve to correspond to the jury box. She also had a list of the entire jury pool that Cesar had annotated with political affiliations and other random facts derived from his Google searching. As Eliza and

Lester asked their questions, Ivy would fill in the chart with notes on each juror. Next to her chart, she had a stack of Post-it notes so that whenever a juror was excused, she could cover their square with the Post-it and take notes on the person who replaced them.

In voir dire, there was no limit to the number of people the judge could dismiss "for cause," but Lester said those were relatively rare. Thus, the weeding out would primarily be done by the eight peremptory strikes allotted to each side. Those strikes could be exercised without stating a reason. The only limitation was a Supreme Court case called *Batson v. Kentucky*, which prohibited the exclusion of jurors on the basis of race. If one side believed the other was behaving in such a discriminatory manner, then it could raise a *Batson* challenge, in which case the striking attorney would have to present a credible, non–race-based reason for excusing the juror that would convince the judge.

Much of the morning was fought on that battleground, as Eliza Wells managed to exclude the majority of Black jurors. But unlike in *Batson*, where every Black juror had been excused and an all-white jury selected, Eliza was smooth enough to allow two people of color, one Black and one Asian, to stay, while also excusing one white juror to make it look good.

Lester wasn't having it, though, demanding to be heard outside the presence of the jury. He was steaming mad as he made his accusations of prejudice. "It's outrageous, Your Honor. This is *Batson* all the way. The state is clearly exercising its strikes on the basis of race."

Eliza responded with just as much righteous fury. "What's outrageous is Mr. Williams's outlandish and completely unfounded accusation."

Judge Bingham raised a hand to call for silence. "Have a seat, Mr. Williams. Let's hear the state out."

Ivy saw Lester mouth the word *bitch* as he sat down.

Judge Bingham indicated he was also concerned about racial bias. He asked Eliza to put on the record her rationale for each strike. The Hatchet Lady was completely unfazed. She stood there before Lester and Judge Bingham, two Black men, and without the slightest hint of concern, rattled off a litany of very credible-sounding reasons why she had excused the selected jurors.

Judge Bingham frowned while he thought it over. Ivy had a feeling she knew what was going on in his head. Rather than exercising her strikes periodically throughout her questioning, Eliza had waited and done them all in one batch. If the judge found that a single juror had been dismissed unfairly, then he could allow that one juror to stay on. But because Eliza had exercised her strikes en masse, the only remedy would be to strike the entire panel and start jury selection all over again. Judge Bingham, mindful of the jurors' time, was loath to do that.

"I cannot find that there has been a constitutional violation at this point," he said. "But I will be closely watching the state's conduct throughout the remainder of voir dire."

"That's fine, Your Honor," Eliza said. "I was actually about to pass the questioning to Mr. Williams. The prosecution is satisfied with the panel as currently constituted."

"Very well," Judge Bingham said. "Bailiff, please bring the venire back in, and the jury will be with Mr. Williams for additional questioning."

When the jurors returned, Lester shook off his anger over the failed *Batson* challenge and gave them his high-watt smile. He introduced himself and Ivy and motioned for Sonia to stand. Her stomach had grown so out of proportion with her petite frame that Ivy had to help her to her feet. Lester reminded the jury of her name and put his arm around Sonia like a proud father, a not-so-subtle endorsement of her character.

Judge Bingham had been strict with the attorneys that they were not to discuss the facts of the case during voir dire and could not do anything to "stake out the jurors" with questions like "If we prove X, will you find Y?" Their questions were to be limited to the jurors' backgrounds and their ability to follow the law impartially. Because the prosecution went first and had already covered those issues, Lester used his questions to impress upon the jury just how high a burden of proof the state had in a criminal case.

"In this trial, the state is going to have the burden of proving *each* and *every* element of the charged crimes *beyond* a reasonable doubt. It's the highest evidentiary standard there is. Now, some people think that's just too hard."

Ivy noticed that every time Lester mentioned the burden, he used the words *hard* or *high*. He also used his hands to demonstrate the balancing scales of justice and shot one hand way up in the air and the other way down low to emphasize just how overwhelming the state's evidence needed to be.

"I mention this," Lester said, "because some people worry that the burden on the state is just too onerous, and they have difficulty applying that hard, high burden. Now, has anybody here ever had any concerns about the reasonable-doubt standard placing too high a burden on the state?"

Two jurors raised their hands. Lester thanked them for their honesty and their courage to speak up. "Mr. Yost, I saw you raise your hand. Tell me what kind of concerns you have."

Mr. Yost, a retired schoolteacher who wore a dark toupee that stood in stark contrast to the gray hair around his ears, said, "The reasonable-doubt thing just seems really tough, you know? Like, a lot of times, you're ninety-nine percent sure, but there always has to be some doubt."

Lester smiled like he couldn't have said it better himself. "Being a juror is hard," he said. "No two ways about it. The question is 'Can you do your civic duty and follow the judge's instructions and decide this case based upon what the law is and not what you think it should be?'"

Mr. Yost said he could.

"You're sure, now? Remember, there's no wrong answers here, as long as they're honest answers. If you are selected to this jury, will you be able to hold the state to that high, hard burden of proving *each* and *every* element of their case *beyond* a reasonable doubt?"

Again, Mr. Yost said he could.

Lester moved on to the other juror who'd raised her hand, a nurse who was staring at her phone. "How about you, Ms. Parker?"

"Me?" Ms. Parker looked up suddenly.

"Yes, Ms. Parker. Now, I'm not saying this is gonna happen, because we feel very good about our defense in this case, but how are you going to feel if, after all the evidence is in, you think it's possible, or maybe even very likely, that the defendant is guilty, but you still have some *tiiiny* little doubt? Are you gonna be able to follow the law and find the defendant not guilty?"

"Objection!" Eliza shouted.

Judge Bingham beckoned for the attorneys to approach. Ivy tagged along to be a fly on the wall during the sidebar. Fuming, Eliza said Lester was overstating the law and also staking out jurors, getting them to commit to a not-guilty verdict if they had any doubt whatsoever.

"That's the law, last time I checked," Lester said.

"It has to be a *reasonable* doubt," Eliza shot back, "not just some conjectural, theoretical doubt."

Judge Bingham silenced them. "I think the defense is due a little latitude," he said.

Ivy recognized what he was doing. The judge had given the prosecution the benefit of the doubt on the constitutional challenge, so he was evening the playing field by letting Lester indoctrinate the ju-ry with his defense-friendly view of the law.

As they walked back to counsel's table, Ivy heard Eliza Wells mumble, "Jackass," under her breath.

When the questioning resumed, Lester spent a few more min-utes beating the reasonable-doubt drum before moving on to anoth-er topic.

"I'd like all of you to take a look at the state seal on the wall over there. Engraved on it is Lady Justice holding her scales, and you'll no-tice she's blindfolded, because justice is supposed to be blind. That means the same rules should be applied the same way to everybody, no matter their color, their gender, their religion, how much money they make, where they come from, or what language they speak. Can everyone here agree that justice should be blind?"

Twelve heads nodded in unison.

Lester said, "I'm not getting into any facts of the case, but I am al-lowed to tell you that my client, Ms. Sonia Cabrerra, is an immigrant to this country. She came here from Guatemala, and she doesn't speak English real good. Now, I know people have all kinds of opin-ions about immigration and things like that, but none of those issues are being decided in this case, so can everyone here agree that even though my client is an immigrant and doesn't speak English, you can still apply the law to her the same way you would anyone else?"

Twelve more nods followed.

"Nobody's gonna hold it against you," Lester said. "Again, there's no wrong answers here as long as we're being honest. Does anyone have any concerns whatsoever that they might not be able to treat my client the same way you would someone who looks and talks just like you do?"

No one raised their hand, but Lester wasn't done. He went down the line, asking the jurors individually until he had a firm commit-ment from each. Ivy realized Lester wasn't really expecting anyone to admit to bias. He just wanted to throw down the gauntlet and make it a personal challenge for each juror to go out of their way to treat Sonia fairly.

Once he was done, Lester spent twenty minutes on the presumption of innocence. "I'm gonna let you in on a little secret," he said. "The reason we're here today is because my client was arrested and charged with a crime. Now, a lot of people understandably think that means she's probably guilty. That's human nature. We want to trust the police and the prosecutors and hope they get it right. But the law says you can't do that. And this isn't Lester Williams talking. The judge is gonna instruct you that you have got to *presume* the defendant is innocent. You've got to put your natural instincts aside and presume, right now, that Ms. Sonia Cabrerra has been wrongly accused, unless and until the state proves otherwise by meeting that high, hard burden of proof we've been talking about."

Eliza Wells tried again to object, but Judge Bingham overruled her without allowing for a bench conference. He then permitted Lester to go down the row, asking each and every juror whether they could presume, right then, before hearing any evidence, that Sonia Cabrerra was innocent.

After that, the judge called a lunch break, which afforded Lester and Ivy some extended time to confer about who they should strike. They stayed in the courtroom while everyone else left in search of a restaurant. Cesar brought them sandwiches from a nearby deli along with some bad news. "All I can tell you is the lady is for-real sick. Like can't-get-out-of-bed sick. My guy swears it's legit. We just have to hope she gets better overnight."

Lester expressed his ongoing skepticism, but Ivy was encouraged that there had not been a request for more money, which she would have expected if they were being scammed. They'd just have to stay the course and hope for the best. Ivy tried to get Lester back on track by talking through the copious notes she'd taken on the prospective jurors. She thought they should dismiss six, hoping to get a more diverse pool.

"Did you see who else was sitting in that gallery?" Lester asked, referencing the fact that the remaining venire was also predominantly white. "Just keep in mind that the replacement can be worse than the person you kick. The goal isn't to cherry-pick people who are perfect. It's just to boot the ones you can't live with."

After some additional discussion, they settled on four jurors they would strike once the afternoon session began. That would leave them with four peremptory strikes in case the replacements turned out to be stinkers.

When court resumed, Lester announced their strikes. The clerk called the names of four people to take their places, and the questioning went back to Eliza Wells. After talking just to those four for about thirty minutes, she used a peremptory strike on one of them and got another dismissed for cause—a white hipster who'd been active in the Black Lives Matter protests and freely admitted he believed police were likely to lie in order to get a conviction.

Eliza's strikes brought two more jurors. Once she passed on them, Lester got to talk to the four newbies. He reiterated the points he had made before then used two more strikes. Thus, the process repeated, Eliza and Lester alternately striking jurors they perceived as too advantageous to the other side.

Eventually, they reached an unspoken compromise on white male jurors with an engineering or science background. Such people were prevalent in Wake County because of the area's multiple universities and medical facilities as well as its proximity to the Research Triangle Park, the home to dozens of major technology- and science-based companies. Ivy understood the attraction of such jurors to Eliza, as she thought they would tend to lean toward the conservative, law-and-order side of things. But she didn't get why Lester wanted them. During one of their whispered conferences, he explained his theory that "the nerds" would require a high standard of proof. "These guys want everything to add up like an equation. If we can point out some discrepancies, it might be enough to hang them."

Ivy deferred to Lester's judgment but didn't feel confident about the jury they'd picked: seven men and five women; four Republicans and two Democrats; and six who were either independents or unregistered. Nine jurors were white, two were Black, and one was Asian. None of them looked anything like Sonia.

Lester wasn't elated with the draw, either, but at least he had a sense of humor about it.

Sonia had worn headphones throughout the proceedings so everything could be simultaneously translated for her. Lester tapped her shoulder then motioned to Marisol, the translator, who sat in the first row behind them. "Tell Sonia to take a good look," he said. "That right there is a jury of her peers."

CHAPTER 36

Shortly before four o'clock, the jury was empaneled, and Judge Bingham called a brief recess. The break couldn't have come at a better time because Ivy had been nervously sipping water all afternoon and felt like her bladder was about to explode. She was squeezing her legs together as the jurors filed out of the courtroom. Then Judge Bingham asked the lawyers if there were any other issues that needed to be discussed before opening statements.

"None from the state," Eliza said.

Ivy was officially on deck for the opening, so that was her time to respond. She hated to prolong things, because her body was telling her to make a mad dash for the ladies' room, but she needed to address something. "Your Honor, for planning purposes, I was wondering if the state has an estimate as to how long their opening will be."

Only an hour of court time remained, and Ivy was hoping the state would use all that time, thus pushing the defense's opening to the following morning. The reprieve would allow time to find out if they could get the Guatemalan medical records. In which case, Ivy could do the presentation she'd prepared.

Judge Bingham gestured to the prosecutor.

The always-wily Eliza Wells was noncommittal. "Well, that depends. How long does the defense need for its opening?"

Ivy knew precisely how long and wished it were longer, but Lester was adamant she limit her opening to fifteen minutes max. "If you can't explain your case in that amount of time, then you need to go do something else for a living," he'd said. "Plus, that's all the attention today's ADD, iPhone-addicted Twitter-heads can handle anyway." Consequently, Ivy had prepared an opening statement she could deliver in exactly fourteen minutes.

"Oh, I don't know," she lied. "I'm guessing the defense will probably need about half an hour. Maybe we should plan to go tomorrow."

"I doubt that will be necessary," Eliza said. "I plan to keep my remarks brief."

Fuck.

"Well," Judge Bingham said, "we'll just see how far we get. I'll see you all back here in ten minutes. We stand in recess."

Eliza had a satisfied smirk on her face as Ivy scurried past her down the aisle of the courtroom and shot through the door out into the hall. Ivy made a dash to the bathroom to do her business then decided to take her time, just sitting on the toilet, twiddling her thumbs, hoping an extra five minutes or so could make the difference in whether the defense could run out the clock on the first day.

At ten minutes past the hour, Ivy finally returned to the courtroom. She feared she was about to get a tongue-lashing for being late, but Judge Bingham simply said, "Are we ready to proceed, Ms. Collins?"

"Sorry, Judge. There was a line for the ladies' room."

He didn't seem upset. "I understand. But I would still like to see if we can get both openings in today. So, Mr. Bailiff, if you would, sir, let's please go ahead and bring in the jury."

Ivy took her place next to Lester and Sonia.

Lester leaned over to whisper, "Did you fall in?"

"No. Just taking my time," Ivy said.

"Okay. Well, make sure you're ready for what's coming. I've already warned Sonia. No matter how bad Eliza whips our ass with her opening, you can't let it show. The jurors see everything, so at all times, we have to look like we think we're winning. Anything Eliza says is exactly what we thought she would say, and it doesn't bother us at all. Got it?"

"Got it," Ivy said.

But she didn't have it, not even close. Eliza's opening was overwhelmingly powerful. She laid out the state's case succinctly and convincingly, infusing it with a smoldering sense of condemnation that bubbled like a volcano about to erupt. She showed the jury pictures of Hugo in all his adorableness then put on a pair of oven mitts to take hold of the skillet grate seized from Sonia's house and reenacted how the state contended the defendant had held Hugo down while torturing him with the hot metal, searing it into his side.

By the time Eliza was done, the jurors looked ready to drag Sonia into a back room and inflict some eye-for-an-eye justice all by themselves. Ivy found herself wishing that trials, like youth sports, had a mercy rule, where they'd just go ahead and call it once the rout was on. She felt completely demoralized and knew that it showed all over her face.

How can I possibly follow that?

Once Eliza took her seat and the dust had cleared from all the truth bombs she'd dropped, Ivy realized that the only thing worse than the quality of the state's opening was the fact that it had been delivered in just twenty minutes.

She whispered to Lester, "I thought the state usually droned on for at least an hour." Watching celebrity trials, Ivy had seen openings take hours, even days.

"That's TV law bullshit," Lester said.

Judge Bingham spoke. "Ms. Collins, Mr. Williams, does the defense wish to give an opening?"

Panic ravaged Ivy's body. Cold sweat poured down her back. "What do we do?" she whispered. "My opening is all about Hugo being burned in Guatemala. Should we—"

"You never mention anything in opening unless you're one hundred percent sure it will come into evidence."

"Even if we don't get the record, we could still have Sonia testify about it."

"If all we have is Sonia's testimony, then I'm not so sure we should put her on the stand," Lester said. "I certainly don't want to commit to it right now."

"Then what?"

Lester turned up his palms. "I'll do the archer opening unless you've got something better."

"Ms. Collins?" the judge asked. "My understanding is you'll be handling the opening for the defense. Is that correct?"

The statement was a polite way of saying, "Move your ass."

"Actually, Your Honor..." Ivy hesitated. Her sense of dread was momentarily balanced by pride, as she knew that any self-respecting trial lawyer wouldn't give up a chance to address the jury without a fight. But there was no way she could do it. She'd memorized her opening like a speech, had every little bit down pat. There was no way she could change it up on the fly without devolving into a babbling fool. "Uh, actually, Mr. Williams is going to do the opening."

Lester shrugged like it was no big thing. The Truth stood and gave Ivy a little wink before strutting confidently into the well of the courtroom. He got really close to the jury box, much closer than Eliza had, taking a more intimate approach. Whereas Eliza's style was shock and awe, Lester's was more like the guy at the end of the bar, spinning a tale.

"I want to take y'all on a trip, all the way back to merry old England," he said. "The place where our legal system comes from. 'Cause, see, back then, there was this archer who was known to be the best archer in all the land. No one could outshoot him. He was a legend. But then one day, this archer's out riding around and comes across this village, and everywhere he looks, he sees targets. There are targets painted on trees, on bales of hay, on the sides of buildings, everywhere. And on every single one of these targets, there's an arrow sticking right smack-dab in the middle of the bull's-eye. Not a single miss. Not even by a hair. Well, this archer is blown away, because even with all his skill, he's not that accurate and consistent."

Ivy had absolutely no idea what the hell Lester was talking about, but she had to admit he was a great storyteller and seemed to have the jury's attention. His friendly delivery also seemed to have calmed them some from the emotional state in which Eliza had left them.

"So the archer asks around, wanting to know who has managed such exemplary feats of marksmanship, and the townspeople call upon the young man responsible. This boy comes forward, and it's obvious that he's a little slow, right? Like, not very bright. And he acts real awkward—kind of goofy, you know?"

Lester jerked about in a highly offensive barrage of spastic gestures that had half the jury laughing and the other half covering their eyes. Ivy was so embarrassed that she wanted to run and hide, but Lester was either oblivious to or completely unconcerned about the unease he had caused.

"So the archer realizes this little boy is the village idiot. And he demands to know what is going on. 'How is it,' he asks, 'that this weird, silly kid can hit the bull's-eye every single time?'"

"'It's simple,' the boy says. 'All I do is I shoot an arrow, and wherever it lands, then I go and paint a target around it.'"

The jurors all laughed. When they were done, Lester made his point.

"You see, in this case, the defense intends to demonstrate that the state has done the same thing as that boy. Their case will look real impressive at first, but by the time the defense is able to take you to the bottom of things, you'll see that what's really happened here is that the state started with a conclusion, then they painted their case around it. And by the time you have heard all the evidence, we believe you will find that, in reality, they have missed the mark big-time."

With that, Lester returned to the counsel's table and winked again at Ivy like he'd just won an award or something. His entire opening had been pure argument. He had not forecast a single fact of evidence. Lester hadn't mentioned the Guatemalan medical records or the basis of any defense. He hadn't even mentioned any of the witnesses. Yet somehow, amazingly, Lester had delivered the perfect theme for what the defense hoped to show: that the seemingly open-and-shut case was a total misunderstanding.

After Lester sat, Eliza Wells pounded on the table and bellowed, "Objection!"

Judge Bingham looked up, surprised. "The openings are now complete, Ms. Wells. What's the nature of your objection?"

Eliza stood, appearing far more disheveled and uncertain than Ivy had ever seen her. She pointed at Lester with her mouth agape. "He just called me the village idiot."

The jurors burst out in uproarious laughter. Even Judge Bingham had to bite his lip to suppress a smile.

"Well, why didn't you object earlier?" he asked, snickering.

Eliza remained silent for a moment, as though searching her soul for an answer to that very question. "I wanted to hear the end of the story," she admitted.

Again, the jury cracked up.

The prosecutor's pale skin blushed. A woman as deathly serious and coolly sanguine as Eliza Wells wasn't used to being laughed at. The judge called the courtroom to order and overruled the objection. Eliza sat and angrily paged through her trial notebook. Ivy feared the embarrassment would only fuel the hot-running prosecutor's already-considerable fire.

Without further ado, Judge Bingham dismissed the jury for the day, instructing them not to discuss the case or perform any outside research.

Once they were gone and the court was in recess, Ivy looked at Sonia, who seemed mystified, unsure how to feel about all that had occurred. Ivy squeezed her hand and smiled. There was no telling what would happen, but somehow, despite all their disadvantages, they were about to leave the courtroom having survived the first day.

CHAPTER 37

Any optimism Ivy felt after day one of the trial was completely obliterated on the morning of day two. She and Eliza Wells had just submitted their briefs to Judge Bingham, who was quietly reading them when Cesar entered the courtroom and approached the defense table.

"Bad news, boss," he whispered.

Lester, who was on the opposite side of Ivy, leaned over so he could hear.

"I just talked to the PI in Guatemala. His contact has COVID. She's real sick and won't be able to set foot in that hospital for at least ten days."

"Fuck," Lester grumbled. "This trial will be over way before then."

Ivy felt her stomach drop. That meant doom.

"Did he con us?" Lester asked. "You think there ever really was a lady? Or a record?"

"I believe him," Cesar said. "He knew the date and the name of the boy's grandmother."

"Doesn't mean anything," Lester said. "He could have just dug into it enough to figure out what he needed to tell us so we'd send more money."

"I really don't think so," Cesar said. "He'd be asking for more cash if it was a con."

Lester still looked pissed.

Ivy felt desperate. "What do we do now?" she asked.

"Take our beatdown," Lester said.

Ivy looked over at Sonia, thinking about what a conviction would mean for her.

Lester nudged Ivy's elbow. "Listen," he said. "Growing up, there was a rule that if you ever got jumped by a bunch of guys and knew you were going down, then you picked out one of those motherfuckers and inflicted as much punishment on him as possible."

Great, Ivy thought. *Another fight metaphor.* "What does that mean?"

"It means whatever witness they put on the stand first, I'm gonna tear him a new asshole."

A shuffling of papers at the bench alerted them that Judge Bingham had finished reading through the briefs and was ready to announce his ruling.

"Thank you, counsel, for laying out your arguments and research on this matter so thoroughly," he said. "Having reviewed them, I have to agree with the defense that the case of *Washington v. Crawford* is controlling here, and it would be a violation of the defendant's Sixth Amendment rights to admit the video statement of the alleged victim if he is not going to testify live at trial."

Ivy pumped her fist underneath the table. It was likely a Pyrrhic victory, given the news they'd just gotten from Cesar, but she'd been up until three in the morning, working on that brief, and it felt good to win one small battle over Eliza Wells, even if it would have little effect on the outcome of the war.

Judge Bingham wasn't finished, however. Always looking for a way to give something to each side, he said, "Ms. Wells, that means you have a choice. I'll allow the admission of the video but only if you can make a firm commitment that the boy will testify."

Eliza didn't need time to think about it. "He'll testify, Judge."

Of course he will, Ivy thought. *Anything to get that heart-wrenching video in front of the jury.* That really blunted the effect of the judge's ruling. Eliza would be permitted to show Hugo's taped interview in its entirety, allowing the state to essentially present his testimony unchallenged for the majority of the trial, during which the jurors' views would become fixed. At the end of the state's case, she could put Hugo up on the stand briefly just to affirm what they had already heard. The defense would then have to walk the tightrope of cross-examining a child, whom they couldn't be overly aggressive with because of his age.

"Is there anything else we need to address before we call the jury in?" Judge Bingham asked.

With no other motions or legal issues to confront, the judge summoned the jury. Once they were situated, Eliza Wells called her first witness.

"Your Honor, the state calls Detective James Reed to the stand."

That was expected. The prosecution was tasked with laying out the entire case for the jury. Thus, Lester had said, it was common to start with a police officer who could tell the story from start to finish.

Detective Reed placed his left hand on the Bible and raised his right one as he swore to tell the truth, the whole truth, and nothing but the truth, so help him God. He was a handsome man in his forties, a little over six feet tall, with an athletic build and sandy blond hair.

Eliza started by going through Reed's background and experience. He was understated in his responses, speaking with a quiet confidence, and Ivy could see that the jury instantly believed and trusted him.

If this is the witness Lester's going to tear into, he'll really have his work cut out for him, Ivy thought.

After Eliza finished with the preliminaries, she drew first blood in the case by going straight for the jugular: the video. Detective Reed was the one who'd arranged for Hugo's TEDI Bear evaluation, and he was able to describe it as part of his investigation, thus introducing it to the jury. Lester repeated the defense's objection to the video, but that was pro forma, done solely for the purpose of preserving the issue for appeal. The objection was noted and overruled, after which the damning tape rolled for the jury, as did the tears from several of the jurors.

Sonia had to look away during the playing. She had been instructed by Ivy not to do this, to make no reaction whatsoever, but she was unable to control herself. She became red-faced with what Ivy believed was anger over Hugo's lies, but that could have played to the jury like shame. *This is not good.*

When the video mercifully came to an end, the judge called for a ten-minute recess to let the jurors compose themselves, which only further cemented the emotional impact of Hugo's harrowing tale in their minds.

After the trial resumed, Detective Reed took the jury through his process of obtaining a warrant and the search of Sonia's home. Eliza, who was old-school, eschewed the technology commonly used in modern courtrooms, like smart boards and overhead projectors, opting instead for several large blowups she set on a series of tripods. That allowed Detective Reed to get off the stand and look like a trusted teacher as he walked the jury through the photos. Each of the four sat on its own easel, creating a kind of wall of evidence. The first blowup was of the computer printout Hugo had identified, showing the type of skillet that had been used. It had his childish signature written at the bottom. Second was an enlarged photo of the actual skillet recovered from Sonia's kitchen, which was an exact match, brand and all. Third was a picture of a tape measure extended over the skillet grates to show the spacing between the metal bars. Fourth was a photo of the scars along Hugo's side, with the same tape measure in the foreground to establish that the spacing of the scars roughly matched that of the skillet grates.

All the engineers and science guys Lester had been so eager to have on his jury were nodding along. The case was adding up just fine for them, Ivy thought. *As simple as two plus two.*

Once Detective Reed finished with the photos, he returned to the witness stand, but Eliza left the blowups in place to make a continuing impression upon the jury. Lester asked if they could be taken down, since it appeared that the prosecution was finished with them, but Eliza said she might return to them later in her examination. That was bullshit but a sufficient excuse for Judge Bingham to allow them to remain in place.

As a result of the prior ruling excluding Sonia's alleged confession about the broken arm, Eliza skipped over that part. She instead asked Detective Reed whether he had conducted any additional interviews with Hugo after the search of the defendant's home.

"Yes."

"And what, if anything, did you learn?"

"Hugo also told—"

"Objection! Hearsay," Lester said, leaping out of his seat like a jack-in-the-box at the utterance of the word *told*.

Ivy knew it was a little risky to keep opposing Hugo's out-of-court statements. The objections were certain to be overruled, and they ran the risk of alienating the jury, who would want the information and generally disliked interruptions. It also made it look like the defense was afraid of the evidence, which of course was true. Against a less experienced attorney, frequent objections might fluster the opponent and cause them to move on too quickly, glossing over or completely skipping key facts, but Eliza was unflappable. Therefore, the only reason Ivy could figure that Lester was continuing to object was simply to preserve the issue for appeal.

"Your Honor," Eliza said, sighing, "this has already been ruled upon."

Lester, aware of the dilemma of objecting too much, offered a solution. With his million-dollar smile and easy manner, he said, "I'm sorry, Judge, but the rules require me to keep objecting for appeal purposes. But if you'll grant me a continuing hearsay objection to any out-of-court statements made by Mr. Cabrerra, then I'll be very happy to just sit down and shut up."

The jurors all smiled at Lester. Ivy could tell they liked him.

"How about that, Ms. Wells?" Judge Bingham asked.

Lester's proposal presented Eliza with her own dilemma. Granting a continuing hearsay objection would greatly improve the flow of her presentation, but it would also ensure the appealability of the issue, negating any opportunity she might have with a higher court to argue it had been waived. Getting a conviction at the trial court level, however, was much more important than setting up the appeal. Judges in North Carolina, including appellate judges, were elected. And if they wanted to get reelected, they had to avoid any decisions an opponent could use to label them as "soft on crime." Thus, the chance of ever getting a conviction overturned on appeal was remote, no matter how egregious the errors at trial.

Eliza wisely agreed to the continuing objection then repeated her question. "Detective Reed, what did you learn from your subsequent interview with the victim?"

The detective told the jurors how Hugo said his mother had previously twisted and broken his arm, which was met with requisite looks of repulsion among the jury. Detective Reed then recounted how the police had obtained medical records from Memorial Hospital confirming that Hugo was previously seen there for a spiral fracture to his arm.

"No further questions," Eliza said. She started to remove her easels and blowups.

But Lester, who had previously been so eager to have them taken down, said, "Please leave them up. I think I may use them."

CHAPTER 38

In law school, Ivy's trial advocacy professor had taught some basic rules for cross-examination. First, the questions should always be leading, requiring a yes-or-no response. You didn't ask someone, "Where were you on Tuesday night?" You told them, "On Tuesday night, you were at home, weren't you?" Second, to keep the adverse witness from arguing or explaining, each question should be limited to a single undeniable fact that the lawyer could prove independently with documents or a prior statement. That way, the witness either had to agree or else get impeached in front of the jury. Third and perhaps most important, you never, ever asked the witness a question you didn't already know the answer to.

During the Cabrerra trial's first cross-examination, Ivy quickly learned that Lester did not follow any of those rules.

"Deeee-tect-ive Reed," he began, "there's a whole lot you left out, isn't there?"

Detective Reed appeared unsettled by the question. "I'm... not sure... what you mean."

"Uh-huh," Lester said. "Well, we'll just see about that." Lester approached the tripods displaying the state's exhibits. "Let's start with what's behind door number one, shall we?" Lester pointed at the enlarged computer printout. "You stood up here in front of this jury a minute ago and told them that this printout right here is a picture Hugo Cabrerra identified as the skillet he was burned with. Isn't that right?"

"Yes, sir."

"But that isn't true, is it, Detective?"

Detective Reed looked confused. Ivy was as well. She had no idea where Lester was going with this.

"It absolutely is true," Detective Reed said. "The victim was asked to identify a picture of a skillet that looked like the one he was burned with, and this is the picture he chose out of a stack of about fifteen or twenty."

Lester wagged his finger. "Hold up now, Detective Reed. That is *not* the question that was put to Mr. Cabrerra, was it?"

Detective Reed looked at the prosecutor then the judge before answering. "Yes, it was, sir. We all just watched the interview."

"We all watched it, then *you* mischaracterized it," Lester said. He read from the notes he'd taken during the video. "What was asked was, and I quote: 'Look at these and tell me if any of them look like your mother's.' Not 'Can you show us a picture of the skillet you were burned with?' Isn't that right? We can replay that portion of the video if you like."

The point seemed minor to Ivy, a distinction without a difference. Detective Reed thought so too.

"Those may not have been the exact words, but the victim had just told the interviewer his mother burned him with her skillet and was then asked to identify a picture of what his mother's skillet looked like, so I think it is effectively the same thing."

Lester wagged his finger and smiled like he knew something no one else did. "Detective Reed, he said his *mother* burned him with a skillet grate, right?"

"Yes."

"He wasn't able to tell you exactly when it happened, though, correct?"

"No, he wasn't certain of the date."

"And when the doctors examined him, they weren't able to say how old the burn scars were. Is that right?"

"That's correct. They said it was impossible to tell from a scar precisely when the burn was inflicted."

"But it's clear that it wasn't something that just happened, because the burn had already healed and turned into scars, right?"

"The burns had turned into scars. That is true."

"So," Lester said, "Mr. Cabrerra reported being burned by his 'mother' sometime in the past. Am I right?" Lester put finger quotes around the word *mother*.

Ivy was getting more and more concerned that Lester was just freestyling without any plan and was consequently reiterating some very, very bad facts. Detective Reed took advantage of the opportunity.

"Yes, sir. He reported that his mother had burned him with a hot metal grate, basically branding him like he was a cow or something."

The last little piece of commentary conveyed the most emotion Detective Reed had shown up to that point. He appeared annoyed with Lester's antics and took the opportunity to twist the knife in deeper. Lester's next question only made it worse.

"That is my point. He said his 'mother' did that, right?" Again, he made air quotes.

"Right."

Ivy's poker face failed her in that instant. She looked down, unable to watch.

Then Lester said, "But you never asked him which 'mother,' did you?"

Ivy wanted to shoot upright but managed to control herself. Instead, she simply turned her head and looked at the jurors, who were all staring with rapt attention.

Detective Reed looked confused but then played the question off as a joke. "As far as I know, everybody only has one mother."

Juror number five laughed.

Lester wasn't amused. "That's not true of Mr. Cabrerra, though, is it? He's had two moms, right?"

Detective Reed got the first inkling of where Lester was going but still did a good job of keeping his response confident sounding. "The victim was raised for a period of time by his grandmother, but he—"

"Not just a period of time. Most of his life, right?"

There, Eliza lodged her first objection, asking that counsel allow the witness to finish his answers before interrupting with a question.

Judge Bingham agreed. "Let the witness finish, please, Mr. Williams."

"By all means," Lester said. He made a grand gesture to Detective Reed.

The detective then said, "The victim was cared for by his grandmother when he was young, but almost two years ago, he moved to the US and has been living with his mother, who is the defendant. He only has one mother."

"Biologically, sure," Lester said, "but we're talking about language here. Words. Words used by a scared little eight-year-old kid who was on camera, under the bright lights, answering questions in front of cops and therapists and a bunch of strange adults he'd never met before."

"Objection," Eliza said. "Argumentative."

Judge Bingham sustained.

Lester moved on to his next question, which was a zinger. "Isn't it true that Mr. Cabrerra often referred to his grandmother as his 'mother'?" Again, he curled his fingers.

Detective Reed took a few moments to page through the report he'd been allowed to reference during his testimony. "I'm not sure about that," he admitted.

"Not sure?" Lester asked incredulously. "So let me get this straight. You've got an eight-year-old boy who tells you he was burned by his mother at some point in the past—we don't know when—and you don't even bother to ask him which mother he was talking about before you go and slap this poor little pregnant lady in handcuffs?"

Eliza objected again, but that time, she was overruled. Detective Reed looked at her like he wanted some direction.

"She can't answer for you," Lester said.

Judge Bingham piled on too. "The witness will answer."

Having been chastised by the judge, Detective Reed threw a little shade on the psychologist who had actually conducted the interview. "It is true that the interviewer did not specifically ask that question."

Lester wouldn't let him off the hook, though. "You didn't ask it either, did you?"

"I was trying not to interfere in the interview."

"But you're the lead detective, right?"

"I am."

"And you were present during the interview, weren't you?"

"I was."

"And when the interviewer asked Mr. Cabrerra to identify a picture of what his mother's skillet looked like, rather than the skillet he was burned by, you didn't say anything about it, did you?"

"I was there as an observer," the detective said. "I did not want to interfere with the interview."

"Riiight," Lester said. He seized hold of the first two blowups—the printout and the photo of Sonia's matching skillet—whipped them off the easels, and dropped them to the ground as though he'd just obliterated that part of the case. Then he moved on to the two photos with the tape measure that matched up the spacing between Sonia's skillet grill and Hugo's scars.

"Tell me, Detective, how many other skillets did you measure in addition to the one in this picture here?"

Again, Detective Reed looked confused. "That was the only skillet recovered from the defendant's home."

"Maybe that was the only skillet the defendant had, but there's lots of skillets out there with removable grates, right?"

"I don't know how many, but I'm sure there are others."

"And the spacing between the grates on all the skillets is kind of standard, right? Otherwise, your hot dog or whatever would fall right through."

Detective Reed looked again at Eliza Wells. To her credit, the prosecutor made no attempt to prompt him.

"I... don't know," he conceded.

"Is it safe to assume you didn't fly down to Guatemala and do any measurements of any skillets or grills Mr. Cabrerra's other mother down there had?"

Eliza objected to the reference to an "other mother," but Judge Bingham overruled.

"We did not inspect any other grills or skillets," Detective Reed admitted.

Lester took the last two blowups off their easels and dropped them to the floor with a satisfying clatter. The naked tripods remained there like skeletal edifices of the state's case, suddenly stripped of all its meat.

"Now let's talk about this broken-arm business," Lester said. "You told the jury you had some subsequent interviews with Mr. Cabrerra, but you conveniently skipped over how you got onto this whole arm thing to begin with, right?"

Eliza Wells shot to her feet, looking furious as she objected. "Your Honor, may we approach?"

Judge Bingham waved for counsel to come forward. When they huddled around the bench, he switched on a fan to drown out their whispered voices.

Eliza spoke first. "Judge, the defense is attempting to bring out this whole alleged mistranslation issue when they are the ones who moved to have it excluded."

Judge Bingham nodded. "That's what it sounded like to me too, Mr. Williams. You are the ones who took the position that the whole confession about the broken arm was inadmissible."

"Inadmissible for them," Lester said, "but not for us. If we want to point out how slipshod and sloppy the police investigation has been, we should be allowed to."

"That's ridiculous, Judge," Eliza said. "If the confession hadn't been ruled inadmissible, we would have gone over it on direct. To have it excluded so we don't talk about it then let Mr. Williams bring it out for the first time on cross is sandbagging. It makes it look like we were hiding something when we weren't."

"She's got a point, Mr. Williams," Judge Bingham said.

Lester responded, sounding as innocent as an altar boy. "Your Honor, it was not my plan to proceed this way, but I had no idea Detective Reed was going to testify the way he did, totally skipping over the whole grandmother-slash-second mother issue. So now this police screwup about the broken arm seems to be another example of making some assumptions that were then used to pressure and influence the boy into giving them a statement confirming what the police erroneously thought happened. They opened the door to this."

Eliza looked like she was about to spit nails, but Judge Bingham stopped her before she could speak.

"You don't get to have it both ways, Mr. Williams. You wanted the confession out, and it's out. I do not believe the prosecution has done anything to sufficiently open the door for bringing it back in."

Nice try, Ivy thought. She was realizing that nearly every decision in trial was a double-edged sword. The defense had moved to exclude the confession because that was necessary to try to get the broken-arm charge dismissed. But there could have been some advantages to leaving it in because it was such a dramatic example of how the police could get things wrong. When the motion to dismiss had been denied, they could have withdrawn the motion to exclude, but that ran the risk of angering the judge for having wasted his time hearing the issue. Moreover, Lester and Ivy were still concerned with how bad the confession sounded when presented by the state and were afraid that the jury might not be totally convinced it was a mistranslation.

What Lester had just attempted would have been perfect if it had worked. Keeping the prosecution from bringing up the statement so he could reveal it first on cross would have made it look like an admission by the state that the confession was bogus and Eliza was trying to hide an example of shoddy police work.

Lester didn't let the near miss dishearten him, however. He was the first to turn back from the sidebar. At the perfect time when neither the judge nor Eliza could see him, he drew back on an imaginary bow and fired an invisible arrow at the jurors.

They all smiled at him as Lester broke another rule Ivy had been taught: Never end your examination on an objection. Lester didn't seem bothered by that conventional wisdom, though, as he ended his cross by pointing at Detective Reed and simply saying, "To be continued."

When he came back to the defense table, Ivy congratulated him on a great job. "I feel so stupid for missing it," she said. "How did you know Hugo also calls his grandmother his mother?"

Lester winked at her. "I have no idea if he does or doesn't. But it sounded good."

CHAPTER 39

After Eliza Wells had used Detective Reed's testimony to provide an overview of the state's case, Lester and Ivy assumed she would then move through her witnesses chronologically. First would be the school counselor who had contacted authorities, followed by the psychologist who'd conducted the TEDI Bear interview, then the doctor who'd previously treated Hugo for his broken arm. Hugo would likely be saved for the grand finale.

Initially, Eliza proceeded as expected. She called the school guidance counselor, Estelle Garber, and conducted a direct exam that was short and straightforward, eliciting a description of the horror Ms. Garber felt upon discovering Hugo's scars. Estelle said Hugo had been quite reluctant to reveal how he got them but eventually named his mother as the one responsible. From that point on, Ms. Garber had turned things over to the authorities and thus had little more to add.

Lester and Ivy had not planned a specific cross-exam for Ms. Garber, so Lester handled it based upon some notes he'd made while she was testifying. His demeanor when questioning her was much less combative than with Detective Reed. Lester established that Hugo had been a student at the school for over a year, and there had been no prior concern about child abuse. He also reiterated with Ms. Garber what the jury already knew from Detective Reed: that the burn marks were not fresh and it was impossible to determine from the scars exactly when the burning had occurred. Ms. Garber also admitted that she was unaware that Hugo had been separated from his mother for the first six or so years of his life, during which he was cared for by his grandparents.

"I take it, then, that you didn't know Hugo also refers to his grandmother as his mother."

"I was not aware of that," Ms. Garber said, falsely assuming Lester knew what he was talking about.

It kind of worked. Maybe Ivy was being overly optimistic, but she thought the jury was questioning whether Hugo may have confusingly described an event that had happened years earlier, perpetrated by his grandmother, and that some overzealous social workers and Keystone Cops, while in a rush to judgment, had arrested the wrong woman.

But after Ms. Garber was excused, Eliza Wells strayed from the predicted plan by skipping over the psychologist and jumping to the physician who had treated Hugo's broken arm. For that witness, Eliza had blowups of some impressive-looking X-rays of the spiral fracture, which Dr. Killen said was "usually indicative of a twisting injury."

That was Ivy's first opportunity to speak in front of the jury. She kept her cross-exam of Dr. Killen simple, remaining seated at counsel's table, where she read from prepared questions.

"Dr. Killen, you testified that a spiral fracture in a child Hugo's age is most often the result of a twisting injury, but it is possible for a child to suffer a spiral fracture from a fall, isn't it?"

Ivy had three medical journal articles at the ready to prove she was right about what she'd just said, but they proved unnecessary, as the doctor agreed with the point without a fight.

"Yes. Particularly where the child has put their arm out to try to brace themselves during a fall, it is possible to get a spiral fracture."

Perfect, Ivy thought. "And whenever a child shows up at the hospital with an injury like this, one of the things that the doctors and nurses are trained to look for is signs of abuse. Isn't that right?"

"It is."

"If you suspect abuse, you report it, right?"

"We're required to," Dr. Killen said.

It was going much easier than Ivy had thought. The doctor was truly a neutral witness who was not interested in doing anything on the stand other than testifying honestly and getting out of there as soon as possible. Ivy only had one more question.

"And in the case of Hugo's broken arm, neither you nor anyone else at the hospital reported any suspicion of abuse. Correct?"

"That is correct."

"Thank you," Ivy said. "No further questions."

Boom. That felt pretty good. Ivy was actually proud of herself.

"Not bad," Lester said. "Got in and out and made your points. Good job."

"Thanks," Ivy said. She would have liked to bask in the glow of Lester's compliment a little while longer, but her attention was drawn to Eliza Wells, who was packing up her exhibits. "Why doesn't she ever redirect the witness after our cross-exams? There are things she could do to counter some of the points we made."

Lester shrugged. "Part of it is her style, I suspect. Eliza's approach is that everything the defense does is bullshit and not worth her time. She ignores it and implicitly suggests to the jury that they should as well. But I think she's also just gotten a bit cocky over the years. She's not used to people putting up this much of a fight."

It made Ivy proud to think they were giving Eliza more resistance than she was used to. She turned and gave Sonia a little side hug before the deputy came to lead the pregnant woman away.

As the courtroom cleared out, Cesar came forward to join the defense team from where he'd been camped out in the rear of the gallery, taking notes on juror reactions and other things the attorneys were less able to observe from their vantage point. "Juror number six thinks you're cute, boss," he said to Ivy. "His face lit up when you started asking questions."

"Well, at least I've got something going for me." Ivy was feeling self-conscious about her courtroom prowess. Although her cross-exam of the doctor had gone okay, she wished she could throw the script aside and mud-wrestle with a witness the way Lester had.

The three moved from the courthouse down to Barrister's for dinner and drinks and to discuss what work needed to be done that night. Lester assigned Ivy with preparing the pro forma motion to dismiss they'd make when the state rested its case. The motion was necessary to preserve issues for appeal but had no chance of being granted. Lester told Ivy not to stress over it, but she knew she'd be up all night researching it anyway, wanting to have some kind of plausible argument and maybe some case law to support it.

"You know," Lester said, taking the first sip of his third whiskey, "I'll bet you the reason they didn't put the shrink on today was so they could prep her to respond to some of the smoke we've been blowing up the jury's ass."

Ivy agreed. "I think the whole thing about Hugo calling his grandmother 'Mom' kind of threw them for a loop."

"It's playing with the jury, though," Cesar said. "The first time you brought that up, they all started looking at each other like 'What the hell? Did you hear that?'"

Lester swirled his drink. "Yeah, it was fun while it lasted, but they'll probably blow it out of the water tomorrow. What will be interesting is if the shrink and Hugo come off as too rehearsed, like they're there to argue the case instead of just telling the truth." Lester started to take another sip but paused, holding the glass a few inches from his lips. "Hey, Ives." He set the glass back down. "I know we talked about letting you be the good cop who would do kind of a gentle cross-exam of Hugo, but I think maybe I need to take that one too. Might need to tear into his ass a little."

Ivy knew she should act disappointed, but it was hard to hide the relief she felt. "That's fine if you want to do it," she said. "But it's risky to be too aggressive with him. The jury will feel protective over someone that young."

"Yeah," Lester agreed. "But without the medical record, our only chance may be to swing for the fences and see if we can get Hugo to admit he was lying."

Ivy didn't think such admissions happened very often, but Lester was probably right that going for one could be their only shot. "Okay. Fine. You want the cross, you got it. I'll give you my notes. I've got pages of questions written out."

Lester didn't look interested. "Sure. I'll look at them. I don't like using too many notes, though. Kind of stifles the flow, you know. You'll know you're a trial lawyer the day you can put all that stuff away. At some point, you'll just feel it. Instinct will take over."

Ivy didn't think she would ever reach that stage.

Lester could tell that something he said had upset her. "Why the long face?"

"It's nothing," Ivy said. "It's fine."

Lester didn't let it go. "Come on, now. None of that. What is it? You're mad I want to cross Hugo?"

Ivy shook her head. That wasn't it. She wanted to win the case, and if Lester crossing Hugo gave them the best chance to do that—which it did—then that was what should happen. "I'm just disappointed that I'm not up to it. Makes me think maybe my dad was—"

"You can squash that shit right now," Lester said. "You've been great in there. My God, you prepped this whole case."

"Prepped, yeah. But you've been the one doing all the high-level stuff. There's no way I could do what you do."

Lester put down his drink. "Well, goddamn, girl. I've only got three decades of experience on you. I should be a little bit better at this, don't you think?"

Ivy shrugged. Lester had a point. Experience was a factor, to be sure, but he also possessed a natural charisma that Ivy didn't think she'd ever be able to match. She pointed at the drink menu on the table. "Barristers," she said, reading the name at the top. "In England, they've got that clear divide between the lawyers who go to court and the solicitors, the lawyers who work behind a desk. The planners. People who do *prep work*."

"Well, this is America, Ivy. Who gives a shit what they do in England?"

"I'm just saying maybe there should be that clear divide. Maybe I'm just not cut out for this."

Lester waved her off. "You're being too hard on yourself. The way you handled that doctor today was on point. I couldn't have done it any better. And the pretrial motions—cross-examining a cop like you did. Shit, six months out of law school and going toe-to-toe with a fucking destroyer like Eliza Wells. That was straight fire."

"Yeah, boss," Cesar said. "You're being way too hard on yourself. You're doing good."

Ivy wasn't sure whether they were just being kind or maybe she had been doing better than she'd given herself credit for. "You're not just blowing smoke?"

"Hell no," Lester said.

"No way," Cesar added.

"In fact," Lester said, "forget what I said earlier. The Hugo cross is all yours. You got it. I have total confidence."

"No, no, no." Ivy wasn't about to screw up the case to give herself an ego boost.

"I'm serious," Lester said. "You've already got it locked and loaded. You'll probably do a better job than I would anyway. Let's just stick with the original plan. Do a soft, respectful cross of young Hugo, and stick to the facts that fit our theme. Stuff he can't hide from. That's really probably the best strategy."

She found herself wishing she hadn't said anything and just left the cross-examination of Hugo in Lester's capable hands. But the Truth had his mind made up.

"You're sure?"

"Absolutely. I'm not touching it," Lester said and mimed washing his hands.

CHAPTER 40

On day three of the trial, Eliza Wells called Dr. Patel, the psychologist who'd first interviewed Hugo. She was an Indian woman with long, dark, gray-streaked hair that was woven into a three-strand braid. Like Detective Reed, she was clearly very comfortable on the stand, and her testimony provided numerous opportunities to replay clips of the damaging video. Then, just as Lester had predicted, Eliza started using Dr. Patel to shore up any damage previously inflicted by the defense.

"Dr. Patel, there has been a suggestion in this trial that when Hugo referred to his mother abusing him, he may have actually been referring to his grandmother, who he previously lived with in Guatemala. What is your response to that?"

"It's ridiculous."

"Why do you say that?"

"Because I have talked to Hugo about his family history—as recently as yesterday, in fact—and he is very consistent in referring to his grandmother as his grandmother and his mother as his mother. It's also quite obvious when considering the context of what he has described. For instance, when talking about the burning incident, he tells me he was in the kitchen in his mother's trailer. His grandmother in Guatemala did not live in a trailer. So there's no ambiguity there. And when he talked about the broken arm, that is something he said happened before the burning, and it is clear from the medical records that Hugo was living in the US when his arm was broken. So there is absolutely no question that Hugo has identified the defendant, Sonia Cabrerra, as the abuser."

Game, set, and match, Ivy thought.

"Thank you, Dr. Patel," Eliza said. "No further questions."

Ivy looked at Lester, hoping he had something up his sleeve. The Truth was stroking his chin, pondering.

"Counsel, would you like to cross-examine?" Judge Bingham asked.

"Just one moment to confer, please, Your Honor." Lester leaned over and whispered to Ivy, "She'll be expecting us to cross her on how she conducted the interview, poke holes at little mistakes, and take a few digs at her qualifications, right?"

"Yes," Ivy agreed.

"You've seen her testify. How successful do you think that will be?"

"Not very," Ivy admitted. Though she had put together an exhaustive list of every problematic aspect of the questioning or everything that could be made to sound problematic, in the end, it didn't amount to much. Dr. Patel was highly qualified and had conducted her interactions with Hugo professionally.

"That's what I thought," Lester said. "I think I may go another way. Something they won't see coming."

"Like what?"

Lester smiled. "Well, since Eliza got our expert excluded, I'm thinking I'll just use hers."

"Counsel?" Judge Bingham prodded. "Are we ready to proceed?"

"Yes, Your Honor." Lester cleared his throat. "Dr. Patel, can you tell the jury what histrionic personality disorder is?"

Seeming taken aback, Dr. Patel paused long enough for Eliza Wells to object and ask to approach.

Ivy followed Lester to the bench and listened in as he and Eliza argued their points.

"Judge," Eliza said, "we have already been through this in pretrial motions. The defense expert's opinion that the victim suffered from histrionic personality disorder was excluded. Now defense counsel is trying to backdoor it into the case with the state's expert."

Lester said, "The expert was excluded, Judge, but not the possibility that Hugo suffers from the disorder. And the only reason our expert got bounced was because he didn't get the opportunity to interview young Hugo. Dr. Patel has had that opportunity, and I think it's fair to ask her about any assessments she might be able to make."

Eliza came back at him quickly. "It is obvious what defense counsel is doing. Dr. Patel has expressed absolutely no concern whatsoever about Hugo suffering from any personality disorder. But Mr. Williams will ask her a lot of suggestive questions to make it sound like the boy has been diagnosed with one, the same way he did with all the nonsense about Hugo supposedly referring to his grandmother as his mother."

The judge gave Lester an accusatory look, but it didn't cow him at all.

"I don't think it was nonsense, Judge, and it's something we are likely to get into very soon. But regardless, the point is that Dr. Patel is the psychologist that the state has put forward as their expert to opine that Hugo is a victim of child abuse, and I should have wide latitude to cross-examine her about any psychological issues that could otherwise explain Hugo's account."

Eliza said, "Judge—"

"The objection is overruled for now. You can continue with your questioning along these lines, Mr. Williams, and we'll see where it takes us. But I'm going to be watching for anything that smacks of a baseless parlor trick. And I will go ahead and instruct you that you are not to refer to any diagnosis made by the defense expert who was excluded. I also have concerns about attempts to backdoor the opinion that was kept out."

Lester gave the judge the Scout's honor sign. "Wasn't planning to do that at all, Judge. I just want to see what this lady thinks."

"Very well," Judge Bingham said. "Let's proceed."

As they walked back to the counsel's table, Ivy whispered to Lester, "I hope you know what you're doing."

"Me too," he said then turned to address the witness. "So, Dr. Patel, histrionic personality disorder. What is it?"

"It's part of what's referred to as Cluster B personality disorders. Those include borderline personality disorder, narcissism, and anti-social personalities."

"How does it manifest?"

Dr. Patel shifted in her seat. "Grandiosity, attention-seeking behavior, shallow, superficial relationships, sometimes depression. There are many ways it can manifest."

"But it's fair to say that the word *histrionic* is used because these are people who tend to be theatrical."

"That's true."

"In other words, they're actors. People who can put on a performance. Correct?"

Dr. Patel took her time in answering, obviously trying to figure out where Lester was headed with his questioning. "That can be true. Yes."

"And like narcissists, people with histrionic personality disorder are charmers, right?"

"Yes, they can be."

"They can manipulate people to get what they want."

"Yes, oftentimes."

Lester was reading over the disclosure that his excluded expert, Dr. Eli, had created. Ivy, like Judge Bingham, was concerned that Lester was looking for a way to bootstrap Eli's diagnosis into evidence, perhaps by getting Dr. Patel to declare that Hugo had never been diagnosed with the disorder so he could confront her with the report showing that indeed he had. But Dr. Patel made no such erroneous statements, and Lester stayed safely in the realm of hypothetical questions that were permissible so long as the judge considered them relevant.

"Is it fair to say that people who suffer from histrionic personality disorder are largely driven by a fear of abandonment?" Lester asked.

"Yes."

"Would you agree that a person with histrionic personality disorder tends to feel comfortable only when they are the center of attention?"

"That is the classic presentation."

"And as soon as they aren't the center of attention, they believe they are going to be abandoned, right?"

"Yes," Dr. Patel said a half second before Eliza objected.

"Overruled," the judge said. "But let's get somewhere soon, Mr. Williams."

Lester gave the judge a thumbs-up before continuing. "When a person with histrionic personality disorder feels like they're about to be abandoned, they can really turn on somebody pretty quickly, can't they?"

"That can happen."

"They can be vindictive and even make up lies about them, right?"

"Yes," Dr. Patel replied.

Eliza objected again, and Judge Bingham announced that he had lost his patience. "Mr. Williams, if you have a way of connecting this line of questioning with the present case, it's time to do it."

"Yes, sir," Lester said. He dropped Dr. Eli's report onto the table, ready to engage the witness without notes. "Let's talk specifically about young Mr. Cabrerra. He was basically abandoned by his mother for the first six years of his life, right?"

Ivy wished Lester had found a nicer way of putting that. "Abandoned" was pretty harsh and completely robbed Sonia's situation of context. But Lester wasn't one for subtlety.

"My understanding is that the defendant was very young when she had Hugo, and so he was raised by his grandparents until he was six then moved here to the United States to be with his mother."

"During the time Hugo was living with his grandparents, he never saw his mom, right?"

"That's my understanding."

"Fair to say he didn't form the normal mother–child attachments, then?"

"Objection. Calls for speculation," Eliza said.

Lester responded with a chuckle. "This is their expert, Judge. If her opinions are now speculation, then I move to strike her whole testimony."

"Overruled," the judge said. "The witness can answer."

Dr. Patel smiled. "I think it's safe to say that during the time Hugo and his mother were separated, they were not forming the normal attachment."

"Right," Lester said. "During the time Hugo was with his grandparents, they were basically the only parental figures he knew. Correct?"

"At that time, yes."

"And he was basically an only child then, right, soaking up all that good Grandma and Grandpa attention?"

"I don't believe there were any other children living with them."

"So," Lester said, looking at the jury, "not only was Mr. Cabrerra abandoned by his mom at birth, when he was six, he was also ripped away from his grandparents, who were the only parents he'd known up to that point, right?"

"That's... basically correct."

"Then," Lester said, getting really dramatic, "his grandparents died not long after that, right?"

Dr. Patel acknowledged the fact.

Lester said, "That's got to be pretty traumatic for a kid. Wouldn't you agree?"

"I would."

"And trauma is thought to be one of the causes of histrionic personality disorder, right?"

Eliza Wells was on her feet again, objecting.

"Overruled," Judge Bingham said. "Please answer, Dr. Patel."

The doctor swiveled to face the jury. "Trauma is generally thought to be a cause or at least a risk factor for histrionic personality disorder."

"Specifically trauma that causes a fear of abandonment, right?"

Dr. Patel nodded her answer. When the judge told her she needed to use words so that the record was clear, she said, "Yes."

"Now," Lester said, "when Mr. Cabrerra got to the US, he was an only child with his mother, right?"

"That's true. There were no other children living with him."

"And he lived with his mother as an only child for over a year without any reports of suspected child abuse, right?"

"Uh..." Dr. Patel thought for a moment. "A little over a year, yes. That's true."

Lester walked behind Sonia and put his hands upon his client's shoulders, drawing everyone's attention to her very pregnant belly. "But Hugo's not gonna be an only child much longer, is he?"

Eliza Wells made another attempt to object that was overruled.

The witness agreed though stated she wasn't clear whether Hugo would have known about his mother's pregnancy before the abuse allegations were made.

Lester liked that answer just fine and passed the witness.

Eliza decided to redirect for the first time in the trial. She asked Dr. Patel whether she believed Hugo suffered from histrionic personality disorder. "Or any personality disorder, for that matter?"

"No," Dr. Patel said.

"Therefore all these questions about histrionic personality disorder are completely irrelevant, aren't they?"

Lester's objection to that question was sustained, but Eliza seemed satisfied she had made her point. She excused Dr. Patel from the witness stand then asked the judge if they could recess early for lunch. "My final witness is not presently in the courthouse, Your Honor."

The judge agreed. He dismissed the jury and instructed everyone to be back by one o'clock.

Once they were in recess, Lester and Ivy both looked at each other.

"Final witness," Ivy said.

That could only be one person.

CHAPTER 41

Ivy watched with intense anticipation as the victim's advocate led Hugo into the courtroom. She was surprised by how much he'd grown since the video interview she'd watched so many times. Hugo looked a couple of inches taller, and his wavy, unkempt hair had been replaced by a short, slicked-down cut with a right-side part. Hugo's glasses were different, too, the round sky-blue rubber frames having been replaced with rectangular metal ones that made him look like a little engineer.

Eliza got up from the counsel's table and went to meet Hugo halfway down the courtroom aisle. In a surprising show of affection, she took the boy's hand and walked him the rest of the way to the stand.

Once the boy was sworn in, Eliza conducted a brief and straightforward examination. Hugo confirmed that everything he'd said in the video was true and made it absolutely, unequivocally clear that when he described the abuse inflicted upon him by his mother, he was in fact referring to the defendant, Sonia Cabrerra, whom he dramatically pointed out to the jury.

The whole time, Sonia fidgeted and squirmed in her seat. She seemed even more nervous than Ivy, who had a white-knuckle grip on the pages of questions she'd typed out.

Lester had told her to try to stay loose, trust her instincts, and read the moment rather than following a script, but that just wasn't how Ivy operated. Her eyes went to the page as she started in on the cross, exactly as prepared.

"Mr. Cabrerra," she began. Just deciding what to call the boy had been a matter of debate among the defense counsel. Lester said they should call him Hugo, the way his mother would if she was angry, and go after him like a scolding parent. But Ivy was more comfortable with the formal greeting. It was less familiar and deemphasized his youth, which probably wouldn't make an iota of difference with the jury, but it made Ivy feel more comfortable, so that was what she was going to do, dammit. "You were raised by your grandparents for the first six years of your life. Correct?"

The question was safe to start with but also slightly overreaching because it was actually five years and ten months that mother and son had been estranged. That was one of the reasons Ivy posed the inquiry first as a test to see if Hugo was going to be the kind of witness who would quibble over irrelevant details.

He did not. In fact, the boy didn't even look at her. He kept his eyes focused on Eliza as he spoke meekly into the microphone. "Yes, ma'am."

Okay, we're off and rolling, Ivy thought. She continued, "So during those first six years of your life, you really had no relationship with your mother, right?" The question was basically a reiteration of the prior one, but Ivy wanted to see if she could get the boy into a rhythm of simply agreeing with her. That was the way she had been taught. Just get the witness in the habit of spitting out one-word answers—preferably Yes—and it was like the attorney was testifying.

"Yes," Hugo said.

So far, so good. Ivy kept going. "Then when you were six, you came to the US to live with your mom, right?"

"Yes."

"Your mom, who was basically a stranger to you at that point, wasn't she?"

The boy's focus remained completely upon the prosecutor as he gave another one-word answer. "Yes."

"And when you came to live with your mom, you were then separated from your grandparents, right?"

"Yes."

"Up until that point, your grandparents were basically the only parents you'd ever known. Correct?"

Ivy thought she might get an asked-and-answered objection on that one, but Eliza made no move to protect her witness or disrupt Ivy's momentum. *That must be their strategy,* Ivy thought. *Have Hugo appear as demure as possible to get maximum sympathy from the jury.* She could see Eliza arguing during the closing, "You saw that poor boy." He wasn't there to sell the state's case. He was just a sweet, innocent child, telling the truth.

Ivy thought about changing things up to counter the strategy, but that called for too many mental calculations for her to make on the fly. She did considerably soften her voice, however, when she asked her next question. "And shortly after you moved to the US, you learned that your grandparents had passed away. Correct?"

"Yes."

"I'm very sorry," Ivy said. "That must have been extremely traumatic for you."

She was hoping to draw some emotion out of the child. The defense had insinuated he suffered from histrionic personality disorder, so getting him to act out on the stand would have been helpful, but Hugo showed no visceral reaction at all.

"Yes," he said flatly.

"You then lived with your mother for approximately two whole years before you first made your allegations at school, saying she'd abused you, right?"

"Yes."

At that point, Ivy began to suspect that her trial advocacy professors were wrong. Getting one-word agreements from the witness might be nice and tidy and allow you to argue whatever you wanted in closing, but it also sapped the examination of the human drama it took to engage the jury. If a witness argued, the jury might conclude that he doth protest too much, but the way Eliza had prepped Hugo was allowing his examination to pass almost as a nonevent.

She was about to move on to her next question when Hugo interjected for the first time. "But… there was abuse." Something about the way he said it sounded different, like he was speaking with a different voice—perhaps his true voice.

"My question," Ivy said, trying not to sound overly assertive, "is: Isn't it true that you lived with your mother for about two years before you ever accused her of abuse?"

Hugo didn't answer at first. He looked at Eliza, who made no effort to signal him.

Ivy waved to get the boy's attention. He looked at her with a cold, blank stare. There was something oddly dissociative about it. He was looking at her while not looking at her at all. Meanwhile, Sonia continued to make noises of discomfort, moaning and shifting in her seat.

"Yes," Hugo said. His voice had regained his flat affect.

In planning her cross, Ivy had expected Hugo might bring up the broken arm at that point as evidence that the abuse predated his complaints. If he had, then Ivy was prepared to point out that the medical records indicated he broke his arm by falling and the hospital didn't report any suspicion of abuse. She would also point out that when Hugo accused his mother of burning him, he didn't say anything about the broken arm until later prompted by police. But since Hugo hadn't gone there, Ivy decided she shouldn't either.

Instead, she focused on the burn allegations. "By the time you first told the people at school that your mother had burned you, those burns had already turned into scars, right?"

Hugo hesitated like he was thinking through this response. Ivy had an inkling he was resisting an urge to argue.

"Yes," he said.

"So it's not like you were burned then went in and complained about it the next day. Correct?'

Another pause followed. "That's correct."

"And in fact, you weren't able to tell authorities exactly when the burning took place, right?"

"Yes."

At that point, Ivy knew Lester would start freestyling to get the boy talking. "What are we talking about here? Years, months, weeks, days?" He might be able to get him to say something that didn't make sense that he could use to trip him up—like it had just been a couple of days earlier, too soon for scars to have formed, or at a time or place they could prove was impossible. That would have been the right thing to do, but Ivy didn't think she had it in her.

Lester leaned over and whispered, "Ask him: Isn't it true that it wasn't until you found out your mom was pregnant that you accused her of abuse?"

Ivy had thought about that, but the question violated one of the rules she'd had ingrained in her about cross examination because she didn't know the answer to it. There was nothing in Hugo's prior interviews about it, so if he denied having knowledge of his mother's pregnancy at the time he accused her, there was nothing in the record Ivy could use to impeach him.

"But we don't know whether Hugo knew she was pregnant."

Sonia had told them she wasn't certain whether Hugo knew. She said she had not sat him down and told him but thought he may have overheard her and Juan arguing about it.

"So what?" Lester said. "We know she was pregnant. Medical records and simple math can show that. The jury will assume it's true."

Just then, Sonia made a groaning sound that was loud enough to draw juror attention. Ivy gently shushed her as she thought about what Lester said. There was a way to craft the question that would fit the cross-examination rules she'd been taught.

"Mr. Cabrerra, isn't it true that it wasn't until your mother became pregnant that you accused her of abusing you?'

Hugo paused. He turned and looked at Ivy, whose pulse quickened. The boy clearly wanted to say something about that. She could feel it. It was the first unscripted question she had asked, so she started immediately planning how to follow up. If he said no, she'd push him and try to make him look like a liar. *If medical records show that it was shortly after your mother first had her pregnancy confirmed that you first accused her, would you say that was just coincidence?* If he said yes, she'd try to emphasize the psychological trauma. *So it was after your grandparents died and this new mother you'd recently been reunited with became pregnant, such that you would no longer be an only child, that you accused her of abuse.*

Ivy wasn't sure which would play better. It was the first moment of real drama, as the boy continued to hesitate before answering. She could feel the jurors leaning forward in anticipation. The suspense was eating Sonia up as well, as she started squirming like mad. Ivy tried to squeeze Sonia's hand beneath the table, but she pulled away. Then to Ivy's horror, her client actually stood, shooting up so quickly that Ivy was afraid she was about to go after Hugo. But Sonia made no forward movements. Instead, she clutched at her stomach and released the harshest of sounds, something between a shriek and a moan.

Not until Ivy felt the splash of wetness against her lower leg and saw the damp stain spreading across Sonia's yellow dress did she understand what was happening.

CHAPTER 42

The courtroom erupted into chaos after Sonia's water broke. Judge Bingham instructed the bailiff to call an ambulance, but the female deputy assigned to guard Sonia assured him that wouldn't be necessary. She had a cruiser that could get Sonia to the hospital much faster. The judge declared the court in recess for the remainder of the day while the deputy and Ivy helped walk Sonia out of the courtroom, a feat made more difficult by the deputy's insistence that she be handcuffed.

"Marisol, we need you to come too," Ivy said to the interpreter.

"But I've... I can't. It's not..."

"Please," Ivy said. "We need your help. Don't make Sonia go through this without being able to communicate."

The translator reluctantly agreed to tag along. As they were just about to exit the courtroom, Ivy looked back at Lester.

"Go," he said. "Take care of her."

The four women—deputy, prisoner, lawyer, and translator—made it down the hall and piled into a courthouse elevator that took them to an underground garage where the judges and law enforcement got to park. There, the deputy led them to her cruiser. Ivy sat in the back and held Sonia's hand.

Sonia told Marisol she'd been feeling mild contractions all morning that she assumed were false labor, but it appeared that she'd been laboring for hours. The deputy drove fast, her lights and sirens allowing them to cut through traffic. But once they arrived at Memorial Hospital, they ran into a wall of bureaucracy. The check-in nurse had seen plenty of pregnant women before and found the situation much less alarming than the four haggard women on the other side of the desk did. The deputy and Ivy tried to answer the questions necessary to have Sonia admitted. Meanwhile, a man came around with a wheelchair, but Sonia told Marisol it hurt too much to sit.

After ten minutes that felt like an eternity, they finally got Sonia into a room, and things seemed to calm down. They'd made it in time, thank God. The labor nurse started checking Sonia's vitals and hooked her up to a fetal monitor while the deputy unshackled one of her wrists and secured the cuff to the bed railing. The nurse continued examining Sonia and announced that she was at eight centimeters, which she explained was a transition phase of intense contractions, but it wasn't quite time for delivery.

Fortunately, the doctor on call was one who had seen Sonia before in some of her checkups. He came in with a Spanish translator, which was how they'd been forced to communicate with Sonia in the past, and was thankful to discover they would have Marisol's services.

Sonia's breathing slowed. She was in between contractions and so happy to see a doctor she recognized that she started to cry. With Marisol's help, the doctor answered some of her questions. Sonia wanted an epidural, something that had not been an option during Hugo's delivery. The doctor confirmed she was still at eight centimeters and said there should still be just enough time to get anesthesia in there. He went to the computer and put in the order for the epidural. "Someone should be here in a few minutes to administer it," the doctor said.

Sonia, via Marisol, asked if she could go to the bathroom.

"Sure," the doctor said. "I'm just going to check on a few other patients, but I'll be back when it's time to deliver."

The deputy uncuffed Sonia, and the nurse disconnected her from the fetal monitor before helping her to the tiny lavatory inside the hospital room.

Ivy wasn't sure whether she should stay or go. She turned and looked out the window, staring down onto a gravel courtyard, wanting to give Sonia some privacy because the deputy insisted the bathroom door be left open.

Sonia was in there for several minutes, moaning, then started chattering excitedly in Mam.

"What's she saying?" the nurse asked.

Marisol said, "She feels like she has to push."

The nurse was alarmed. "Hold on. Tell her not to push." She raced into the bathroom. "Tell her to lean back."

Marisol did.

"Oh my God," the nurse said. "She's crowning. We need to get her back in the bed."

The nurse and Ivy helped get Sonia into bed, where the deputy handcuffed her to the rail.

"Is that really necessary?" Ivy asked. "I don't think she's going to try to make a run for it."

The deputy, a husky white woman with thin, straight hair and lots of freckles, said in a raspy country twang, "It's the policy."

"Come on," Ivy said. "Have a heart."

The deputy stared at her for a moment then nodded and undid the cuffs.

Ivy turned to Marisol. "Please tell Sonia everything is going to be okay. She's in good hands. I'm just gonna—"

Sonia didn't wait for the translation. As soon as Ivy started to pull away, Sonia seized her by the wrist. "Please stay," she said.

This was definitely something law school had not prepared Ivy for, but she couldn't say no. "Okay." She brushed Sonia's hair off her forehead and smiled at her. "It's okay," she said. "I'll stay."

CHAPTER 43

Colel Cabrerra was born at 4:17 p.m., exactly forty-two minutes after her mother first arrived at the hospital. She weighed a healthy eight pounds, three ounces, and was twenty inches long. It was the first time Ivy had ever witnessed the miracle of birth, and she realized the truly miraculous part was that any woman was willing to go through it all. The pushing, the screaming, the tears—it seemed like pure agony—followed by a moment of sheer joy as the nurse placed the baby on Sonia's chest for some skin-to-skin contact.

Marisol eventually had to leave, but Ivy remained, watching as the infant slept peacefully within the embrace of her mother's right arm—the left had been reshackled to the rail of the hospital bed.

Ivy dozed a little herself until the nurse came in to check on them. She moved the baby to a bassinet so Sonia could rest. Ivy could tell she was beyond exhausted. The young mother soon fell fast asleep, even snoring a little. Ivy had just taken out her phone and started scrolling through emails when there was a knock on the door. The baby began to cry, and Sonia shot up in bed.

In walked another sheriff's deputy, an older Black man, followed by a tall, slender white woman with corkscrew-curly blonde hair. She wore a navy-blue pantsuit.

Ivy stood, placing herself defensively between the interlopers and her client.

"I'm Melissa Talbert with Social Services," the woman said. She held out her hand.

Ivy made no move to shake it.

"Ivy Collins," she said. "I'm Ms. Cabrerra's attorney."

The woman smiled apologetically. "I'm very sorry to have to be here under these circumstances," she said. "But we have to take custody of the child."

"The hell you are," Ivy said.

She stepped to her right, blocking them from the baby's bassinet.

Sonia cried out in her broken English, "What is…? What happening?"

"Ma'am, you'll need to step aside," the deputy said.

Ivy didn't move.

The deputy placed his hand on her shoulder, ready to move her if necessary.

"Ivy!" Sonia shrieked. "What is…?"

"I'm really very sorry," the woman from Social Services said. She nodded reluctantly to the deputy, who grabbed hold of Ivy and moved her to the side. Sonia shrieked like a wild animal as the woman began wheeling the bassinet out of the room.

"At least let her hold her one more time," Ivy pleaded.

The woman paused. "I'm sorry," she said. "If I do that, then we end up in a tug of war for the child and hurt the baby. It's better this way. Hopefully, this will only be temporary."

"No!" Sonia screamed, followed by angry Mam rantings. She thrashed violently in the hospital bed. Ivy was afraid Sonia might break her shackled wrist as she reached out so desperately with her opposite arm, grasping in vain for her child.

Unable to do anything else, Ivy went to her client. She seized Sonia in a bear hug while the baby was wheeled from the room. "We'll get her back," Ivy promised, based upon nothing but a foundationless desire that it would prove true. "Trust me. This will only be temporary. We'll get her back."

Sonia stopped thrashing and wailed. Her tiny body trembled with torment. Her face was drowning in tears.

Ivy grasped Sonia by the shoulder and forced her to make eye contact.

"We will get her back. Do you understand me?"

Sonia swallowed hard. "I understand," she said. "Thank you. I understand."

The nurse came in, apologizing profusely for what had just transpired but insisting they had no choice in the matter. The doctor had prescribed some calming medicines for Sonia that, after administered, eventually allowed her to cry herself to sleep.

Ivy slipped out into the hall and called Lester. She told him about all that had happened.

"Damn, those bastards move quick."

"How did things wrap up in court?" Ivy asked.

"The judge wants to see us back in the courtroom in the morning," Lester said. "Wants to have a status conference to figure out where we go from here. I'm thinking maybe we should move for a mistrial. That would give us more time to see if this medical record actually exists."

Mistrying the case would mean starting all over months down the road. Judges were loath to do it, but in their case, it was a possibility.

"There's no way," Ivy said. "Sonia will refuse. It will just mean more time she's away from her baby."

"If she gets convicted, she ain't getting that baby back anyway," Lester said. "We need to win first and worry about timing second. I think mistrial is our best bet at this point. With the delay, we might be able to get a medical record that makes a difference. Or maybe Eliza won't feel like starting all over and will offer us a better deal."

Ivy tried to think. Sonia would never agree to a mistrial that would delay things indefinitely. They needed to win, and they needed to do it now, not in a do-over trial.

"Instead of a mistrial, do you think the judge would give us a continuance?" Ivy asked.

"Yeah, under the circumstances, I'm sure he'd let the jury stay home for the rest of the week and come back on Monday. Give Sonia some time to recuperate. But why? What are you thinking?"

Ivy hesitated, wanting to make sure she was willing to go through with what she was about to propose. "I'm thinking," she said finally, "that would be just enough time for me to fly down to Guatemala."

CHAPTER 44

The state would never pay for a factfinding trip to Guatemala, but Ivy didn't care. She was resolved to go and would pay for it herself, whether she ever got reimbursed or not. To her surprise, Lester actually agreed to front the cost, giving her the use of a firm credit card for the first time ever, saying, "Coach. No extra bags. Budget hotel. Got it?"

"Got it," Ivy said.

Then Cesar insisted on going too. Ivy initially tried to talk him out of it, worrying that he wouldn't be able to get back into the US. But Lester—by challenging the calibration of the breathalyzer—had actually managed to get Cesar's DUI charge reduced to reckless driving, and Cesar was feeling very good about his U-Visa prospects.

"Trust me, boss. All I need is a certification from the cops, and I'm home free. After Guatemala, I'll just go stay with my family in Mexico for a little bit. Be back here in no time. Besides, if you're going to get that record, you're going to need my help."

That last part was definitely true. Ivy would have a hard time accomplishing her Central American mission without a translator who possessed Cesar's finesse and smooth-talking ways.

Thus, the following morning, the two caught a Delta flight to Atlanta, from which their connection took them to Guatemala City. Ivy was surprised by what she found there and a little ashamed of herself. She'd expected jungles and thatched huts, but Guatemala's capital turned out to be a major metropolitan area that was actually several times larger than Raleigh. The streets were lined with familiar hallmarks like Starbucks, McDonald's, Burger King, Papa Johns, Panda Express, nail salons, movie theaters, and major hotel chains.

Not until the bus ride through the countryside toward Huehue-tenango did the experience begin to match her expectations. There, she gazed for hours out on impoverished villages while listening to crying babies during the long, hot, air-condition-less ride. They also passed multiple transports filled with soldiers bearing machine guns, prompting reminders from Cesar about how the area they were entering was notorious for cartel violence.

When they finally reached their stop, Cesar and Ivy got out and ate a quick lunch at an open-air chicken restaurant, where multiple birds were turned on spits over a charcoal fire pit. From there, they had a thirty-minute walk to the hospital, traveling down cobblestone streets through a quaint town that was a mixture of beautiful, ornate Spanish-style architecture and the type of urban blight that only occurred in the complete absence of regulation.

The hospital was much smaller than what Ivy had imagined, a one-story rectangular building half the size of a typical big-box store. Equally as unexpected was the exterior color: electric blue. Inside, the lobby was subject to post-COVID security. Masks were not required of the patrons but were worn by the staff, including the receptionist, who sat behind protective glass.

Cesar addressed her with a smile. Ivy didn't understand much of what he said but saw him hand over an affidavit they'd obtained from Sonia establishing her status as Hugo's mother. He also handed the girl a subpoena Ivy had drafted and signed. It had absolutely no legal effect in Guatemala, but it was official looking.

The girl behind the desk was truly a girl. If she was twenty, then Ivy was a grandmother. As the receptionist and Cesar went back and forth in Spanish, Ivy thought about how strange it was that the gatekeeper to Sonia's freedom could be this young person in what seemed a remote part of the world.

She was about to ask Cesar what the girl was saying when he slapped the front desk in frustration.

"What?" Ivy asked.

Cesar pointed angrily at the young woman. "She's got it pulled up right there on her computer but says she's not allowed to give it to us."

"But we explained why Sonia isn't listed as Hugo's mother."

"I know. But she says the lady who handles all the record requests is the one who has to approve it, and she's out sick."

Sick. The PI must have been telling the truth. He had bribed the records person, who had come down with COVID before she could give him the record they so desperately needed.

It didn't matter. There was no way Ivy was going to take no for an answer. They had come too far to be denied.

"Offer her money. Tell her we'll pay her whatever she makes here in a month if she'll just give us the record."

"I'll try it," Cesar said.

As he approached the reception desk again, there was a loud commotion outside, with shouting. Then the front doors burst open, and three military police came in, struggling to support a fourth who was badly wounded, his shirt soaked with blood.

Ivy and Cesar stood aside. The receptionist came around the desk to help the military police as they put the man in a wheelchair, then the entire group disappeared behind a set of double doors.

"Holy shit!" Cesar said.

Ivy was shaken by the scene, too, but not enough to take her eyes off the prize. The receptionist was gone, but her computer was not, and she and Cesar were all alone there in the lobby. Ivy couldn't pass up the opportunity. Without a moment's hesitation, she ran around to the other side of the reception desk and wiggled the mouse to wake the computer from its spiral-patterned screensaver.

Cesar didn't miss a beat. "Hurry," he said. "I'll guard the door."

Ivy stared at a database that was all in Spanish, but it was still on a page where Hugo Cabrerra's name appeared. The text was in blue, and when Ivy hovered the mouse above it, the arrow turned into a pointy-fingered hand. The name was a hyperlink. One click would open the record Ivy had prayed existed.

She paused to say another quick silent prayer that she hadn't come all that way for nothing, that she wouldn't click on the record only to discover that Hugo had been seen at the hospital for a random illness that had no bearing on Sonia's case.

"Hurry," Cesar said, looking over his shoulder at the double doors.

Ivy pressed the mouse button. The screen went dark for a second, and Ivy was afraid the computer had frozen, but it was just an old, slow processor. The monitor lit back up. Listed across the top was a date of service from several years prior, though it took Ivy a second to realize that because the numbers for the month and day were reversed from what she was used to. Below that were more numbers that appeared to be vitals. As Ivy scanned the screen, she heard voices from the other side of the lobby doors.

She scrolled down, looking for some kind of narrative description, and found a paragraph that she guessed was the history, but it was in Spanish.

"Cesar, come read this for me."

While he made his way over to her, Ivy pulled out her phone and took a picture of the screen.

The hallway voices grew louder.

"What's it say?"

Cesar read aloud. "Patient is a five-year-old male. Received burns to flank from leaning against a hot grill that had been set against a wall to cool."

Ivy's heart probably skipped several beats in that moment. She almost couldn't believe it. This was it. The Holy Grail. The smoking gun. The magical piece of evidence that could win the case and set Sonia free.

Given more opportunity, Ivy might have cried, but there was no time.

"See if you can print it," she said.

An old Epson printer was on the desk next to the computer. Cesar clicked the printer icon at the top of the screen. The printer buzzed to life, but the paper advanced painfully slowly. While it buzzed and whirred, there was a mechanical clicking noise across the room. The autolock on the lobby doors had disengaged.

"Come on!" Cesar said.

Ivy ripped the paper from the printer just as the double doors opened. Standing there was the receptionist, followed by two of the military police officers. Cesar tried to play it cool, but Ivy saw the receptionist's eyes immediately read the situation. She pointed at them, and Ivy sprinted for the door.

"*Policía! Policía!*" the woman shouted.

Ivy burst through the double doors and had just tasted fresh air when she felt a viselike grip seize her shoulder.

CHAPTER 45

The officer pulled Ivy back and pushed her up against the wall of the hospital while another pointed a machine gun at her and yelled something in Spanish.

"Jesus, don't shoot!" Ivy screamed. She dropped to her knees with her hands in the air. "It's just a sheet of paper!"

The girl from the front desk came running outside, yelling in Spanish as well. She snatched the medical record from Ivy's fist, ripping it in the process. Meanwhile, another officer frog-marched Cesar outside with his hands already cuffed behind his back.

"Cesar, please tell them it's okay," Ivy said. "Tell them we can pay. Whatever we need to. Just find out how much. We can pay them."

Ivy remembered what Sonia had said about how the justice system worked in Guatemala. But when Cesar translated her offer, it did not go over well. The officer who'd seized her had a dead, grayed-out eye that he somehow fixed on her all the same, with a look of furious insult. The next thing she knew, she was also being handcuffed, and both she and Cesar were shoved into the back of a police car that sped into traffic, hauling them off to God knew where.

"Shit, Ivy," Cesar said. "They say they're going to charge us with attempting to bribe an official in addition to theft and computer fraud."

"I thought that's how it works here. Tell them I didn't mean any harm."

Cesar tried to convey that to the two officers, who shouted back something angry. "They said that's what the cartels do. Try to buy everyone off, but they aren't like that. I think we offended them."

"Great."

"I think we should just keep quiet," Cesar said.

"Well, where are they taking us?"

Cesar leaned forward so Ivy could see the handcuffs shackling his wrists. "Where do you think?"

Ivy felt panicked chills throughout her body. "Oh Jesus. This cannot be happening." Her mind filled with images from every show she'd ever seen about Americans imprisoned in foreign countries: *Midnight Express, Brokedown Palace, Locked Up Abroad*. It was nearly enough to set off a full-blown panic attack, but at some point, Ivy's fear turned into anger, and she went into what Cesar would later refer to as "stage-four Karen mode." She loudly demanded her phone call, an attorney, her right to remain silent—which she clearly was not exercising—and immediate access to the US consulate. She was an American and a lawyer, goddammit, and was not to be treated in such a manner.

The police were not impressed. Rather than acquiescing to Ivy's demands, they locked them in a holding cell in the basement of the local police station. There, pale-yellow bars with peeling paint confined them in a six-by-eight space that had a moldy concrete floor and smelled like urine. The dungeon wasn't air-conditioned, and it had to be at least ninety degrees down there, with sweltering humidity. The police had also confiscated their belongings, including Ivy's phone, which contained the photo of the medical record they had come there to get. Ivy hadn't had a chance to view it before the arrest, and since the paper copy had been seized and destroyed, she could only hope that the digital picture was legible.

"We need to get in touch with Lester," she said.

"What the hell's Lester going to do?" Cesar asked. "He can't help us down here. It's not like the Truth has an international law department."

"Well, what do you suggest?"

Cesar leaned back against the damp stone wall. "I suggest we do nothing. Every time we try, things just get worse. So let's just sit here and shut up, and eventually, they will come and tell us what the deal is."

Ivy thought that over but not for long. "Fuck that," she said. "I want my phone call."

She stood and yanked on the bars of the cell door, which had just enough shimmy to make a clanking sound. "I demand to see someone! I am a US citizen and demand to see someone now!" Her voice echoed throughout the basement but to no avail. No one even bothered to come downstairs and tell her to shut up.

While Ivy yelled, Cesar lay on the steel bench with a finger firmly inserted into each ear. When she started growing hoarse and couldn't scream anymore, she turned her ire on him.

"How can you just lie there?"

Cesar rolled onto his side to face the wall. "It's not like I'm going back anyway," he mumbled.

"What?" Ivy wasn't sure she'd heard him right.

"Nothing," Cesar said.

Ivy seized him by the shoulder and forced him to turn and face her.

"What did you say?"

Cesar sat up and sighed. "I said, 'It's not like I'm going back anyway.'"

"What are you talking about? I thought you said you and your immigration attorney had everything worked out."

"Yeah, we do. But the cops wouldn't sign off on my U-visa certification, so my only options were to wait and get deported, in which case I'd be subject to a ban, or voluntarily depart and hope I could somehow qualify for some other immigration status in the future. So here I am, voluntarily departed."

Ivy couldn't believe what she was hearing. "I thought he said you had a good case."

Cesar shrugged. "I would have if the cops had signed off on it. But it's totally within their discretion. No way to make them do it."

More arbitrary "discretion" over life-altering decisions. The notion made Ivy sick. "There has to be a way," she insisted.

"No. My attorney says the police were suspicious of whether the break-in was legit. They saw through Lester's little scheme. I was afraid if I pushed it any further, it would blow up in his face."

Ivy wasn't totally shocked to hear that. Getting robbed the day after receiving a deportation notice was as suspicious as hell. But she wasn't going to let Cesar just roll over and accept his fate.

"Let's just get married, then."

Cesar pointed at her. "That right there is why I didn't tell you. I knew you'd bring that nonsense up again. I'm not going to have you risk your license and everything else committing fraud for me."

Ivy stammered, searching for a response.

Cesar stopped her. "Look, it's not like I'm dying. I'm just going to go live with my aunt in Puerto Vallarta. There're far worse things. Believe me. Plus, Lester can legally employ me again as long as I'm working from Mexico. I'll just be on Zoom. The way everyone's working remotely these days, it will be like I never left."

Cesar was putting on a brave face for her benefit, but she could see the hurt in his eyes.

"Lester knew about this?"

"Yeah," Cesar said. "He just wanted me to wait until after Sonia's trial was over to tell you. I was already making plans to leave, but when this trip came up, I knew you could use my help and decided it would be easier to just rip off the Band-Aid. I'll get my cousin to come by your place and gather up my stuff later."

"And Lester let you go through with this?"

Cesar shrugged. "What choice did he have?"

Ivy didn't know the answer to that but wasn't going to just passively accept this fate.

"Can you try in Spanish to get somebody's attention and tell them I just need to get my phone call?"

"I'll try. But who are you going to call?"

Ivy took a moment to swallow her pride before answering.

"I'm calling my father."

CHAPTER 46

On Sunday morning, the guard opened the cell door, pointed at Cesar, and said, "*Vamos.*"

Ivy's heart soared. "Oh, thank God." She wasted little time in stretching her weary bones before trying to follow Cesar out of the cell. But the guard raised a hand to stop her and said something Ivy didn't understand.

"Why just me?" Cesar asked. The guard nodded behind him, where heavy footsteps could be heard descending the stairs.

Ivy's father stepped into view. He seemed comically large next to the short police officer, like an aristocratic ogre in his Polo shirt, cargo shorts, and designer deck shoes, ducking his head to pass through the low hallway in that dark underground dungeon.

"I'd like to talk to my daughter alone," he said.

Cesar looked back at Ivy.

"It's okay," she said. "Go on."

If the situation had been reversed, Ivy suspected she'd probably make a mad dash up the stairs and out into the sunlight, but to Cesar's credit, he lingered. "You're sure?" he asked.

"I'm sure."

Her father looked like he had some sharp words he'd like to hurl at Cesar as he reluctantly moved toward the stairs, but he limited his commentary to a seething glare that he maintained until both Cesar and the guard were out of sight.

"Thank you for coming," Ivy said, hoping to get things with her father off on a positive note.

Charles Collins III pointed toward the stairs. "You are not marrying that boy," he said then raised a hand to stop Ivy from responding. "And before you start calling me a bigot or whatever other slander you're inclined to throw my way, this has nothing to do with race or religion or any other constitutionally protected category, okay? This is about the simple fact that I have only laid eyes on this young man twice in my life, and both times, the police were involved."

Ivy took a beat before saying anything. She reminded herself to stay calm. She needed her father's help, and it was not the time to provoke him—which was easy to do. He'd obviously been able to pull the strings necessary to get Cesar released, which meant she'd surely be free to go, too, as soon as he gave the police the thumbs-up.

"Fine. I won't marry him. Can I leave now?"

Charles seemed surprised by how easily she'd given in. "Just like that?"

"Is this attorney–client privileged?" Ivy asked.

"It can be."

"Okay," Ivy said. She decided to come clean with her father and explained that the engagement to Cesar had been purely for immigration purposes.

"I'm not sure what bothers me more," he said. "That you were attempting to commit immigration fraud or that you lied about it just to bother me."

"It wasn't about you, Dad. I was just trying to help out a friend. Anyway, he turned me down. Wasn't willing to go through with it."

"Good for him."

"Yeah, well, he came down here to help me on a case, and now he's stuck with no way to get back into the US."

Charles Collins shook his head. "Ivy, what in the world have you gotten yourself mixed up in?"

"A litigator has to be willing to get their hands dirty," she said.

Her father didn't blink at having his own words thrown back at him. "What is that supposed to mean?"

Ivy gave her father a cursory rundown of the Sonia Cabrerra trial and how she and Cesar had come there to obtain a medical record that proved her client's innocence.

"My God, Ivy. Why didn't you just say something to me? Maybe I could have helped. There had to be a better way to go about it than this."

Given her current circumstances, Ivy found that point hard to argue with.

"Well, what's done is done," she said. "The only question is whether you can get me out of here so I can get back and finish this trial and help an innocent woman go free."

Her father smiled, and Ivy thought she detected a tiny glint of pride in his eyes.

"In that regard, I'm prepared to offer you a deal," he said.

"We're negotiating?"

"Life is a negotiation, Ivy."

She resisted the urge to roll her eyes while simultaneously realizing that she was a lot more receptive to life-slash-legal lessons when they came from Lester than from her father.

"Okay, let's hear your offer," she said.

"My proposal is this: Through no small amount of effort, I have pulled some considerable strings to have this situation dealt with. All charges here will be dropped, and you can accompany me home tonight on a flight back to Raleigh."

"What about Cesar?"

"His charges will be dropped as well. He'll be free to go. But he's on his own. Obviously."

The thought of leaving Cesar was breaking Ivy's heart, but she also didn't know what she could do about it. There didn't seem to be any other choice.

"What I want in return is for you to immediately tender your resignation at your current position so you'll stop getting mixed up in this kind of nonsense, then you are to come work with me."

"I thought you said I wasn't cut out for litigation."

Her father let out a deep sigh of frustration. "My goodness, Ivy. You always take me the worst possible way. I mean, is it so wrong for a father to not want his daughter to have to swim with the sharks? Is it so wrong to think that maybe she's a better, nicer person than he is? Well, if so, then I'm guilty. But if you're certain that litigation is what you want to do, then so be it. I'll welcome you aboard my team."

Ivy thought there was a little bit of revisionist history going on with how her father characterized his prior statements, but she also recognized that he was trying, in his way, to extend an olive branch. Instinctively, she wanted to take it. She would relish the opportunity to prove herself to her father. But she also didn't want to stop working for Lester.

Getting out of jail and getting back to Sonia's case was paramount, however. If she accepted her father's terms, she could leave immediately and, assuming the photo she'd taken of the medical records was legible, there was still time to win the case.

"I've got one additional term," she said.

"Ivy, quitting is not up for discussion. You—"

"I'll quit," she said. "I need to finish this trial, but as soon as it's over, I'll quit. The only additional thing I'm asking is that you call your buddy, the district attorney, or whoever it is you know in the police department and get someone to sign off on a visa certification for Cesar."

"A what?"

Ivy explained to her father how U-Visas worked, and although it involved a lengthy immigration process, the first and most crucial step was to get law enforcement to certify that the applicant had been the victim of a qualifying crime.

"Ivy, you overestimate me. I can't just—"

"This part isn't up for discussion, Dad. Cesar is a great guy. The best. He deserves it. And I know you can make it happen if you really want to."

Charles Collins III sighed again and turned up his palms. "I'll try," he said. "I can't guarantee a result, but I will make some calls."

That's something, Ivy thought. At least it was enough for her conscience to permit her to stick her hand through the bars and watch it disappear inside her father's meaty palm.

CHAPTER 47

As soon as Ivy got her phone back, the first thing she did was look at the photo she'd taken of Hugo's medical record. The image was dark and pixelated around the edges with a glare from the computer screen, but with some manipulation of the editing feature, adjusting the contrast, she was able to settle on a definitive image of the relevant text. Ivy immediately sent it to Lester with a message that she'd be getting in late that evening and would meet him at the courthouse in the morning.

Lester immediately texted back. *Do you have a paper copy? Something with an official seal or affidavit of authenticity?*

Ivy felt a pang in her chest. She'd hoped Lester would know how to deal with all that.

No, she texted back. Then she added, *I guess I would have to testify to authenticate it.*

A cold sweat broke out on her skin as she thought about how that would go, being placed under oath and having to explain to a judge how she'd stolen the record from a Guatemalan hospital.

Her spirits were lifted, however, by Lester's follow-up text. *Don't worry about it. We'll figure something out. This is big-league stuff, Ives. You really brought this one home. Great job!!!*

That vote of confidence warmed her heart as Cesar accompanied Ivy and her father to the airport. He'd managed to book a flight to Mexico City that left an hour after hers. From there, he'd take a bus to the town where his aunt lived and stay there until his visa came through.

She and Cesar hugged at the gate for a long time after Ivy's flight was called. She couldn't help crying, afraid that she might never see her friend again.

"Come on now, boss," Cesar said. "It's not goodbye forever. I'll see you soon."

"Right," Ivy said, despite her fear for his immigration prospects. Cesar had such a positive attitude about it all that Ivy didn't want to ruin it.

"Now, go set our girl free," Cesar said and kissed her forehead.

Ivy wiped the tears from her eyes. "Thank you. For everything."

"You are welcome. But you tell Lester I deserve some kind of hazard pay or something."

"Will do."

Ivy hugged him again one last time before joining her father on the plane.

Once they landed at RDU, made it through customs and immigration, and were safely back on US soil, Ivy's father tried to persuade her to return home with him for the evening, saying how relieved her mother would be to see her. Ivy declined, citing her need to be in court the following morning, but promised to call or come by soon.

When she got back to her townhouse, the first thing she did was take a thirty-minute shower to scrub off all of the Guatemalan-jail funk. Then she put on her fuzziest pajamas, set her alarm, and went to bed early. The house felt ominously quiet without Cesar there, and Ivy had so many emotions running through her that it would have been insomnia inducing under normal circumstances, but she was so exhausted from barely sleeping during her detention that she had no trouble drifting off.

The next morning, when she showed up to the courtroom, Lester and Eliza were both already there, huddled together, looking over something she assumed was the medical-record photo Ivy had obtained. Before she could join them, she noticed someone else in the courtroom as well. In the back row, slid all the way down into the corner of the room, was her father. He gave Ivy a little wave, which she returned as she passed down the aisle and heard Eliza cackle with laughter.

"You'll never be able to get that into evidence," she said. "It's either inauthentic or stolen. And where the attorney has participated in the theft, the evidence is patently inadmissible. This changes nothing."

Lester threw up his arms. "Goddammit," he said. "We shouldn't have to get it into evidence. Your job is to see that justice is done. You should dismiss the case."

"Fat chance," Eliza said. "How do I know you didn't fake this?"

"For the love of God, woman," Lester said, "have a heart."

"You first," Eliza fired back.

Ivy felt an eerie sense of calm as she entered the conversation. She was still shaking off the deep sleep from the night before and feeling the remnants of her dreams. It made something about what she was doing there seem kind of preordained, like she was watching herself without thinking. All the normal nerves and stress were gone.

"We'll just ask for a continuance," Ivy said. "Or a mistrial. With Sonia giving birth and this record that exonerates her, there's no way the judge is going to let you convict. He'll give us whatever time we need to get this authenticated. The case is over, Eliza."

It was the first time Ivy had ever addressed the prosecutor by her first name. Either that or the easy confidence in Ivy's voice shook the ADA. Ivy could see it in Eliza's eyes.

"Damn right," Lester said.

Eliza jutted her jaw and gazed over toward the prisoner hold as Sonia was being led into the courtroom by the same deputy who'd driven her to the hospital the week prior. Sonia looked like hell. The strain of childbirth followed by the trauma of losing her child to Social Services had turned her into a zombie, a functioning body with a murdered soul. Ivy went and sat down next to her and patted her knee. Sonia leaned her head on Ivy's shoulder as the lawyer stroked her hair.

Marisol had just arrived. She sat down next to them and translated when Ivy said, "It will all be over soon, Sonia. The prosecutor knows the truth now. She knows that Hugo lied about you. His scars came from something that happened when he was in Guatemala and you were in the US. And if Hugo lied about that, then he must have lied about the broken arm too. Ms. Wells will do the right thing."

Eliza huffed, but Ivy could see her wheels turning. The medical record changed everything.

"Final offer," Eliza said. "I'll dismiss count one on the burns if she'll plead to count two on the broken arm."

Lester responded instantly. "Hell no."

"Wait a second," Eliza said. "I'm not finished. I'll also recommend a sentence of time served. Your lady will go home today."

That was a really good offer. A sentence of time served meant not only that Sonia would immediately go free but also that she could probably avoid deportation as well.

Lester turned to Ivy. "It's your call."

"But it's still a felony," Ivy complained. "She could still lose custody of Hugo."

Eliza's face softened at the mention of the boy. "You know, Hugo's doing really well now. He's being fostered by a great couple who are spoiling him rotten. His grades are good. There have been no behavioral issues at school. He's really thriving. And once there's an official finding of abuse, he'll be eligible for SIJS."

"What's that?" Ivy asked.

Lester answered, "Special Immigrant Juvenile Status. It's a visa for abandoned or abused kids that lets them stay here legally and eventually become citizens."

Suddenly, Ivy realized that had been the whole point all along. It was why Eliza had never been willing to consider any serious plea negotiations. The state needed the felony conviction for immigration purposes. Ivy could instantly see how the whole thing might have unfolded between social workers and therapists, overzealous do-gooders who took something Hugo said and ran with it, unintentionally rewarding him with attention and candy and who knew what else, the more graphic and extreme his allegations became—all the while hoping to help the child with some special immigration program. *How many times,* she wondered, *did Hugo go over his story, letting it snowball with embellishments, before it was first captured on camera?*

The whole time, Marisol had been translating for Sonia, who blurted something out.

"She says she'll take the deal."

Ivy viciously shook her head. She tried to quiet them, but Sonia was talking, and Marisol was translating. "She says she did break Hugo's arm. He was running away, and she was angry. She grabbed and pulled too hard."

"Stop!" Ivy commanded. "We can talk in private."

But then Sonia said loudly in English, "I." She pointed to herself when she did then seized the air in front of her in a tight fist and made a vicious twisting motion. Her expression was a mixture of anger and sadness and also determination as she said firmly, "I break."

CHAPTER 48

It was too late for Ivy to do anything about it. Sonia had confessed. Eliza had heard it, and twenty minutes later, Judge Bingham did as well when Sonia pled guilty on count two of the indictment. With the services of Marisol as certified Mam translator, the judge took the defendant through the allocution, a series of questions to assure she understood what she was agreeing to and the consequences of her guilty plea. Ivy and Lester stood on opposite sides of their client. When the judge asked if she was "in fact guilty," Sonia answered yes without hesitation. A tear formed at the corner of Ivy's eye, and she wiped it away with the back of her sleeve.

When it was over, Sonia was permitted to hug each of her lawyers before being taken away for processing. Ivy held her for a long time. When they separated, Ivy looked Sonia in the eyes.

"Is it true?" she asked. "Did you really break Hugo's arm?"

Legally, the answer would make no difference at that point, but Ivy needed to know. Marisol translated, and Sonia answered in Mam.

"She says she wanted Hugo to have a better life. Now he'll have it."

Before Ivy could ask what she meant by that, the deputy placed her hand on Sonia's shoulder. "Time to go," she said.

Ivy barely had time to wave goodbye to Sonia before she was whisked away, behind the slamming steel door of the prisoner hold.

"She can still get her daughter back," Lester said. "Social Services will watch her like a hawk for a while, but ultimately, I think those two will be fine."

Ivy hoped that was true. She dropped down in her chair, exhausted, overwhelmed, and consumed with worry over the uncertain future Sonia still faced. She would be released later that day with no money and no home to go to and would continue living under the specter of potential deportation if she was ever picked up by ICE. But at least she would have a fighting chance. She still had hope.

"Well, I guess that's it," Lester said.

The Truth immediately started working two cell phones, talking to Maria on one and an insurance adjuster on the other. Ivy knew what an economic burden it had placed on the practice for Lester to basically close the office for more than a week in order to try Sonia's case. She thought at first that he was going to leave without even saying goodbye when he took note of Ivy's glum expression and paused his calls.

"Why don't you take the rest of the day off?" he said to her. "You've earned it."

"Thanks," Ivy said. She struggled for a way to quickly broach the topic she needed to raise with him—to tell him she'd agreed to quit her job and go work with her father.

"Thank you," Lester said. "This is the most fun I've had practicing law in a long time, Ives. We'll have to do it again sometime."

"Yeah, Lester, about that. I don't—"

"Now, don't start with all that woe-is-me, pity-party stuff. You made your bones on this one, Ives. You're a trial lawyer, all right."

Ivy still didn't feel like that was the case. "I didn't even get to finish my cross of Hugo," she said.

"So what? You getting that medical record like you did. That's the kind of stuff that wins cases a hell of a lot more than making some great speech or beating up on a witness."

Ivy shrugged. Maybe he was right about that, but still, she would have loved to be able to command a courtroom the way Lester could.

"All that stuff about natural ability is bullshit," Lester said. "I mean, look at me and Eliza. We're totally different in how we approach this thing. At the end of the day, there's one quality and one quality only that makes you a trial lawyer."

"What's that?' Ivy asked.

Lester gave his high-watt smile. "It's the sick, perverse, fucked-up desire to do it. And you, my friend, are fucked up."

Ivy placed her hand atop his. "Thanks, Lester."

He winked at her and began to leave. Ivy started to call after him, but he was already working his phones again, and she decided she could wait to talk to him later. He made eye contact with her one last time when he swiveled around to back through the courtroom doors, and Ivy heard him say, "That offer is insulting. It would be malpractice for me to settle the case for that."

Throughout the morning, Ivy's father had been waiting patiently in the corner of the courtroom. Now that Lester was gone, he approached, smiling at his daughter. "You looked pretty good up there," he said.

Ivy shrugged. "Thanks. It wasn't exactly how I was expecting things to go."

"It never is."

He gently pushed up her chin. "Hey, I've got some good news for you. The certification for your friend—I should have it by the end of the day."

Ivy immediately felt half the weight she'd been carrying being removed from her shoulders. A certification meant that Cesar had cleared the biggest hurdle toward getting his U-visa. There would still be a long process ahead, but the chances of his being able to return were very high. Ivy hugged her father tightly. "Oh my God. Thank you."

Charles Collins III seemed awkwardly confused but pleased by his daughter's sudden show of affection—the first time she'd hugged him in years. "So," he said, "should I... um... expect to see you at the office in the morning?"

Ivy looked up at her dad, the big, strong, intimidating man, and took a step back.

"You know, Dad, about that. I—"

"Ivy Collins, you've made a commitment."

"I know. I know. I'll honor my commitment. I'll quit my job and come work for you. And I'll resent you for coercing me under duress to agree to that. Or..." Ivy employed her cute voice. "*Maybe* you let me out of my commitment, I keep my job with Lester, and in exchange, I'll agree to wipe our slate clean."

"Meaning?"

"Meaning I'll consider the possibility that I could have taken you the wrong way at times, and whatever hurts or slights I may have felt in the past, I'll do my best to look past them and give you—us—another chance."

Charles Collins III bit his top lip and shook his head. "So we're renegotiating? Is that it?"

"Life is a negotiation, Dad."

"So it is," he said, smiling. Her father took a deep breath. "You're sure this is what you really want to do?"

Ivy didn't hesitate. "I'm sure."

"Well, I'd hate to miss out on a candidate of your talent, but I have to admit you were pretty impressive up there, handling something like this at your age. And if staying in your current position gets me a clean slate with you, then I'd have to say that is good and sufficient consideration."

He held out his hand. "You've got a deal."

Ivy hugged him instead. She buried her face in his massive chest then felt her father kiss the top of her head.

When they parted, Ivy's father stiffened and straightened his jacket. "Could I... at least take you to lunch?" he asked.

Though it was a nice offer, Ivy really wanted to be alone with her thoughts for a while and try to process all that had occurred.

"Honestly, Dad, I don't think I could eat right now. I kind of just want to sit here by myself for a bit."

Charles nodded knowingly. "The posttrial hangover. Takes a while to get over it. How about dinner, then? I'm sure I could persuade your mother to make that pasta dish you like. You could... tell us all about the case."

"That sounds great," Ivy said.

With the promise of a family dinner date, father and daughter said their goodbyes. After that, once Ivy was alone in the courtroom, she plopped into her chair at the counsel's table and soaked up the silence. She smelled the wood of the table and chairs, the railing, and all the benches. She took in the front of the courtroom, the jury box, the well where the attorneys stood and faced the jury during openings and closings, the high judge's desk, the lonely witness chair, and the cluttered clerk's area with its stacks of papers.

It bothered her how anticlimactic everything seemed, how all the other lawyers and court staff could just go on about their business as though it were any other day. Ivy was determined not to do that. She would stick with Sonia for the long haul, whether she was paid for it or not, and do what she could to help with all the challenges that lay ahead for her. Ivy wouldn't rest until Sonia got her baby back.

So consumed was she by her thoughts that Ivy didn't even realize she was crying again until Eliza Wells entered from a private side door to retrieve a folder she'd left behind. Ivy quickly sat up and wiped her eyes.

The prosecutor considered her curiously. "You really thought she was innocent, didn't you?"

"I still do," Ivy said.

Eliza smirked, wrinkling her forehead. She looked different to Ivy in that moment. The mystique was gone. Instead of *wise* and *formidable*, the words *worn* and *cynical* came to mind.

Eliza tipped her folder in Ivy's direction. "Hang in there, counselor. Once you've been doing this as long as I have, you'll get pretty calloused to the whole thing."

Ivy thought about that for a second, about how much pain and heartache and injustice that kind of indifference—especially from those in power—could cause.

She stood to face her adversary for one last time. "Well," Ivy said, "I guess we're all guilty of something."

Acknowledgments

I would like to thank Lynn McNamee and her team at Red Adept Publishing for their editing expertise and production support. Thanks also to my agent, Mark Falkin, and beta readers, Scott Blackburn, Steve Daugherty, Bill Floyd, Lynn Fairchild Hawks, J.G. Hetherton, Phillip Kimbrough, Eryk Pruitt, John Rasinsky, and Casey Stegman. Finally, a special thanks to Bert Diener, who first told me the archer story and was brave enough to actually use it in trial.

About the Author

Russell W. Johnson is originally from West Virginia, spent his middle and high school years in Pennsylvania, and currently lives in North Carolina, where he is a practicing attorney and fiction writer.Russell holds an undergraduate degree in English and history, with a minor in creative writing, from West Virginia University and a juris doctorate from the University of North Carolina at Chapel Hill.(Seriously, he really holds them. He gets those diplomas down off the wall at least once a day and struts around, shoving them in people's faces, saying, "How you like me now, suckas?")

Read more at https://www.russellwjohnson.com/.

About the Publisher

Dear Reader,

We hope you enjoyed this book. Please consider leaving a review on your favorite book site.

Visit our site to find more quality books!

Read more at https://RedAdeptPublishing.com.